By Sandra Thompson

CLOSE-UPS

WILD BANANAS

Wild Bananas

Wild Bananas

A novel by
SANDRA THOMPSON

The Atlantic Monthly Press
BOSTON / NEW YORK

FIRST EDITION

LIBRARY OF CONGRESS CATALOGING IN PUBLICATION DATA

Thompson, Sandra.
   Wild bananas.

   I. Title.
PS3570.H6436W5   1985   813'.54   85-47788
ISBN 0-87113-032-7

BP

Published simultaneously in Canada

PRINTED IN THE UNITED STATES OF AMERICA

For Larry

Wild Bananas

BARRY picks me up to carry me over the threshold. "Oof," he says and kicks open the door.

I didn't think Barry could carry me. He is the smallest man I have ever slept with. He lets me down inside the front hall, then collapses against the wall. His suit is too big for him, and he seems to hang there in it.

"Whew," he says. He looks up past me into the living room. "Hi, Mel. Hi, Patsy."

A man about Barry's age, twenty-three, is walking across the living room towards us in his jockey shorts. With him is a woman about the same age wearing a pink peignoir and a chiffon cap that has little bows all over it. She thrusts towards me a bottle of pink champagne. The man Barry called Mel, who is big and burly, envelopes Barry in a bear hug. "Congratulations, Feldman," he says.

"Yeah, congratulations," the woman, Patsy, says. She has a sweet smile and resembles a Pekingese.

I look at Barry. Maybe he will tell me who these people are. But he's talking to Mel.

"Come in," Patsy says. "What am I saying. It's your house. Do you guys want something to eat?" I follow Patsy into the kitchen of Barry's apartment. She opens the refrigerator door. "We've got some leftover tunafish," she says. She takes out a saucer with something yellowish in it and lifts it to her nose. "Yuck. It doesn't look too good, does it, Mel?"

Mel is at her side, opening the bottle of champagne.

Patsy takes out a half-empty can of Chun King chow mein. "I could heat up some of this," she says. "Or do you

3

want a piece of pie?" She takes out a half of a store-bought chocolate cream pie with a round indentation on the top where the tunafish saucer has been sitting on it.

"Do you eat this kind of stuff often?" I ask Patsy.

Mel loosens the cork on the champagne. I've heard about people getting their eyeballs popped out by flying corks, so I cover my face with my hands. The cork sputters about an inch from Mel's fist and falls to the floor. He pours champagne into four jelly glasses. The one I get has Archie and Veronica and Betty and Reggie on it. When I was a kid, I identified with Veronica. She was rich and beautiful and she got everything she wanted even though she wasn't nice like Betty.

"To the Feldmans!" Mel says.

We all take a sip of champagne. It tastes like Lik-m-aid.

"When did you guys get married?" Patsy asks.

"This afternoon," I say.

"Great," Mel says. "How about a game of Hearts?"

"Oka-a-y," Barry says, the last syllable drawled out lazy, the way I like it.

The apartment looks different than it did six weeks ago, the last time I flew down from New York to visit Barry. A card table has been set up in the middle of the living room. Barry and Mel pull the dining-room chairs over to it. Mel starts shuffling a deck of cards.

I take off my shoes and drop them on the carpet. I've had them on since the wedding. They are too tight and pinch. My feet show red through my nylons.

"This is our new dining-room table," Patsy says, patting the top of the card table. "Do you like it?"

"It looks like a card table to me," I say.

"We got it with the Blue Corn stamps Mel's mother gave us," Patsy says.

4

"Oh," I say.

"This is all our furniture. Except the bed, but it won't be delivered until next week."

"Is it being delivered here?" I ask. I had never seen or heard of Mel and Patsy before tonight.

"Hey, we found an apartment," Mel says to Barry. "We can move in as soon as the bed is delivered." He smiles a broad smile and spreads his hands across the air. "So we'll just be here with you two Feldmans for one more week."

"How long have you been here?" I ask.

Mel drops his hands and looks at Barry. "Feldman, didn't you tell your wife we were here?"

I'm staring across the card table at Barry. "I don't know, baby," he says. "Didn't I tell you?"

Patsy smiles a sweet and kind of sad smile at me. "Mel is going to law school with Barry," she says. She sounds like she's talking to a child. "They were at the University of Miami together. Barry said we could stay at his place until we found an apartment." She turns to Barry. "You should have told your wife, Barry."

"I knew you wouldn't mind, baby," Barry says.

Mel deals the cards. He and Patsy and Barry pick up their hands. Mel and Barry pick through their cards without looking up once. My cards lie in an untidy pile on the table in front of me.

"All r-i-i-ght," Mel says. He looks at me and the *right* fades away. "Feldman," he says. "Your wife isn't picking up her cards."

"I hate Hearts," I say.

"Feldman, your wife says she hates Hearts."

Barry looks at me. "You never told me that, baby."

Barry looks pale and tired. No one made it easy for us to get married. I bring my foot up into my lap and rub the instep where the shoe pinched. The corridor in the Birmingham airport was so long, the little heels of my shoes clickclacking beside Barry's wing tips, shuffling slightly slew-footed. I wanted to cry out in pain. I deserved to have shoes that fit. It was my wedding day.

"Come on, baby," Barry says. "Just one game, okay?"

"All right. But I'm not going to try to win."

We play five games of Hearts. Mel wins three. Barry wins two.

"Let's go to bed, Mel," Patsy says. "I've got to get up for work tomorrow."

"A couple more hands," Mel says and starts dealing.

At midnight, Patsy tugs at Mel's sleeve. "Mel, come on. I have to be at work at eight tomorrow."

Mel stands up. "Okay. I win for the night seven to six." He takes out a pen and writes something on the inside of a matchbook cover. "I'll just keep a record of the score, and we can continue tomorrow night." Mel takes a deep breath. "Good night, Feldmans," he says.

Barry and I pick up our suitcases that are still by the front door where we left them when he carried me inside.

"What are they doing here?" I whisper to Barry.

"I told Mel they could stay here until they found a place."

"Why?"

"Where else would they stay? They don't have any money."

Barry and I knock into each other as we carry our suitcases through the bedroom door. "Well," Barry says, flinging his free arm across my shoulder, "let's see what sex is like now that it's obligatory."

I lie in bed next to Barry, my feet throbbing. Barry is sleeping, one arm slung across the pillow, his mouth open. He looks too young to be married to anyone. The white curve of his bare, slender shoulder glows in the light from the terrace outside. He is breathing softly, sprawled across the bed. The angular lines in his face have slackened. Mel's and Patsy's voices come from the bedroom across the hall, carrying the intimacy that voices have when words are muffled beyond meaning. I wish I could go and sit at the foot of their bed and listen. I need to know how it's done, how to talk to someone after you've married him.

In the morning, the blue draperies pulled across the picture window turn the sunlight blue. The whole room looks blue. Barry is lying on one elbow, smoking a Lark. The lower half of his slim body curves gracefully into the blue sheets. He looks like some kind of merman.

"Good morning, baby." He leans over and kisses the inside of my elbow. "I've been thinking. You've got to start looking for a job."

"Now?"

"Well, not today. Maybe tomorrow. The two hundred my dad sends me every month isn't enough bread to live on."

I reach across Barry's chest and take one of his Larks. The first drag jolts, then firms my outline. I blow smoke into the blue room.

"Feldman. That a Jewish name?"

I am sitting across the desk from the vice-president of the Mutual Protection Life Insurance Company in downtown Birmingham. He is interviewing me for a job as a claims examiner. The way he says "Jewish" rhymes with "Hirsh." I nod.

"You Jewish?"

"My husband is."

"What church do you go to, Mrs. Feldman?"

"My family was Methodist."

The man across the desk smiles at me. "I trust you still go to your own church, don't you?"

"I'm an agnostic," I say.

"You ought to go to church, no matter. God keeps track. What line of business is your husband in?"

"He's in law school."

"Over at the Appalachia School of Law? The Harvard of the South. Lawyer's a good job for a Jewish boy. He's not one of them working for the N double A C P, is he?"

I know I don't have to answer. If I keep my mouth shut, and even if I don't, I have the kind of face that is beyond reproach.

"I see you're from up North, Mrs. Feldman. Do you intend to participate in any civil rights marches while you're down here?"

"I hate crowds," I say.

"I beg your pardon."

"I don't like crowds."

"Well, I am telling you, Mrs. Feldman, that if I see you on the television or any other way find out that you are involved in any of them civil rights demonstrations, you will not have a job here at Mutual Protection Life."

Outside the Mutual Protection Life Insurance building, Barry is pulled up at the curb in his white Chevy Supersport. He reaches across the front seat and swings the door open. The car radio is on, and he's tapping his index finger in the air along with the melody to some tune.

When I get in, Barry leans towards me and forms an arc around me with his arms. He is smiling. He gives me a big smack on the cheek, then leans back against the door on his side of the car and says, "Wel-l-l-l-l?"

I bring one of my feet into my lap and take off my shoe. Then I throw it to the floor of the car. I take off the other shoe and throw it. I watch my toes wiggle around in my nylons.

Barry takes my foot into his hand and rubs it. "Did you get the job, baby?"

I take my foot back. I look around at the red leather upholstery in the Supersport, at Barry smoking his Lark, tapping his fingers on the steering wheel. "What do we need this car for? It looks like it belongs to a pimp. Let's sell it and get a Volkswagen."

"This is a better car, baby."

"So what? All a car is for is to get from one place to another. What difference does it make which is better?"

"I'll have to think about that," Barry says. He turns the key in the ignition, then turns it off again. He looks at me. "Well," he says. This time the *well* is not long and lazy and smiling. "Did you get the job or not?"

"Uh huh."

"Uh huh or uh uh?" Barry turns the key in the ignition, presses down on the accelerator, and pulls away from the curb.

"Uh *huh*."

"Really? That's great!"

"It is?"

"Yeah, sure. How much?"

"I got the job because I used to be Methodist."

"I didn't know that was a marketable skill," Barry says. "How much?"

"Sixty."

Barry thinks for a minute. "Do you think sixty is the best you can do? Patsy makes eighty-five."

"Patsy has shorthand and steno. I have Shakespeare and Sartre."

"Right." He pauses, reaches over and ruffles my hair. "We sure could use that extra twenty-five, though." Then he laughs. "Uh, you save France, I'll wash up."

It's Mel Brooks, our favorite line. The 2,000-year-old man said it to Joan of Arc.

"My wife got a job," Barry says to Mel and Patsy. Mel is sitting at the card table, a hand of Solitaire dealt out in front of him. Patsy is in the kitchen.

"Congratulations," Patsy says.

Barry sits down across from Mel at the card table. Mel picks up his cards and deals out two hands of Gin. I throw my shoes down on the carpet.

"Thanks," I say to Patsy.

"We'll have to celebrate," she says. "I'll make stuffed cabbage."

After dinner, Mel and Patsy and Barry and I sit down at the card table. Mel takes the matchbook out of his pocket and announces, "Steingut, twenty-four; Feldman, twenty-two." He pronounces the twenty-two carefully, putting emphasis on the second *two,* looking right at Barry with a big smile.

That means in the six days Barry and I have been married, we have played forty-six games of Hearts with Mel and Patsy, and neither Patsy nor I has won one game. Patsy doesn't win because she is kind of stupid, and she doesn't know how to play cards. I don't know why I don't win.

We're on our second game when Bruce and Susie come

in. Bruce is wearing one of his tight knit shirts and his pointy Italian loafers. Susie's blond hair is tumbling over one eye, and she's looking down. Her hands are thrust into the pockets of a long sweater she's wearing over her jeans. Susie and Bruce and Barry and I would hang out together when I came to stay with Barry in Birmingham, first for the weekend, then a week, then three. They're our best friends and this is the first time we've seen them since Barry and I got married. So I figure she could look a little more celebratory.

"How ya doin', Grease," Barry says to Bruce.

"We just got back from the Beach, man," Bruce says. "The Boom Boom Room."

"Wild bananas," Barry says. "Was anybody playing in Miami? Ira Sullivan or anybody?" He starts rapping on the card table with his fingers and scatting in his high breathless voice.

Bruce turns to Mel. "Another Jew-boy in B-ham. What law school did you flunk out of, Steingut?"

"Did you catch Ira?" Barry says.

"Come on, Feldman, let's finish this hand," Mel says.

Bruce goes into the kitchen and pours our bourbon into our glasses. "What have you got to mix this stuff with?" he calls out.

"There's some Kool-Aid in the refrigerator," I say.

Barry turns to me. "Shit, I asked him twice if anyone was playing in Miami."

Bruce passes out drinks that are muddy purple from the bourbon and the grape Kool-Aid mixed together.

Susie is sitting in the corner of the couch, flipping through a copy of *Playboy*. "How was your trip?" I ask her.

"All right," she says without looking up.

Bruce pulls a chair up to the card table and leans over

towards Mel. "Nobody just decides to come to the Appalachia School of Law in Birmingham, Alabama. You're got to flunk out of someplace else first, man. This is the end of the road."

Mel looks at the hands lying on the card table. "Okay, Feldman. Since you're losing twenty-four to twenty-three, I'll be generous and call this one a draw." He turns to Bruce. "Appalachia is the only law school I got into that wasn't in North Dakota."

"You must be dumber than I am," Bruce says.

"Mel isn't dumb," Patsy says. She looks insulted and scared.

"Mel thought the library at the University of Miami was on the handball courts," Barry says. He starts to giggle.

"What were you doing there, Feldman? It looked very much to me like you were playing handball."

"I played my way right out of the University of Miami law school," Barry says. "I never could have made it there. There were too many distractions."

"You don't have that problem here," I say.

"Yeah," Barry says. "But you could die here. I was dying here, baby." He looks at me and smiles. "You saved me."

"Let's get some atmosphere in here," Bruce says. "Susie and I just got back from the Beach."

Susie doesn't look up from her *Playboy*.

Bruce goes over to Barry's three-piece portable cardboard stereo that he got for his bar mitzvah. "Nice set you got here," he says. He puts on "The Girl from Ipanema." I gave Barry the album before we got married.

"Stan *Getz?*" Barry says. "Shit, Grease. Getz isn't happening. How about Bill Evans? Or Herbie? Paul Bley? Miles, even?"

12

Bruce leaves on the Stan Getz. Then he goes around the living room, turning off lights. When he gets to the lamp on the end table where Susie is flipping through *Playboy*, she says, "Come on, Bruce. I'm reading." She grabs his arm to stop him from turning off the lamp. He brushes her hand away and turns off the lamp, anyway. She sits in the dark, looking down at the magazine in her lap.

Bruce pours more of the bourbon into his glass and comes over to the card table. "Are the grades posted yet?" he asks Barry.

"I don't know."

"You must have been up at school since you got back. Are the grades posted yet or not?"

"I don't know," Barry says. "I didn't look."

"You didn't look?"

"I forgot."

"He forgot. Will you drive me up to the school tomorrow? If I didn't pass Torts, I don't need to unpack."

"Okay."

"You'll give me a ride?"

"How did you get to school all last semester?"

Barry gets up and pulls me up with him. We play around at dancing. He dips me down to the floor. We hang on each other and shuffle around one corner of the living room, American Bandstand style. Bruce sticks his face in between our two. He says, "I think I failed Torts."

Barry doesn't answer.

"Really, Bruce?" I say.

Barry groans and lets me go. He puts one arm around my shoulder and kind of hangs there, watching me and Bruce. Bruce reaches out his hand to me and flashes a big smile. "Hello, Mrs. Feldman. I see you don't have a vacuum cleaner in the house. No homemaker should be without an Electrolux. Now if you'll sign on the dotted line —"

"Baby, you wouldn't let a grease-ball like him into the house while I'm gone, would you?" Barry says. He's smiling.

I light a cigarette and drink more bourbon. Bruce goes over to Susie and pulls her up off the couch. She doesn't fight him, but she doesn't help him either. The way he has to work to get her off the couch makes it look like she weighs three hundred pounds. The two of them dance, Bruce doing some fancy steps and Susie just standing there, smoking. Patsy has moved her chair next to Mel's. They have their feet up on the card table and are holding hands. The bourbon is making my head mushy. I can hardly make out Mel's and Patsy's faces.

Barry sinks into a chair and pulls me down onto his lap. He kisses me on the neck. "Baby," he says. "You really make me hot."

I blow cigarette smoke into his ear and play with the hair in the V of his sweater, my fingers icy and wet from my glass. I bury my head in Barry's shoulder. His skin is so smooth, so cool. He is moving his hand up and down my back in a slow rhythmic motion. Then it stops short.

"Oh, baby," he says. His voice is high and breathless. "Don't get up, baby." He shifts a little to one side in the chair, closes his eyes for a few seconds, then opens them. "Whew," he says. Now he's smiling.

"How did you do it?" I ask him.

"I imagined my mother's face. When I was a kid and got a hard-on looking at girlie books in the drugstore, I closed my eyes and imagined my mother's face, and the hard-on went away."

Bruce comes over and puts his arm around Barry. "It's all over," he says. "I failed Torts. I know it."

I get up and go over and sit down next to Susie on the floor. "What did you and Bruce do in Miami?" I ask her.

She doesn't say anything.

I stare at our four legs stretched out in front of us on the carpet. Hers are pale and soft around the ankles. Mine are deep brown in diamond-patterned nylons. The diamonds dance up and down. I jiggle the ice around in my glass and blow some smoke rings.

"I just broke up with Bruce in the car on the way over here," Susie says.

"What happened?" I say.

"I just don't love him, I guess. You know I slept with Barry New Year's Eve, don't you? I told Bruce, and he's not being cool about it. I mean, it was over a month ago and he's still fighting with me about it. He says he feels like he's being compared to Barry all the time."

I picture the burning end of my cigarette plunging through the dark into Susie's white ankle and held there while her skin smolders. "Oh," I say.

"If I had really loved him, I wouldn't have slept with Barry, Bruce says. I don't think I ever really loved Bruce. I liked hanging around with you and Barry. Barry's great.

"Bruce tried to slug me tonight. You wouldn't stay with Barry if he tried to slug you, would you?"

"I don't know. It depends."

Susie is one or two inches away from me on the carpet. I could grab the hoop of her pierced ear and rip it out through the fleshy lobe.

★   ★   ★

"Do you think Susie is sexy?" I ask Barry. Mel and Patsy are sleeping in the bedroom across the hall. I can hear Mel snoring. Barry is lying on his back in the dark with one arm flung over his forehead.

"I think I'm drunk, baby," Barry says.

"Do you think she's sexy?"

"Who?"

"Susie."

"Not especially."

"Not especially?"

"She's kind of fat."

"That doesn't bother Bruce."

"Oh, she's okay for Grease, baby, but not for me."

"Then why did you sleep with her New Year's Eve?"

"Did she tell you that? That pisses me off."

"Why didn't you tell me?"

"I don't know, baby. It wasn't important."

"It's important to me."

"No one else was in Birmingham. She came over with a bottle of champagne, and we watched the ball go down on TV. You weren't here. Hey, wait a minute, baby. Where were you? Oh, yeah. You were in New York. You told me to call Susie."

"I didn't tell you to sleep with her."

"I didn't want to, baby."

"Then why did you?"

"She wanted me to."

"You slept with her because she wanted you to?"

"Baby, we were watching TV in bed, and she took off all her clothes and started sucking my cock. I didn't want to do it. I don't think I even came."

"You don't remember?"

"It was late. I just wanted to go to sleep."

"Did she stay all night?"

"I don't know. I went to sleep. She was gone when I woke up."

"Did you see her again?"

"Why would I want to do that?"

Barry reaches his hand out to touch my cheek, and I turn my head away. His hand brushes air. "Barry, how could you do it? Susie was my only friend down here."

"You can still be friends with her."

"No I can't."

"Why not?"

"Because I hate her guts."

Barry falls into a drunken sleep. I lie awake and out of the bourbon haze emerges a fall day. Barry and I pull into a parking space at a bookstore on the outskirts of Birmingham. He stays in the car with the motor running. The radio is on. He is smiling. I am wearing jeans and a bandana over my long hair. I walk past the thin spines of the books I have been reading this summer — J. P. Donleavy, André Gide, García Lorca — and pick out a *Better Homes and Gardens Cookbook* with a red-and-white-checked cover like a picnic tablecloth.

My marriage to Barry will be a triumph of ideals and honesty. My body is weightless. Anything is possible. I fly into the parking lot. "I love you, Feldman!" I cry.

After dinner we go to bed on the blue sheets.

"Look," I say. "Your knees are bald." We laugh. We have been together for two weeks, and Barry has rubbed all the hair off his knees.

He pushes me down on the sheets. He pins my arms down, then he makes me slap my face with my hands.

17

"Why are you hitting yourself, baby?" he says. He's smiling. Then he kisses my eyelids, my cheeks, my ears. He throws the sheer salmon top of my baby-doll pajamas over my face and slips into me. As he moves on top of me, he is not heavy, he is smooth, and through the salmon veil I watch him, his eyes open, staring at something beyond me, and I feel chosen.

"Promise me we'll never lie to each other," I say when we're lying side by side, feeling the cool air from the window flow over our separate bodies.

"Why would I ever lie to you, baby?" he says.

I can't think of one reason why.

The next morning, I wake up when Mel and Patsy jump onto our bed.

"Guess what?" Patsy says. "Pizitz just called. Our bed is being delivered today." She looks at Mel. "Just think, honey, our very own bed."

Mel is shuffling a deck of cards. "How about a few rounds of Hearts before we move out?" He starts dealing the cards onto the blue sheets.

"We've got to pack, Mel," Patsy says.

"That will take a couple minutes." He looks at his watch. "The bed is not being delivered until this afternoon. It's ten o'clock now. We can play until noon."

I reach over Barry for a cigarette. "I just woke up," I say.

"That's the best time to play Hearts," Mel says.

At noon, Mel has won five hands and Barry has won five. Patsy gets up and pulls at Mel's T-shirt. "I don't want to miss the delivery truck, honey."

Mel is dealing out another hand. He lights a cigarette.

"Steingut, twenty-nine; Feldman, twenty-eight. Delivery trucks are never on time."

At 1:15, Patsy says, "I'm going to pack, Mel." Her voice is so high it sounds like it's going to break. She goes across the hall to the other bedroom.

"How about three-handed?" Mel says. "We can play Patsy's hand face-down."

I get out of bed and stretch. Mel deals out two hands of Gin to Barry and himself.

At 1:30 Patsy is in the hall outside the bedroom with her coat on and a suitcase in each hand.

Mel and Barry go into the living room and collapse the four legs of the card table, then carry it out to the parking lot and put it in the back seat of Mel and Patsy's secondhand Mustang.

Barry and I stand in the front door and wave good-bye. Patsy smiles and waves from her seat. Mel pauses at his side of the car before he gets in. His arm lifts up in a swift arc. "Good-bye, Feldmans," he yells.

He gets in the car and starts the engine. The Mustang begins to pull away. I don't know why I feel so sad all of a sudden. Fifteen feet out of the parking lot, the car stops. Mel's head appears over the roof of the car. "Come on over tonight," he yells. "We'll play a couple rounds of Hearts."

Smoking and drinking bourbon and Kool-Aid, Barry and I are lying naked on the blue sheets, a deep subterranean blue because all the lights are out except Barry's tensor lamp on the dresser. Jazz is playing on the radio, the only jazz you can get in Birmingham, Alabama, all week. Ten to midnight Saturday night. Barry says he's a hardcore jazzer, and jazz is what we are all about, even though I don't know anything about jazz. When Barry got out of college, he drove his beat-up Valiant straight to San Francisco to hear Denny Zeitlin at the Trident. All summer he jammed in the bars at night and when summer was over, his father bought him the Supersport and sent him to law school. I married the Barry who drove across country to hear a good tune, even though I didn't know him then.

Barry knows the deejay, Ray Whiteman. His voice is low and syrupy. Ray raps between tunes. He's saying, "The other day I got a call from a man who asked me to play some John Coltrane 'Lush Life,' and I said sure, naturally. The man says, 'You know, I'm a white man.' So I say, 'Hey, buddy, I'm a white man, too, *Ray* Whiteman.' "

"Fucking Ray," Barry says. "He's beautiful."

I reach for my pack of Marlboros. There aren't any left, so I crumple the pack and take one of Barry's Larks. Barry lights it for me, and I blow smoke into his face. I feel warm from the bourbon and the jazz and the blue sheets and Barry's smell of burnt toast and Jade East.

Barry gets on top of me, whispering into my hair. "I love you, baby. You're my wife. You're my family. You're my family, baby. That's so sexy."

The sheets are a deep blue, the spot of light from the tensor lamp shuttles back and forth in the dark as Barry fucks me, his burned toast Jade East smell soaked in sweat. This is why I'm here, but something has been taken away. With one hand I'm clutching onto the side of the mattress to keep myself from being moved.

Later, Barry puts two cigarettes in his mouth, lights them, and hands one to me.

The Lark is a funny-tasting cigarette. "I wish I had a Marlboro," I say.

Barry brushes a strand of wet hair from my forehead. "I'll switch to Marlboros, baby," he says.

A piano piece comes on, and Barry sits straight up on the bed. He sits there listening, not moving. When the tune is over, he says, "That's Denny Zeitlin. He kills me." He pulls the phone onto the sheets and dials.

"Ray," Barry says. "Denny Zeitlin in B-ham. You're too much." Barry laughs his high, reckless giggle. Then he says, "I got married, man. Uh huh. Sally. Gorgeous. To distraction. Yeah. Bill Evans. 'Always.' "

Ray Whiteman's voice comes on. "Hey, my good friend and fellow jazzophile, who's now pursuing jewishprudence, sorry, Barry, uhm, jurisprudence, here in Birmingham, just called and told me he got married. Her name is Sally. He says he loves her to distraction. For Barry and Sally, Bill Evans' 'Always.' " Ray pauses between the syllables in the song title, drops his voice an octave, and swings into the tune.

It sounds strange to hear my name on the radio in Ray Whiteman's molasses voice, announcing my marriage in a city where nobody knows me. Barry is lying on his back, smoking, his free arm flung across my breast. He moves his long, bony fingers on my skin as if it were a keyboard and he were playing "Always" along with Bill Evans. His eyes are closed, and his smile is so pure he looks like Christ or a madman.

At 9:30 the next morning the phone rings, waking me up. Something about Ray Whiteman and the phone goes through my head, and I think maybe he's calling to say there was some mistake last night or something. But it's Mel. "Hey, Feldmans. Come on over for bagels and cream cheese. We can't afford lox."

Mel and Patsy's apartment is unfurnished. The living room is empty except for Mel's law books stacked up on the carpet next to the wall and a thick white leather album that has gold wedding bells and *Patsy and Mel, September 15, 1965* embossed on the cover. The card table, with no chairs, is set up in the dining alcove.

Patsy smiles, looking around at her new home. "Well, what do you think of it?"

"It's nice, Patsy," I say. "It's really nice. Where do you eat?"

"Oh, in bed. Until we get chairs."

Patsy has a sweet smile and a very small head. When she goes out, she looks normal because she wears her hair in a bouffant hair-do. But when we see her, like now, her hair is usually in rollers, and her head looks small.

"My wife is a freak," Mel says, referring to her small head in rollers.

"Mel!" Patsy looks stricken.

"Just joking, honey," Mel says.

Mel and Barry go into the bedroom and start playing Gin on the electric blanket. Patsy and I go into the kitchen to get the bagels and cream cheese.

"We couldn't afford a furnished apartment like yours," Patsy says, "because Mel doesn't get any money from his father like Barry does. We have to live on my salary."

"But the apartment is really nice," I say.

Patsy turns and looks around. She looks lost. "I don't even have a candy dish," she says. "I'm married, and I don't even have a candy dish."

"What's that?"

"You know, a candy dish. A glass dish you leave out with candy in it."

"Oh." I don't recall ever having seen one.

At 5:00 Barry picks me up at the Mutual Protection Life Insurance Company, and we drive straight to the Piggly Wiggly. Barry wheels the cart while I walk beside him. He leans over, kisses me on the cheek, and smashes into a pyramid of canned soups. We are looking for something for dinner.

Barry knows how to cook one thing: hamburgers with chopped onion and Worcestershire sauce. I don't know how to cook anything. Barry and I start up one wide, long aisle, the shelves of groceries fanning out on both sides. In front of us a short, squat woman is picking things from the shelves, looking at them, and then putting them back or tossing them into her basket. I wonder what she is looking at. I walk down the aisle with Barry pushing our empty cart.

"What did your mother cook?" Barry pauses, then says, "Never mind."

He doesn't want to have anything to do with my mother, for good reason. I ignore the "never mind" and say, "She cooked steak and lamb chops. I don't know how she did it. We never discussed it."

"We can't afford steak or lamb chops."

The woman with the cart in front of us is at the meat counter. She is picking up cellophane-wrapped packages that have some parts of chicken in them. I pick one up, too. "Excuse me," I say to the woman. "I was just wondering. How do you cook these?"

The woman turns to me and answers matter-of-factly. "Oh, I just wrap them up in aluminum foil with some butter and Lowry's Seasoned Salt and bake them at three hundred and fifty degrees for one hour."

"Would you write that down, Barry?"

Barry takes his pen out of his shirt pocket where he carries two or three pens and writes the recipe down on the inside of his Marlboro flip top box.

"Thank you," I say to the woman.

She is looking at Barry and me, and all of a sudden she smiles. "Oh, you two are newlyweds. Isn't that wonderful. Oh, Bill," she calls, and a tall man lopes over towards us. "These two young people are newlyweds, Bill. I just gave them my recipe for that baked chicken you like so much." She turns back to Barry and me. "Bill and I have been married for thirty years, and we are as happy as the day we were married."

"That's wild," Barry says.

We round the corner to frozen foods. "Isn't that great," I say.

"Oh, yeah, baby. They're still happy after thirty years."

"I meant about the chicken."

Saturday morning Barry and I are getting ready to go to the Laundromat. We are both inside the walk-in closet, tossing things into the green plastic laundry basket. I only have three things to wear, because I'm waiting for my mother to send my clothes. Barry and I got married in kind of a hurry.

"Barry, if I could wear your pants and a shirt, I could wash all of my things," I say.

"Sure, babe." He plucks a shirt from the closet and looks at it. "Hmmmn," he says. "I'd say blue is your color."

Barry tosses me the blue shirt and a pair of slacks. I put on the shirt, but I can't pull the slacks past my hips. "I guess this wasn't such a good idea," I say.

"I'll start wearing my shirts for two days, so you won't have to iron them so often," Barry says. He sniffs at the underarm of one and throws it into the basket. "I hate wearing a shirt twice."

"Who ironed them before?"

"I sent them out. We can't afford that now."

"How much did it cost?"

"A quarter a shirt. It adds up."

"Barry, do you remember that song, 'Leader of the Laundromat?' It was a takeoff on 'Leader of the Pack.' The girl is in love with this guy who drives the laundry truck and when he crashes, there's dirty laundry all over the highway."

"Nope. I don't listen to rock, baby. You know that."

"It's real funny."

"It sounds funny, baby."

The laundry basket is full. Barry squats down to pick it up. I look at myself in the mirror over the dresser. Barry says I look like Donna Michelle, the Playmate of the Year. She has big breasts, of course, and a face hard with makeup. In the mirror in Barry's shirt, I look more like Barry than like Donna Michelle.

Barry puts down the laundry basket. "Where's my keys, baby?"

"I don't know," I say, but look around the surfaces of the room and see them on the dresser. I pick them up. They feel heavy and solid in my palm. I wonder why Barry has so many keys. I don't have any. I start to hand them to him, but draw back my hand. "Barry, let's get out of Birmingham. Let's just leave. Let's move to New York and live in the Village."

Barry throws his Torts book into the laundry basket on top of the blue sheets. "How would we live, baby?"

"I don't know. I could get a job. You could play piano in a cocktail lounge or something. We could go to hear Bill Evans. He's probably at the Vanguard right now. There are radio stations that play jazz twenty-four hours a day."

"Come on, baby. Give me the keys."

"Barry, listen. I have the five hundred from my father, and you have the bonds from your mother. We can sell the Supersport."

Barry holds out his palm for the keys. I give them to him. He picks up the basket of laundry like a weight lifter, legs wide apart, knees bent. "It's only two more years, baby. I'll be a first-rate shyster. We'll live in Miami and buy a sailboat."

On the way out with the laundry, Barry balances the basket on one hip and sweeps up the mail from the living-room floor. There is a *Village Voice* and a thick envelope from Barry's father. Barry tosses them on top of the laundry.

At the Laundromat, I stare at the front page of the *Village Voice,* then at the row of Bendix commercial washing machines. The *Village Voice* looks odd to me here in a Birmingham, Alabama, Laundromat. I had sent Barry the subscription while I was living in the Village. I thought he would like the jazz column, but he didn't read it. "Do you want me to renew the subscription?" I ask him.

Barry looks up from the letter from his father. "What, baby?"

26

"Do you want me to renew the subscription to the *Village Voice*?"

"If you want to. It has mostly stuff about New York, though, and we don't live there."

I turn the pages and look at the ads for places I can't go to. I check the jazz page to see if Bill Evans is playing at the Vanguard. He's not. I put the paper down and through the porthole watch our laundry slosh around inside the machine.

"Look at this, baby," Barry says. He hands me two articles cut out of the Miami newspaper. One is about local politics, and the other is about a Florida Supreme Court judge. "I wish he wouldn't keep sending me these things," Barry says.

"What did your father say in the letter?"

"Oh, he said to say hi to you."

"What else did he say about me?"

"He said he hoped my being married didn't interfere with my studying."

"That's nice," I say. "What else?"

Barry doesn't say anything.

"Did he say anything about kicking five thousand years of history in the face?"

Barry holds the letter with the tips of his fingers and shakes open its folds. He clears his throat. " 'Dear Barry, I'm pleased you and Sally were able to find a suitable one-bedroom apartment' blah blah blah —"

He lets out a low whistle. "That's about it, baby."

I reach for the letter, and Barry hands it to me. I skim over a few paragraphs about Barry's family and see my name again at the end of the letter: "As you know, I am gravely disappointed in your marriage. I concede that Sally is an attractive, intelligent girl, but you two kids have an attitude that you can do as you please. But the world will not let you.

"You are married now, and I accept Sally as a member of our family as I would accept any girl you chose as your wife. If you continue to do well in school, I am certain my disappointment will steadily decrease. Even now I look forward to the day that you pass the Florida bar, and the three of us are celebrating together."

I stare at Barry's father's neatly typed letter. "I guess we're not going to hear Bill Evans at the Vanguard so soon," I say.

Barry shakes his head. "He's got me by the balls, baby."

Barry and I are asleep when the telephone rings. Barry answers it, then passes the receiver to me. "It's your mother," he says. He reaches for a cigarette, and I mime smoking one, so he'll pass me one, too.

"Hello, Mother."

"How's Mrs. Feldman?" my mother says. The way she says my new name makes my stomach muscles lock.

"Did you send my clothes yet, Mother?"

"Buy new ones."

I take a drag on the cigarette. "You know we don't have the money for me to buy new clothes. I need my clothes. I've been wearing the same three things to work."

"You should have thought of that before you got married."

"Mother, would you please send my things REA Express? All you have to do is put them in a trunk, and they'll pick them up at the house."

"Your father doesn't want me to have anything to do

with you. I had to wait until he went to sleep to call you."

"May I speak to him, Mother?"

"Your father refuses to talk to you. Especially after what happened today. Does this sound familiar to you? 'Baby, I love the hell out of you. I miss your breasts, your thighs, your cunt. I love fucking you, baby.' Shall I go on?"

Barry is sitting up in bed, smoking. One leg is crossed over the other. His legs are bony, but graceful. I motion to him for another cigarette. "You have no right to read my mail, Mother."

"You should have thought of that before you left the letter in your dresser drawer."

I see my white and gold dresser, the drawer open, and the letter: contorted black script on a legal sheet.

"How do you think your father felt when he read it?"

"You showed it to Father?"

"Well, I felt I had to."

"Why did you have to? Why did you have to read it in the first place?"

" 'I love fucking you, baby.' How does that make you feel, you whore?"

"Mother, Barry and I are married. We have a nice apartment. He is in law school, and I have a job. I need my clothes."

"Your father and I don't like short men. How can you stand sleeping with that short man?"

"Barry is five-seven, Mother. I've got to go."

"I think your father broke one of my ribs." She pauses. "He blames me for your marriage."

Step on a crack, break your mother's back. I can't think of anything that rhymes with rib.

"Go to a doctor," I say.

I hand Barry the receiver.

"What a bitch," he says.

"Leave her alone." I can't tell Barry my father hits my mother. I don't want him to know that about me.

He says, "When I answered the phone, she said, 'May I speak to Sally Adams?' "

"I think she's been drinking."

"I'm sorry, baby." Barry reaches for my breast, and I push his hand away.

He turns his back to me. His back is smooth, like a young boy's. I slide down the blue sheets on my stomach and pull the blankets up to my neck. "I'm sorry, Barry. I don't know. I'm sorry. Just don't touch me, okay?"

"What else did she say, baby?"

"She won't send my clothes."

"Make some points with Professor Simpson's wife," Barry says.

Patsy is picking me up to go to a meeting of the Law School Wives' Club. She has her hair teased into a big cloud around her face and is wearing nylons and three-inch heels. I wear nylons, too, but I refuse to wear three-inch heels.

"Are you sure you want to go to this thing?" I ask Patsy. "We could skip it and go to the K mart instead."

"Come on. It'll be fun. There's a speaker, you should like that, and then coffee and cookies."

"Why would I like a speaker?"

"Because you're so intellectual. You're always reading books. Mel thinks you're so smart."

"Yeah, but look what he's got to compare me to." I realize what I just said and say, "I mean, Barry and Mel are always talking about how dumb all these southern crackers are. Anyone else looks smart."

"I know what you meant. Mel thinks I'm stupid. I know that. But I can cook and make eighty-five dollars a week, so he doesn't care."

"It doesn't bother you that he thinks you're stupid?"

Patsy shrugs. "I *am* stupid."

The speaker is Mr. James Roy Porter, a Birmingham attorney. He stands on the stage of the auditorium in front of the thirty or forty law school wives who are sitting with their legs crossed and their hands folded in their laps. He is talking about pornography and how it's bad. He holds up a copy of *Playboy*. "Young ladies," he says, "this magazine is being sold on the newsstands and in the stores in Birmingham, Alabama. Children are forced to see the covers of magazines like this when they go to buy their candy." He opens the *Playboy* to the centerfold of Donna Michelle.

"Barry thinks I look like her," I say to Patsy.

She turns to me. "Maybe your face a little."

It takes Mr. James Roy Porter forty-five minutes to go through his collection of pornography in front of us law school wives. He stacks his books and magazines in one neat pile and puts them back into his briefcase. I think he is finished, but he clutches the empty lectern at its sides and stares straight out at us.

"You fine young women and future mothers of Alabama, I hesitate to show you this last demonstration of filth that is being disseminated throughout our state." He pulls something out from the shelf underneath the lectern, and holds up in front of us a large, glossy magazine. On the cover is a photograph of a Negro man and a white woman, both naked as Adam and Eve, holding hands. Mr. James Roy Porter doesn't say anything for several seconds. Then he turns to the inside of the magazine and spreads it open across his chest. There is a photograph of the Negro man and the white woman kissing.

"This is a magazine they call *Eros,* which is a Greek word for filth. Now what kind of man, if you can call him a man, would print and sell this magazine? Well, I'll tell you. A man by the name of Ginsberg. What kind of name is that, I ask you. And you ought to know that this Mr. Ginsberg and men like him are being supported by the United States government. Any man, woman, or child — and it could be your child — with the price of a copy can have this magazine delivered to his home right through the United States government mails."

"I thought this was going to be intellectual," I whisper to Patsy.

"Sssh," she says.

Mr. James Roy Porter places the magazine solidly on the lectern. "Now we in Alabama know that the United States government does not always have the same interests as the state of Alabama. I think we can say that the United States government is more interested in the Ginsbergs and those other Yankees who are intent on driving the United States of America straight to hell, pardon my French, young ladies, and taking the state of Alabama along for the ride.

"As wives of the future lawyers of our state and mothers of our children, you must enlist your husbands' support in eradicating the pornography that is threatening the lives of every family in Alabama. I thank you. You are fine young women."

"Don't count on it," I say.

"Clap," Patsy says.

We follow the other women out of the auditorium.

"Let's get some cookies," Patsy says. "That's the best part."

Patsy heads for the table set with silver trays of cookies arranged in concentric circles. She looks around at the other women in their nylons and high heels, and when no one is looking, she stuffs a handful of cookies into her purse. "They're for Mel," she says, then takes one from the plate for herself and eats it.

I look for Mr. James Roy Porter. He is standing in the middle of a clump of us fine young women. He doesn't look as tall as he did on stage, and his eyes are hard behind his steel-rimmed glasses. I peel my nametag off my sweater. I don't want to give Mr. James Roy Porter the satisfaction of seeing a name so close to Ginsberg pasted on my chest. When there's a break in the circle, I go up to him.

"*Playboy* publishes some of the best writers in the country," I say.

"Why, how do you do, Mrs. —" I don't supply the end of his sentence for him, but Mr. James Roy Porter goes on, anyway. "I am not talking about the writing in *Playboy*. I am talking about the pictures in *Playboy*. I assure you, ma'am, I do not read *Playboy*."

Mr. James Roy Porter smiles right at me, and I smile back at him. "You should," I say.

Patsy is driving me home. "The point is, Patsy, he should read it. He should at least read the magazine. He only looks at the pictures, he says. That man has seen more dirty pictures than any other man in the state of Alabama."

Patsy reaches into her purse. "Here," she says. "Take one of the cookies I stole for Mel. He should be on a diet anyway. So should I. Take some home for Barry, too. He looks like he's starving to death."

"I give him Carnation Instant Breakfast every morning. Chocolate Marshmallow is his favorite flavor. But, seriously, didn't that creep bother you?"

Patsy sighs. "I don't care about the same things as you. It's just something to do, meet some of the other wives, have some cookies and coffee. I just want Mel to get good grades and graduate, so we can move back to Florida. He'll be a lawyer, and I can stop working. I'll be able to buy a candy dish."

"Is it worth it?"

Patsy looks at me with a funny little smile. "Oh, yeah, sure! Are you kidding?"

"But I don't want a candy dish."

"You don't?"

I stop in the doorway of the examining room. Barry is sitting with his legs hanging over the steel table. A white gown is thrown across his chest. The doctor is standing over him in slacks and a golf shirt. "Come on in, Mrs. Feldman," he says. It seems odd that whenever I hear *Mrs. Feldman,* I nod or get up or if it's a question, say *yes.* I don't know why I am being called into the examining room. Barry is the one who has something wrong with him.

The doctor turns to me and starts talking about Barry as if he weren't right there, sitting between us. He tells me that Barry has developed an infection near his anus where he had a cyst removed two months ago. I nod to the doctor and wait for him to get to the point.

"Now I know your husband is a law student," he says, "and so I'm guessing you might be short on money. The infection needs to be cleaned out every day until it heals. If your husband comes to me to have it done, it will cost ten dollars a visit. But the procedure is so simple, you could do it for him at home."

I don't know what I'm supposed to say.

Barry says, "I don't know, baby. I don't know if I want you to have to do that for me."

I ask the doctor how long it will take to heal, and he says a couple of weeks. I start to make a calculation, but I know the figure is going to come out way too high.

"We're talking one hundred and fifty dollars, baby," Barry says.

I plug Barry's tensor lamp into the socket by the night table, arrange my eyebrow tweezers, a box of Q-tips, a bottle of peroxide, and a box of sterile gauze pads on the night table. Barry is sitting naked on the blue sheets, looking down at his feet. His toes are like his fingers, long and bony, the skin on his feet a light, smooth tan even in winter. I feel a wave of nausea, and I put my hand on the night table to steady myself. For a week, I have been having a sort of *mal de mer*, only there is no *mer* anywhere near Birmingham. I take a deep breath.

Barry looks up. "Are you sick again, baby? Are you sure you're taking your pill?"

I nod.

"Are you sure, baby? Are you sure you haven't missed a day?"

"There are numbers on the dial to keep track."

"Maybe you're one of the one percent, baby. Maybe the pill doesn't work for you."

"I'm not pregnant, Barry."

"How do you know?"

I twist the top off the bottle of peroxide. "Okay, let's get this over with." Barry whirls around at me. It isn't how I meant to sound. It just came out that way.

Barry gets down on all fours on the blue sheets. I shine the tensor lamp onto his ass. The surface of the scar tissue is shiny pink on the edges. In the middle, white pus with a hardened yellow crust. I have been married to Barry for only two weeks. I should be on my honeymoon, lying on a chaise on the beach, sipping a tall drink. I should have a hotel room with a view of swaying palm trees.

I take out a Q-tip and dip it into the peroxide, then run it along the line of pus. Stiff, black hairs are beginning to sprout near the infection. "Don't move," I say to Barry. I press down on the shiny new skin with the fingers of my left hand, and with my right, pluck the hairs with my tweezers the way the doctor showed me. I swab the skin with peroxide, pulling the skin away from the anus. The skin there is red and raw, mushy. I catch my breath.

I tape on the sterile gauze pad, but I know that tomorrow there will be more pus, more hairs. Barry is on his elbows and knees, his head on his hands. I wonder why he doesn't get up. His shoulders are shaking slightly, like a shiver. He's crying.

"I was very careful," I say. I'm still clutching the tweezers in my hand.

Barry swings his legs over the bed and stands in front of me, his symmetrical chest, his bony legs, his perfect penis below the smooth black hair. "You hated doing it," he says. "You hate me."

I pick up the things from the night table and carry them into the bathroom. I did hate it, but I did it anyway. But Barry wants me to like it. I can't like it, so he will make me feel awful. He will make me feel like a walking cyst, a five-foot-four, 110-pound cyst, oozing pus and sprouting hard black hairs.

Barry and I are moving to the other side of town to a one-bedroom apartment that is just like our two-bedroom apartment Barry had shared with a roommate before we got married, only the rent is $75 a month cheaper. The same real estate company owns both apartment buildings, and all the apartments are the same. We don't bother to drive over to see the new apartment. Barry takes it over the phone.

I'm taking all the food out of the kitchen cabinets and putting it into shopping bags. In the back of one cabinet, I find an open box of marshmallow Dixie Pies. "Where did these things come from?" I say. I hold the box above the garbage can.

"I thought I told Darlene to throw all her stuff out," Barry says.

I drop the box into the garbage. "Dixie Pies. Classy."

"What can I say, baby? Darlene was nowhere."

"Do you still see her at school?"

"She's in the cafeteria sometimes, if that's what you mean."

"Do you talk to her?"

Barry laughs his short, unfunny laugh that sounds like a cough. "Baby, I didn't talk to her even when I was screwing her." He takes a grocery bag of food out to the car. When he comes back, I'm standing in the kitchen, smoking a cigarette, flicking my ashes into the garbage can. Barry puts his hands on my shoulders and shakes me. "Baby," he says. "You and Darlene aren't in the same league. She was a lay, that's all. Just another chick. You're so far above any other chick I've ever met, baby. I couldn't love anyone but you."

I look down at the box of Dixie Pies in the garbage. "How could you eat that crap, Barry?"

"I didn't eat them. She ate them."

I thought it didn't get cold in the South, but it's below freezing, and heavy sleet is falling and freezing over the surface of the parking lot. Barry doesn't own any boots, and my boots are somewhere in my parents' house in Chicago. Barry and I slip and slide on the ice between the apartment and the car. We load the trunk of the Supersport with Barry's stereo, his electric blanket, his blue sheets. He throws his law books into the back seat. Barry is shivering in his thin jacket. "I don't know how anyone can survive in weather like this."

I tell him that one night the wind off Lake Michigan froze the nylons to my legs.

"How could you bear it?" he says.

"I was used to it."

Barry leans over the steering wheel of the Supersport, squinting into the sleet-filled windshield. He is driving slow, but the car slides on the icy streets. There are no other cars on the road.

To turn into the parking lot of the new apartment building, Barry has to make a sharp left up a hill for a few feet and then a quick right down a steep hill into the parking lot. The car skids at the bottom of the hill and slides across the parking lot. The brakes don't hold. Barry turns the wheel to the right and to the left, but the car doesn't respond. It slides to a stop, perpendicular to the lines of a parking space, a few inches in front of someone's picture window. The drapes pull back, and two faces look out the window, then the drapes are pulled closed again.

Barry leans back in his seat, his arms rigid in front of him, his fists on the steering wheel. "Shit," he says. He is either annoyed or devastated; I can never tell which.

"Which apartment is ours?" I ask.

He takes a deep breath. After a while, he says, "Eleven."

I look up to the second floor and scan along the line of green apartment doors to find eleven. Bruce is sitting on the balcony in front of the door. The collar of his pea jacket is turned up, and he's smoking a cigarette.

"Guess what," I say to Barry. "Bruce is up there."

Barry groans.

Neither of us calls out to him.

Barry piles his law books in his arms like a load of fire-wood. I lean into the back seat to get a bag of groceries and hear Barry scream. I turn around, and he is on the ice, his law books lying all around him.

"Are you okay?" I'm still holding the bag of groceries.

Barry doesn't move from where he fell. He is leaning on his elbow with his legs to one side. If he weren't shivering, if he were lying on a chaise and not in an icy parking lot in the sleet, he would look casual, graceful, as if he were mod-eling the slacks he's wearing.

"Barry, what's wrong?" I put the bag of groceries on the first stair. It tips over and spills out a box of Cheerios. I kneel down on the ice next to Barry.

Bruce is on his way down the stairs. "Hey, what's happening?"

I don't know, so I don't answer him.

Bruce comes up behind Barry and puts his arms around Barry's chest and lifts him up. A can of tunafish from the bag of groceries starts rolling down the incline of the parking lot.

With Barry in his arms, Bruce looks at me. "Now what?" I shrug.

"Just leave me here," Barry says.

Bruce lowers Barry to the ground. "So what's happening? Did you break your leg? Should we call an ambulance?"

Bruce's face is chapped and wet. Barry's pants are dotted with wet gravel. A jar of olives is starting to roll out of the grocery bag. I bend down and pick it up.

"Don't call an ambulance," Barry says to Bruce.

Bruce turns to me. "If his leg were broken, you'd hear him all the way to Bessemer."

The icy water is running down my hair into my mouth. I can't feel my toes anymore.

"I know what it is," Barry says. "It's my knee. I've had it before."

"Thanks for telling us," Bruce says. He takes Barry under the arms again. "Put your arm around me," he says to Barry. Bruce starts up the stairs, half supporting Barry. I follow them, carrying a bag of groceries.

We get up the stairs and across the balcony to eleven, but we can't go in because Barry has the key.

I put my hand into Barry's pants pocket to find the keys. "I need a set of keys of my own," I say.

"Why, baby?" Barry says. "I'll always be with you."

Bruce props Barry up next to the door, and I open the

door. The apartment looks just like the one we left. Bruce helps Barry inside, and I go back downstairs to pick up the law books and the rest of the groceries.

When I come back up, Barry is lying on the couch. He and Bruce are smoking cigarettes. Barry laughs his unfunny laugh. "It happened once before, when I was playing handball." He pats his knee lightly, then winces. "This knee is keeping me out of Vietnam." Barry looks out our picture window at the sleet. "They've got nice beaches in 'Nam, baby. You could fly down for R and R, and Uncle Sam would put us up in a class hotel in Honolulu before I had to go back to the rice paddies and get my balls blown off. What do you think, baby?"

"You got Four-F on that knee?" Bruce says.

"Yeah. When I left the doctor at the draft board, he said, 'You can stop limping now.' "

"How did you get out?" I ask Bruce.

"Gout."

Barry laughs his reckless giggle. "Gout? Nobody gets gout anymore, Grease."

"Henry the Eighth had gout," I say.

"I have a tendency to get gout," Bruce says. "The night before I went for my physical I ate a few pounds of raw hamburger, five pizzas with pepperoni, sausage, anchovies, onions, and drank a bottle of wine. The next day, my ankles looked like I had sandbags hanging on them."

Barry is laughing his reckless giggle. It looks as if it is going to take him over, but his face turns deadpan. "You didn't want to make that scene, huh, Grease? Dancing in mine fields, getting dropped out of helicopters into rivers full of crocodiles? Flying home to the States over the swamp where you left your arms and legs? How can those guys go over there? How can we sit here and laugh while they're over there? How can things like this happen?"

Barry looks at me as though I know the answer.

"There have always been wars," I say. "I don't know why."

The three of us stare at the empty coffee table. "How did Mel get out?" I ask Barry.

"He's married, and he's in law school," Barry says. "If that doesn't work, his uncle is a shrink." Barry looks up at Bruce. "Hey, Grease, what are you doing here, anyway?"

Bruce's face is still raw red from the cold. "I got a lift. I thought you moved in yesterday. I got my grades this morning."

"Yeah?" Barry says.

Bruce smiles and puts his hand out to me. "How do you do, Mrs. Feldman." He's about to go into his vacuum cleaner salesman routine, but he stops short and throws his hands into the air. "I flunked out of the greatest gut law school in the Confederacy."

"What a drag, Grease," Barry says. "I'm really sorry."

Bruce takes violent puffs on his cigarette and stalks around the living room. "I'm through with this pit city. I'm through with scuzzy Susie." He trips over a bag of groceries.

"I guess I'll make dinner," I say.

Bruce stops and looks at Barry and me. "Susie gave me a Japanese cricket cage for a good-bye present. What the fuck am I supposed to do with a Japanese cricket cage?"

"Make your chicken thighs, okay, baby?" Barry says.

I take the chicken thighs out of the oven and prick their aluminum foil pouches with a fork. Gamy steam hisses through the holes. Bruce comes in from the living room.

He puts his lips next to my ear. "Listen, Sally, if you ever get tired of Barry, call me. I'll give you my number in Miami." He tears the cover off a matchbook and writes his number on it, then slips it into my jeans pocket.

Barry calls in from the living room couch. "You can sleep here tonight, Grease. You can't go back outside in this weather."

I only have four thighs, so I give Barry two, and Bruce and me one.

"Baby, your chicken thighs are out of sight," Barry says.

"Yeah," Bruce says. He picks up his thigh to take a big bite and drops it into an ashtray.

Barry winces.

Bruce picks up the thigh from the ashtray and takes a bite. Ashes stick around his wet mouth.

"Don't eat that, Bruce," I say, but he keeps on eating.

Barry and I are in bed, and I can hear Bruce walking around out in the living room.

"Poor bastard," Barry says. "What's he going to do now?"

"Why did you ask him to stay over?"

"He can't go home in this weather."

"Sure he can."

"How?"

"Cab."

"He doesn't have the bread, baby."

"Why did you drive him to school all last semester?"

"How else would he get there?"

"How else does anyone get there?"

"He would have had to walk ten blocks to a bus."

"Did he ever pay for gas?"

Barry doesn't answer.

"You let him take advantage of you."

Barry lays his hand on my cheek. "What's so bad about that, baby? I didn't lose anything."

"Bruce wouldn't do anything for you. He would screw you if he could."

Barry smiles. "Baby, Grease can be an asshole, but he's a human being. Maybe he'll change. Maybe one day he'll think, 'Hey, Feldman was pretty nice to drive me to school.' Maybe someday it will take hold, and he'll do something nice for someone because of it."

"Or maybe he'll just screw someone when he remembers how easy it was."

"How can you think that way? How can you get up in the morning if you think that way?"

In the morning, I don't feel like getting up, but I have to make breakfast for Barry and Bruce. Barry can put some weight on his leg. He hops into the living room, holding on to furniture. The sleet has stopped, but the sky is gray and empty.

"You'll drive Grease home, won't you?" Barry says to me.

Bruce looks awful. He hasn't combed his hair, and his teeth are stained yellow. "Got any more cigarettes?" he asks me. "I smoked the pack you left out here."

"When are you leaving for Miami?" Barry says.

"I've got to sell my books to get money for bus fare," Bruce says.

"Bus fare?" Barry laughs his unfunny laugh. "Your old man won't swing you the plane fare?"

"Just write to me care of the bottom of my old man's swimming pool," Bruce says.

"He didn't make it easy for you, Grease. I couldn't live the way you did here: no bread, no wheels, no chick."

"Don't rub it in," Bruce says.

"Maybe you don't really want to be a lawyer," I say.

Bruce laughs. "Nobody wants to be a lawyer."

"Well, the world is made up of more than lawyers."

"Right. There's vacuum cleaner salesmen. That's what I really want to be. When I was six years old, my teacher asked me, 'Brucey, what do you want to be when you grow up?' 'I wanna sell Electrolux, bubula,' I said. I am a man with a calling."

"There must be something you can do," I say, but I can't think of anything.

Bruce raises his eyebrows and jerks his head to one side. "You are a beautiful chick, Sally. You're in a different ball game. You've got Feldman to take care of you, and if the next time he slips he breaks his head open, you'll meet some other guy at the funeral."

"Would you do that, baby?" Barry says. "I can't bear to think of you with anyone else."

"Cut it out, Bruce." I'm driving Bruce home, and he has put his hand on my knee. "Barry is your best friend."

"Yeah, and he fucked my chick, too."

I don't say anything.

"Barry could fuck your own mother, and it would come out like an act of mercy. He's the most innocent guy I ever met. How can you stand living with a guy like that?"

Through the windows of the Supersport, from the crest of the hill that slopes down into the parking lot, I look at my new home. The dark pink brick apartments sprawl along

45

the shallow valley. In the far right of the parking lot, enclosed by a chain metal fence, there is a swimming pool. It is empty.

I know without having to look that, besides the living-room picture windows with floor-to-ceiling drapes that face the front parking lot, there are bedroom picture windows with floor-to-ceiling drapes that face the back parking lot. I know that all the living rooms have one couch with six plastic cushions, two end tables with lamps on either side of the couch, one coffee table in front of the couch, two chairs with arms at either end of the coffee table, one dining table and four chairs without arms. The living-room wall has an aluminum panel with little holes in it, and if you turn on the switch, Muzak comes out.

I know that all the bedrooms have one double bed, one night table with a lamp, and one dresser with a mirror over it. The kitchens have appliances of matching colors, stoves and refrigerators, no dishwashers. The bathrooms are white and have two additional switches next to the light switch. One turns on a heater in the ceiling, and the other turns on a fan.

All the living rooms and bedrooms and halls in between have wall-to-wall carpeting, and all the apartments have central air conditioning. The only difference from one apartment to another is the color of the square plastic cushions on the couch. Ours are turquoise.

Through the picture window, I see Barry lying in the corner of the couch, his Torts books splayed on his chest. When I go inside, he spreads his arms wide, meaning that he wants me to enter them for a hug. I pretend I don't notice and toss the car keys on the coffee table. They clank when they hit. I stand in the middle of the living room considering which way to go. I can either walk straight back into the bedroom or sit down in the living room.

The doorbell rings, and Barry looks up at me. "Who's that? Mel just called, and you drove Grease home. We don't know anyone else, do we, baby?"

I go to the door. There's a woman wearing a green bathrobe. She has blond hair in a bubble. "Hi," she says. She stretches her bathrobe across her stomach and lowers her voice, so Barry can't hear. "I've got the curse," she says. "The cramps are something terrible. Do you have some Midol I could borrow? I've been drinking bourbon to kill the pain, but at the rate I'm going, I'll be blind before noon."

"Come on in," I say.

"Oh, I'm Lucinda Ann Blackwell, your next-door neighbor."

"This is my husband, Barry," I say. Barry looks up from his Torts book for a split second. I dig into my purse and get the tin of Midol for Lucinda Ann.

"How do you do, Barry," Lucinda Ann says, then turns back to me. "What did you say your name was? I'm sorry, I swear my brain is already sloshing around in too much bourbon."

"Sally," I say. My name sounds odd to me in this living room with Barry lying on the couch and Lucinda Ann standing in front of me in her bathrobe. "Sally Feldman," I say. It still sounds odd.

Lucinda Ann says she's having some friends over at her apartment later for drinks. Would Barry and I stop by? I say, "Okay." Barry raises his eyes over his Torts book.

★ ★ ★

"Why did you say we'd come over, baby?" Barry says after she leaves. "I don't want to go over there and chew the fat with a bunch of grits."

"Maybe there will be someone to talk to," I say.

"You can talk to me," Barry says.

"We haven't been to a party since we got married."

"That's only been a month."

"In New York, I went out every night."

"I have a Torts quiz tomorrow."

Lucinda Ann's couch cushions are avocado. There are about ten or fifteen people the same age as Barry and I, standing around drinking mixed drinks or beer. The women all have their hair done in bubbles like Lucinda Ann's, and the men are clean-shaven and wear madras shirts and chinos.

"Grits," Barry whispers to me. "Hicks."

Lucinda Ann comes up to us. "Let me introduce you around. Where are you all from?"

Barry just goes over to the couch, sits down with his feet up on the coffee table, his elbow on the end table, and his head on his hand, as though he were waiting for a bus.

So I have to answer for both of us. It's not easy. Where are we from? Barry is from Florida. But I grew up in Chicago, went to college in Ohio, and lived in the Village for three months before I married Barry. I don't feel like I'm from any of those places.

"New York," I say.

"I thought you were a Yankee," Lucinda Ann says.

A man with a crew cut hands me a drink and puts his arm around Lucinda Ann.

"Bobby Lloyd, this is my new next-door neighbor, Sally Feldman," Lucinda Ann says.

"What kind of name's Feldman?" Bobby Lloyd asks. "I never heard of that name before, did you, Lucy?"

"It's probably German," Lucinda Ann says and turns to me.

"You should ask Barry," I say. "It's his name."

There is a squeal of tires in the parking lot, then brakes, a car door slamming, and footsteps bounding up the stairs and across the balcony. A big, blond man with an open jacket comes in, and everyone yells, "Hey, Aubrey!"

Aubrey is carrying a six-pack of Big Cat malt liquor. "Lucinda Ann, turn on the TV. Bill Cosby is going to be on the *Andy Williams Show*."

Lucinda Ann wheels on Aubrey. "I ain't having a nigger in my living room."

Aubrey laughs and goes over and turns on the TV. "Come on, Lucinda. Folks up North have been watching him regularly."

"Well, we are not watching him in my house." Lucinda Ann tries to wedge herself between Aubrey and the TV.

"Hey, Bobby Lloyd, get your woman out of my way." Aubrey sits down next to Barry on the edge of the couch and leans into the TV. Barry leans back away from him. A soap commercial is on. Aubrey looks at his watch and cracks open a Big Cat. "Should be on now."

"It's my damn television," Lucinda Ann says.

Barry sighs and gets up. Everyone is watching Aubrey and Lucinda Ann and the television screen. "Let's go, baby," Barry says. "I've got to study."

I pretend I don't hear him.

"Bill Cosby isn't going to step out of the TV screen right into your living room, Lucinda Ann," Aubrey says.

The commercial goes off, and Andy Williams' smooth,

bland voice comes on behind the names of tonight's guests as they appear on the screen. Aubrey leans further into the screen. He slaps his thigh with his fist. "Damn. This is a damn rerun." He flips off the TV.

"What did I tell you, Aubrey?" Lucinda Ann says. "We are not going to let the Yankees put niggers on our TV screens like they're putting them in our schools. The next thing you know they'd be busting in here with a court order and sitting them down at our dinner tables."

I look around for Barry, but he's not here. He must have gone home to his Torts.

"Why wouldn't you want to eat dinner with a Negro?" I ask Lucinda Ann.

Bobby Lloyd smiles and turns to Aubrey. "What is a *Negro*, Aubrey? I heard of *niggers*, but I never heard of a *Negro*."

"That's what they call them up North," Aubrey says.

"We had niggers in my mama and daddy's house all my life," Lucinda Ann says. "But we didn't eat with our niggers."

Lucinda Ann and I are glaring at each other across the dining-room table. I'm drinking bourbon and Kool-Aid, and she's drinking straight bourbon. "But why wouldn't you want to have dinner with, say, a Negro lawyer just because he's a Negro?"

"There ain't no nigger lawyers in Alabama," Lucinda Ann says.

I look around for Barry, so he can tell me whether that's true or not, but I don't see him. Then I remember he went home. "Well, let's say there was a Negro lawyer. Would you have dinner with him?"

"There ain't none," Lucinda Ann says.

"All right. What about a Negro doctor?"

"Hey, Aubrey," Lucinda Ann says. Aubrey and Bobby Lloyd are standing around the table, watching Lucinda Ann and me. "You got any nigger doctors over at the medical school?"

Aubrey shrugs. "Don't know. Haven't seen any."

"Well," I say to Lucinda Ann. "Let's say for the sake of the discussion that you know a Negro doctor. Would you have dinner with him?"

"I will not sit down to dinner with a nigger, even for the sake of the discussion."

"You're drunk," Barry says when I come home.

I toss onto the coffee table the hardcover copy of *Gone with the Wind* that Lucinda Ann has given me.

"What's that?" Barry says.

"Lucinda Ann said it would explain everything I need to know about civil rights."

" 'Bama dirt farmers," Barry says. "How can you talk to them?"

"There's no one else around."

Barry and I are leaving the apartment. Lucinda Ann's front door is open, and she and Bobby Lloyd and Aubrey are standing out on the balcony, drinking Colt 45. "Hey, Sally," Lucinda Ann says. "Why don't you all come on in for a drink?"

"We're going to dinner," I say.

"With a Negro?" Aubrey puts emphasis on the *gro* and smiles. He has an open smile and very white teeth. He is tall and blond and handsome, if you like that type.

"Grit," Barry says under his breath.

We're going to have dinner at Ray Whiteman's house.

Like Lucinda Ann, I have never had dinner with a Negro. Before Barry and I got married, Ray came to Barry's apartment for a drink, but that was after his show when everyone else in Birmingham was asleep. I was still scared for the minute it took him to get out the front door and into his car.

Now it's broad daylight. "Do you think it's safe to go to dinner at Ray's?" I ask Barry.

I wait for him to answer, but he's staring off into the highway, scatting to some Mancini. I wonder if he heard me. Even if he did, I said it obliquely, so he might think I was kidding. I wanted a serious answer anyway. But I don't get it, so I listen to Barry scat instead.

He uses the Mancini like a diver uses a diving board: to spring from into twists, flips, swans. He holds on to a note so long it wavers, and his face strains to hold it. I watch his face, open and naked in a kind of rapture as each note is born to its short life, its echo in the closed car. When Barry scats, he is so weird and far-away. I like him best that way, but I wish I had someone to talk to.

The Supersport moves through the traffic like a cruise ship. I look at the faces of the drivers in the other cars to see if they can tell that we are going to have dinner with a Negro. Two Negroes, actually. But the drivers are concentrating on the highway or the person next to them in the front seat. Their faces are white and Negro, and then just Negro.

Small brick ranch and two-story houses sit on dirt yards. The houses have a grim, tenacious hold on their land. There are none of the suburban adornments I expect: no trimmed hedges, no initialed mailboxes on the front porches. The man whose molasses voice floats over Barry's blue sheets every Saturday night cannot live here. I wait for the solid brown houses to give way to a glass-fronted high-rise, something sleek and classy, like Ray, like his voice, like his music, like I expect his wife and his marriage to be, like I expected our marriage to be.

"What's the number, baby?" Barry asks.

I reach for the matchbook on the dash and read the address written in Barry's contorted scribble.

We pull into the driveway of a brown brick ranch. Before I can check to see if I've read the number wrong, the screen door opens, and there's a flash of white, Ray's short-sleeved shirt, as he steps onto the porch and walks across the lawn to us.

"Hey, man, congratulations," he says to both of us and shakes Barry's hand. "I didn't think marriage was your bag, Barry. What did you use to hook this guy, Sally?"

"I thought it was the other way around," I say.

Ray smiles his broad, firm, controlled smile. He has a straight nose and slightly slanted eyes, a smooth dark neck against his white shirt. His dark slacks have razor-blade creases. The slacks pull across his slim hips as he bounds up the steps to the porch. Barry and I walk behind him, and Barry has his arm around me, sort of hanging on me. We have to turn slightly sidewise to fit through the front door together.

Ray's wife, Nellie, is moving around the dining-room table, smoothing the napkins at each place setting. Her head is down, her hair pulled back into a bun. When she looks up, she smiles. She reaches out her hand to me and then to Barry. "You had to get married before Ray would invite you home for dinner," she says.

Ray flashes his smile at Barry. "Why would a hipster like

Barry want to spend an evening with us old married folks?"

Barry smiles his lazy, open smile, the one he saves for people he either doesn't know or is crazy about. "How long have you been married, Ray?"

"Ten years in June, isn't it, Nellie?"

"You know it is, Ray Whiteman," Nellie says.

Barry lets out a low whistle. "Wow. Baby, what do you think we'll be like in ten years?"

Nellie's face is pleasant, and she has a slim figure, but her brown skirt and cardigan sweater, her flat shoes, are plain, and, next to Ray, almost homely. Only one electric light is turned on in the living room. There is no sharp distinction between the gray dusk outside the living-room windows and the dim light inside. The living-room floor is bare. There is no furniture except a long beige brocade sofa covered in plastic. I sit down on the sofa, and the plastic sticks to the backs of my knees.

Ray and Barry carry in two of the chairs from the dining room. The chair Barry is carrying waffles at chest level while Ray's rides high and steady until he sets it down.

"Woof," Barry says. The chair skitters to the floor, and Barry sinks into it. "I thought only Jews put plastic on their furniture, Ray," Barry says. "Are you sure you're not Jewish?"

Ray swings around to Nellie. "Do you hear the man?"

"I had to work long enough to buy the sofa, Ray, and I intend to keep it nice until I die." Nellie runs her hand down the shoulder of the sofa. The way she touches it, as though it is dear to her, makes me uncomfortable. I don't feel that way about furniture.

"We have to work long enough to pay for everything," Ray says. "I don't have a rich daddy, like Barry's."

"He's not rich," Barry says. "Just comfortable."

Ray tells us how he was raised by his grandmammy in a two-room shack, how he slept in a bed with his younger brothers and cousins, how he worked a ten-hour shift as a night watchman to put himself through the Negro college, how he's helping his brothers through school, how he's got plans for Alabama politics when the time is right for a Negro, how Nellie has worked since she was married to save for their own young son's education and for the sofa.

I drink gin and tonic and watch Barry, slumped in his chair with his legs crossed, one slim ankle in a dark sock visible between loafer and cuff. He looks small next to Ray. I feel small, sitting on the sofa, lifting my thighs up and down to unstick them from the plastic.

Barry gets up and goes to the bathroom and when he comes back, he says to Ray, "Hey, man, is that a piano you've got in there?"

"Ray, I told you to close the door to the spare room," Nellie says.

"It's not exactly a Steinway, Barry," Ray says. "It's on loan from the elementary school. I play for the school chorus."

"Those are going to be hip kids," Barry says. "You should have seen who played in my elementary school. Mrs. Perkins. She had red hair like crepe paper and her upper arms jiggled when she played. I mean, she did not swing. Well, how about it? Let's play."

The spare room is empty except for the brown upright, its sides scratched and smudged from little kids' shoes and fingernails. Barry sits down on one end of the piano bench and Ray on the other. Barry starts playing "Chopsticks." Ray laughs.

Then Barry turns to Ray. "How about 'Stella'?"

Ray is playing bass, and Barry segues in with some harmony in the middle of the keyboard. Then Barry starts playing all over the keyboard, reaching over Ray, raising himself up slightly off the bench, his head down, his eyes almost closed.

"He's burnin'," Ray says. He gets up and leans against the piano and listens, smiling.

Nellie and I are standing in the doorway. "Let's go on in the living room and finish our drinks," she says.

I want to stay and watch Barry. He looks different, hunched over the keys, his shoulders relaxed, his body immersed in sound. I turn away and follow Nellie into the living room.

I drink gin and tonic and ask Nellie questions about her son. The piano sounds have gone beyond any tunes I can recognize. It's like another language, and I want to understand what Barry is saying.

"Excuse me, Sally," Nellie says. She walks to the spare room and closes the door.

Barry and Ray come back into the living room. Barry's hair is falling onto his forehead and his face is flushed.

"That's some shit you were playing, Barry," Ray says, and claps him on the shoulder.

"Nah. I can't play worth a damn anymore, Ray," Barry says. "That part of my life is over. I don't know, man. I don't think I would have been any good." Barry is looking down at his shoes.

Ray laughs. "Look, man," he says. "You'll be a lawyer before you're twenty-five. I'll trade places."

Barry smiles at Ray and then at me. "I guess I should be grateful," he says.

I shrug.

"You better believe it," Ray says.

Nellie is clearing the dishes off the table.

Ray is looking out the window into the driveway. "What kind of car is that you're driving?" he asks Barry.

"A Chevy." Barry says.

"A Chevy? Nellie, does that look like a Chevy to you?" Ray whistles. "The only man I know with a car like that is a pimp in Atlanta."

"Ray!" Nellie says.

"Barry's hip," Ray says.

"We'll have you over for dinner," Barry says. "You can make your chicken thighs, baby."

"We only have three plates, Barry."

Nellie goes into the kitchen and comes out with a china plate. She hands it to me. It has a picture of Joe Namath on it. "It's not much of a wedding present," she says. "But at least you have four plates now."

"Thanks," I say. "Are you sure you don't need it?"

In the car on the way home, I hold the plate on my lap. I have drunk too many gin and tonics. I'm tired of things not turning out sleek and classy, easy, like the picture I had in my head.

Barry is looking at me with a kind of suspicious smile. "What did you tell Ray, baby? When we left, he congratulated me on marrying a rich chick."

"He asked me how much of my father's money I gave up when I married you."

"And you told him, baby?"

"He asked me."

"How much, baby?"

"What difference does it make?" I open the window to let some air in the car, but Barry starts shivering, so I close it again. I'm thinking about Nellie touching the shoulder of her sofa.

"How much was it?"

"I don't know. A hundred thousand. Maybe two. I don't know exactly."

"You never told me you were talking about that kind of money, baby." Barry sits back against the seat, and he's not smiling anymore. "Maybe you could make up with your old man," he says.

The words hang in the air for so long, I wonder if Barry really said them. Or maybe he was kidding. If I don't look at him, I can imagine his face the way it is when he's kidding: eyebrows arched, eyes dancing, slightly loony smile. I look down at my lap. I rub my finger over the chipped edge of Nellie's china plate. Joe Namath is looking up at me with his crooked smile.

"What do you think? Is there any way you could get him to forgive you?"

"I could divorce you."

"I don't want you to do that, baby."

Barry and I are at the meat counter at Piggly Wiggly, looking for something to eat. Mel and Patsy are coming over for dinner. I pick up a sirloin steak.

"It's only Mel and Patsy," Barry says. "We can have spaghetti and meat sauce."

"Mel and Patsy are our best friends."

Barry picks up a half-pound of hamburger.

"Mel and Patsy are our only friends."

"Baby, that steak is four bucks."

I throw the steak back into the meat bin. "So what? We never go out. We haven't eaten one dinner out since we got married. I haven't bought one thing to wear. We haven't seen one movie. We haven't gone to one bar." I wish I knew more about money, so I could argue better.

"We don't have the bread, baby."

"Why not? We have the bread for an air-conditioned apartment and air-conditioned car, and it's not even hot."

"It'll get hot, baby."

"We went out before we were married."

"But I never liked going to those redneck bars. I just did it because you liked it."

When we get back to the apartment, Barry looks over the living room. "We can't have Mel and Patsy over with the apartment looking like this."

"We can't?"

"Look at the carpet."

I look at the carpet. It's dirty. "So what? They won't care."

"Well, I do. It's a reflection on me. Patsy wouldn't let her carpet look like that."

I go into the closet and take out the Bissel. I consider telling Barry an anecdote about my high-school history teacher who told people his name was Bissel — "like the vacuum cleaner" — and then everyone called him Mr. Hoover, but I decide against it.

We don't have a real vacuum cleaner; it's only a carpet sweeper. I had a toy one just like it when I was a girl, but no one expected me to sweep carpets with it. I run it over the carpet in the living room, then leave it upright in the hall between the living room and the bedroom. I set the table with our three unmatched plates and Nellie's plate with Joe Namath on it. Then I go into the kitchen and start making the meat sauce.

Barry comes into the kitchen and takes a little basket of cherry tomatoes from the refrigerator. He leans against the counter and, one by one, shakes salt onto the cherry tomatoes by tapping the shaker with his long, bony index finger, and pops them into his mouth. There is a little hushed burst, then squish, as he bites into them and the seeds and juice go squirting into his mouth. I'm chopping onions, then garlic, then mushrooms, then green pepper. Barry is halfway through the basket of cherry tomatoes.

"You're not going to leave the vacuum cleaner in the middle of the living room, are you?" he says.

I keep chopping.

"It looks terrible. It looks terrible to have the vacuum cleaner in the middle of the living room."

"It's not in the middle of the living room. It's almost in the hall that leads to the bedroom."

"You know what I mean. You can see it from the dinner table."

"It doesn't bother me."

Barry stops eating cherry tomatoes. His hand is still poised in the air with the salt shaker.

★　★　★

"Hey, Feldman, what's your vacuum cleaner doing in the middle of the living room?" Mel says when he and Patsy walk in.

"What are we having for dinner?" Patsy says.

Neither Barry nor I says anything.

"Hey, what is this, a mime show?" Mel laughs, sprawls on the couch, and takes a deck of cards out of his back pants pocket. "How about a couple of rounds of Hearts before dinner?"

"I'm game," Barry says and sits down in one of the chairs with arms across the coffee table from Mel.

Patsy comes into the kitchen and gives me a bottle of wine.

"That's really nice, Patsy," I say. "We never bring you anything."

"It's the finest," Mel says. "Italian red to go with the spaghetti."

"I could tell it's Italian by the six-pointed star on the label," I say.

"It's the only kind of wine I knew the name of to ask for at the state store," Patsy says.

"Only Governor Wallace would make you buy wine in a state store," Barry says. "In Florida, you can buy it in the supermarket."

"So what?" I say. "We wouldn't be able to afford it anyway." I twist open the bottle cap, then start to pour out four glasses.

"No thanks," Patsy says. "Do you have any Tab?"

"I don't want any wine, either," Barry says. "I've got a Torts quiz tomorrow."

I taste the wine. "It might be better mixed with some ginger ale." I bring out a bottle of ginger ale and pour it into Mel's and my wine. "It tastes a little like sparkling Burgundy this way."

"Yeah," Mel says.

"When did you ever have sparkling Burgundy?" Patsy says to Mel.

Mel smiles and spreads his hands out on either side of his shoulders. "I drink it all the time," he says.

"Are you sure you don't want some wine?" I ask Patsy. "It doesn't taste that different from soda."

Patsy shakes her head.

"It was really nice of you to bring wine, Patsy," I say. "But how come you did? I mean, since you don't drink it?"

"Mel told me to," Patsy says. "I felt like a real degenerate standing in line at the state store, Mel."

Mel reaches into his pocket and pulls out the matchbook where he's keeping score on the running Hearts tournament. "Okay," he says, "Steingut, thirty-seven; Feldman, thirty-three. Let's go." He starts dealing the cards.

"I'm not playing," I say.

Barry looks up at me.

"Hey, Feldman, what's wrong with your wife?" Mel says. "She says she doesn't want to play Hearts."

"Why don't you want to play, baby?" Barry asks me.

Mel looks across the coffee table at me. He has a big smile on his big, open face.

"I hate Hearts," I say. "I have always hated Hearts. I went through four years of college refusing to play Hearts, and that was with friends who one weekend locked someone in their room with them just so they'd have a fourth. I never win, and I'm not playing anymore."

Barry raises one eyebrow and inclines his head slightly towards me.

"Patsy hasn't won a game, either," Mel says.

"Patsy doesn't care if she wins," I say.

"I don't care," Patsy says.

"I like to win," I say.

Mel throws his cards down on the table. "Okay. What game do you want to play?"

"Bridge. But Barry doesn't know how to play."

"Great." Mel gathers up the cards and deals out four hands face up. "We'll teach Feldman how to play Bridge. Feldman, I win the Hearts tournament, thirty-seven to thirty-three." He slides the matchbook across the table to Barry.

"Wait a minute," Barry says. "We agreed to play to one hundred. The tournament was called. No one wins."

"I win thirty-seven to thirty-three."

"The tournament was called. You can't change the rules in the middle of the game."

Mel is smiling. "It was your wife who defaulted."

We all look at each other.

"I win," Mel says.

"No one wins," Barry says.

At the Mutual Protection Life Insurance Company, I sit at a big brown desk in the middle of the middle of three rows of big brown desks. Over every third desk, hanging from the ceiling on a thick chain, is a heavy white glass lamp, the kind you see in banks in western movies. I'm glad I don't have one hanging over my head. Brown draperies hang from ceiling to floor at intermittent spaces along one wall. No one ever pulls them open, so I figure there is nothing behind them but more wall.

I sit at my desk from 8:00 to 5:00 with two fifteen-minute coffee breaks and one half-hour lunch break. I take my breaks and lunch with the other three group hospital insurance claims examiners: Maribel Gateau, from Shreveport, Louisiana, Sheila Stuart, from Selma, and John Crate, from Hueytown. Except at lunch and at coffee breaks, we do not speak one word to each other. Maribel Gateau curses when she hits the wrong number on her adding machine, but that doesn't happen very often, and, besides, it isn't meant for anyone but herself to hear.

Maribel Gateau makes $70 a week because she has a masters degree in English literature from Louisiana State. John Crate makes $65 a week because he is a man. I make $60 a week because I do not have a masters degree in English literature and I am not a man. I do have a bachelor's degree in romance languages from Ohio Wesleyan University, and John Crate does not have any degree at all. Sheila Stuart has a bachelor's degree, and she makes $60, too. I would have thought she'd get a few dollars more than me for not having been born a Yankee, but she doesn't.

Maribel Gateau chain-smokes. Her cigarette doesn't get in the way of her fingers flying over her adding machine though her machine is full of ashes by the end of the day, and she doesn't bother to clean it off. Her eyes are red and her eyelids are puffy. She always looks half-asleep, which she is because she has two small kids at home. She has a husband, too, but he's a schoolteacher who's out of work right now and not good for much at any other time, either.

Sheila Stuart is the same age as I am, twenty-two, and she's engaged to a man who is thirty-seven and has a tractor dealership. She will quit working at Mutual Protection two weeks before her wedding day. That makes her better off than Maribel Gateau will ever be, and we all know it.

John Crate goes to Birmingham Southern College nights.

He has been going for six years. If he ever graduates, he will probably be made a supervisor, even though his fingers move a whole lot slower on his adding machine than Maribel's, and, for that matter, a whole lot slower than mine.

I sit behind my big desk, smoothing the pages of the rate schedule with my left hand and punching the numbers into my adding machine with my right. Hysterectomy: $75. Anesthetic: $35. Hospital room $8 times 20 days: $160. Drugs (at 50 percent): $75. Total payable: $345. Less deductible: $270. I double-check the addition, sign the bottom of the form, and put it on the pile that will go on to Mr. Blocker, the supervisor, for approval. My job ends here.

I am not paid to think about Parmalee Beauregard, twenty-eight, who had a hysterectomy for cancer of the uterus. I am not paid to think about her seven children, all listed dependents on her husband's group health insurance policy, for which $1.20 is deducted weekly from his salary as janitor of the school in Bibb County. I am not paid to note that John Beauregard filed the claim that is now on my desk eight months ago. I am certainly not paid to figure out that his check for $270 is significantly less than the actual hospital expenses which total $850.

It's the end of the day. I punch out $850, then $270, then MINUS: $580. Where is John Beauregard supposed to get $580? And what if one of his seven kids gets sick before the end of the calendar year? He has only $30 left in benefits.

"Bye now, Sally," Sheila Stuart says as she passes my desk.

Maribel Gateau, a cigarette in her mouth, rushes out of the office without saying good-bye to anyone. John Crate is standing with his coat on in the doorway of Mr. Blocker's office, laughing about something. The clock on the front wall is the same big, round clock with black hands that I used to have in my school rooms. I used to sit in Miss Hochstrasser's senior year English class and watch the minute hand's jerky approach to 3:18, when I could escape to my boyfriend's car.

But I'm in no hurry now. The clock says 5:02. Everyone is gone but Mr. Blocker and he's behind the glass partition of his cubicle in the back of the office. Every night Barry is waiting at the curb in the Supersport at 5:00 sharp, but tonight he will be late. He has a Torts seminar, or maybe it's Moot Court, I don't remember. I light a cigarette and stare at my adding machine.

Patsy has a pocket-sized toy adding machine that she takes with her to the Piggly Wiggly to add up the price of her groceries as she goes. Patsy makes $85 a week because she has steno and can type fast. I wonder why I can't type fast. It's probably congenital.

I take a drag on my cigarette and turn on my adding machine. I punch $85 into it. I make $60 a week. I punch $60. Barry gets $200 a month from his father, and that's tax free. I punch $200. We pay $125 a month rent. I punch $125. We pay $75 a month car payments. I punch $75. Barry carries $1,200 in bonds in the glove compartment of the Supersport. I punch $1,200. Barry and I have $500 in our joint savings account that my father gave me when we got married. I punch $500.

A steak costs $3. I punch $3. It costs maybe $6 for Barry and me to go out to dinner. I punch $6. It costs $20 for a pair of shoes. I punch $20. The airplane tickets from Birmingham to New York cost $45. I punch $45 twice. But Barry won't go to New York. I punch MINUS and $45.

66

I punch TOTAL even though I know the figures won't add up to anything.

$2,319.

I flip off the machine, stopping the dull hum. I tear off the tape. I add numbers all day, and sometimes I dream about numbers at night, the adding machine tape stretching across my sleep vision with its neat little black numerals and its round decimal points in between. I crumple the tape and throw it into the wastebasket. I hate numbers.

"Are you working late, Mrs. Feldman?" Mr. Blocker is standing next to my desk. "That's right convenient because I wanted to have a word with you."

He must have figured out that I hate numbers.

Mr. Blocker pulls Maribel's chair into the aisle and sits down across from me. "From time to time we get backlogged, Mrs. Feldman, and we ask the claims examiners to work overtime from five P.M until eight P.M. at time-and-a-half. I'm telling you this because we will be asking the claims examiners to work overtime for the next two weeks. Now, we have never asked a new employee like yourself to work overtime. Generally an employee does not produce for us in his first three months here, so we don't want to pay him extra."

"I see," I say.

Mr. Blocker smiles at me, and I can see the gold fillings in his teeth. "But you, Mrs. Feldman, you have been producing for us since the first week you were here, so we would appreciate having you work overtime with the rest of the claims examiners."

"Thank you," I say.

Mr. Blocker gets up. "You may bring in a sandwich from home for your dinner, if you like."

I make $1.50 an hour, which at time-and-a-half is $2.25. I punch $2.25 into the adding machine. Three hours a day, five days a week, for two weeks. I punch TIMES, then 30. I punch TOTAL. $67.50.

I turn off the machine, tear off the tape, and put it in my pocket. The clock says 5:13. Barry should be here in two minutes. On my way out of the office, I pick up the edge of one of the brown draperies, expecting to see more wall. There's a large picture window with a view of the street. I see the hood of the Supersport turn the corner and move slowly in the traffic towards the curb where Barry always pulls up to wait for me.

For almost two weeks I have been working from 8:00 A.M to 8:00 P.M. When I get out of bed in the morning it's dark, and when I get out of Mutual Protection Life Insurance at night, it's dark again. I only see the sunlight for half an hour at lunchtime, and then it's too bright.

When Barry picks me up, I get in the car, close my eyes, and wait for the numbers to go away. At the apartment, Lucinda Ann is having one of her parties. Aubrey is standing on the balcony. "Hey there, Sally," he says. "How about stopping by for a brew?"

Barry puts his key in the front door. "How does he know your name, baby?"

Inside, Barry picks up the mail from the carpet. He shuffles through the envelopes as if they were a deck of cards. "Who do you know in Oregon?"

"My brother."

Barry raises an eyebrow. "Maybe your family is starting to come around." He hands me the envelope and another.

"This is from the Jefferson County Department of Relief and Security. It's addressed to you."

Barry opens a bill from the Alabama Power Company. "Wow. Eleven dollars. Are you using too many lights, baby?"

"I'm not home all day, Barry."

I go into the kitchen and get a beer. I sit down at the coffee table and open the letter from my brother. I haven't heard from him since Barry and I got married. It's not a very long letter, just a few words in my brother's handwriting jumping the lines on a piece of notebook paper.

"Dear Snow White. Mother says you married some short Jewish guy and moved to Alabama. What happened, did you get tired of your dwarf in the Village?"

Barry comes out from the kitchen, slicing his teeth through a stalk of celery. "What does your brother have to say, baby?"

I read him the letter.

Barry takes it, reads it, then holds it away from him as if it held a terminal virus. "Nice letter," he says. He tosses it on the coffee table. "Nice brother you've got, baby. His sister gets married and he doesn't even say congratulations. He doesn't send his love." Barry laughs his hollow laugh. "He doesn't even sign his name."

He comes around the table and puts his arms around me. "What a fucked-up family you've got, baby. Your father doesn't come to your wedding. Your mother leaves in the middle of the reception. Your brother — what a prick you've got for a brother, baby."

I just sit there.

Barry goes back into the kitchen. He breaks off another

stalk of celery. His teeth make little crisp sounds as they bite into the stalk. He looks over at me. His eyes have a kind of faraway look. "Did you sleep with the dwarf, baby? I mean, I don't remember his name."

"J.D."

"Oh. Well, did you?"

I shake my head *no*. "Why?"

"I don't like to think that you've slept with anyone but me."

"Why not?"

"I don't know, baby. Now that you're my wife, I just wish you were a virgin."

The letter from the Jefferson County Department of Relief and Security says that my test score of 99 puts me at the top of the civil service list and I am hired as a caseworker at a monthly salary of $363. I make a quick calculation: almost $90 a week. I go into the kitchen to get another beer. Barry starts to open his mouth to say something, but then he closes it and just stares at me as I make a triangular hole in the top of the beer can.

Barry is right about my brother. He is a prick. He's right about my mother and father. They are awful. But I love them. Barry thinks I sprung pure and clean from the white sand at the Silver Sands Beach Club where he first saw me, my skin ablaze with Bain de Soleil. Barry doesn't know that I'm like the rest of my family. I'm awful. And I don't want him to find out.

I take a can of tunafish out of the cupboard to make tunafish casserole from a recipe I got from a Campbell's Cream of Mushroom Soup can. But the tunafish can seems heavy, and to sink the can opener into it and turn and turn until it slices full circle is too much. I put the can down on the kitchen counter and take my beer into the living room. I sit down on the couch and light a cigarette. I don't have a brother anymore. I don't have a mother anymore. I don't have a father anymore. It is as though a plane with my whole family on board has exploded in the stratosphere somewhere between Chicago and Birmingham, and I'm the one who put the bomb in the baggage compartment.

The letter from the Department of Relief and Security is lying on the coffee table. I stare at it. I don't want to change my job. I've already changed everything once.

"Aren't you going to make dinner?" Barry calls from the kitchen. "There's a can of tunafish on the counter."

"I'll do it in a little while," I say.

Barry comes into the living room. I reach for the letter on the coffee table and start to put it in my purse. I don't want Barry to ask about it.

"What's the other letter you got, baby?"

I slide it across the coffee table to him.

"Three hundred and sixty-three dollars a month," Barry says. He looks up at the ceiling, calculating with his eyelids. "Hey, that's a hundred a month more than you're making now."

"I know," I say.

"That's great, baby," Barry says.

"It is?"

Barry just looks at me. I've got to say something. "They've already trained me at Mutual Protection. I can't walk out after two months. They need me there. They're behind on their claims. If I leave, they —" I don't know what they'll do.

Barry laughs. "Baby, you don't owe anyone anything."

"I don't?"

"What's for dinner?"

"Tunafish casserole."

"I'm really hungry, baby."

Barry goes into the bedroom with his briefcase of law books. On his way, he flips on the Muzak. He's been doing that. Whatever song is playing through the aluminum plate on the wall has been mashed and strained until the melody sounds a little bit like every other melody I've ever heard, but nothing like itself.

Behind the Muzak, on the other side of the living room wall, I hear the party going on next door. I could knock on Lucinda Ann's door and ask her if I could borrow a cup of bourbon, and she would invite me in. She would probably want to know what I thought of *Gone with the Wind*, though. Lucinda Ann's front door opens and closes, and someone yells down into the parking lot, "Hey, Aubrey!" I can hear Aubrey bounding up the stairs, imagine his loose blond hair blowing away from his forehead.

I could tell Lucinda Ann that I've been working from eight A.M. to eight P.M., and I haven't had time to read *Gone with the Wind*. I could have a bourbon and Kool-Aid and tell some anecdote about something that happened to me in the Village.

I could tell them about stepping out of J.D.'s van onto Bleecker Street on the night of my arrival, my twenty-second birthday, and the streets were thronged with people in Indian print clothes and music was playing everywhere. A girl with hair down to her waist and a beatific smile grabbed my arm and said, "Here, we want you to have this." In her outstretched hand was a silver ring with a turquoise the size of a fingernail. "It's my birthday," I called out after her, but she had disappeared into the crowd.

72

I could tell them about the fourth-floor walk-up I lived in on Sullivan Street with a woman who was a friend of a friend of J.D.'s and whose cats left sooty pawprints all over my sheets and my clothes. I could tell them about catching the subway to get to the bus to go to the airport to learn how to say, "Good morning, Eastern Airlines Reservations and Information," so I could pay for a room the size of our walk-in closet and for my long-distance calls to Barry.

I sit on the couch and consider the possibilities.

I don't notice Barry go into the kitchen, but he comes out with a sandwich. He sits down at the dining-room table and eats without looking at me, which means he has to stare straight ahead at a blank wall.

I take my beer into the bedroom and lie down on the bed in my skirt and sweater. I'll never see my clothes again. I'll probably never see my brother again. I'll never see my father again. I'll never see my mother again. I'll never see my friend Miranda in Taos or J.D. in the Village. I'll never see the White Horse Tavern or Washington Square or Googie's Bar or the old Italian men who sat on the sidewalk with their German shepherd in front of the Social Club next door to the apartment where I was staying, in the place of someone who was staying someplace else.

I'll never see the bum who slept in the gutter in front of the apartment. I'll never step over him again. He may be dead. They may all be dead.

I wake up in the morning lying on top of the blanket with my skirt twisted around my hips. Barry is asleep under the covers on the far side of the bed. His portable alarm clock on the night table says 6:00. I get out of bed and tiptoe into the bathroom. I look at my face in the mirror. My mascara and eyeliner are smudged around my eyes. I look like a blind person or someone who got slugged in both eyes.

I pull my sweater over my head and look at myself in my blue lace push-up bra. Barry thinks I look like Donna Michelle. I'm always hearing I look like someone else.

"The Department of Relief and Security is a misnomer," says Jeannetta Cardwell, my supervisor, from behind her big desk. "There is nothing secure about the relief anyone gets here."

Mrs. Cardwell has a chipmunk face and little white teeth with spaces in between. She is wearing her hair on top of her head in a flat brown muffin. "Governor Wallace changed the name to suit the old folks. I was partial to the Public Dole myself."

"I see," I say. I look past Mrs. Cardwell to the window behind her desk. Hanging on the building across the street is a sign that says *Bail Bonds No Money Down.*

"You are right lucky, Mrs. Feldman," Mrs. Cardwell is saying. "We are going to put you in the nursing homes. You will have a caseload of only three hundred and fifty." Mrs. Cardwell smiles at me, her dry top lip sticking to her gum.

"Only three hundred and fifty?" I say.

"Why yes. The Aid to Dependent Children and Home Relief caseloads are eight hundred." Mrs. Cardwell looks down at my application. "You're from Chicago? I've got one beer-drinking cousin in Chicago. I don't believe we ever did have a Yankee working here before." Mrs. Cardwell takes a long look at me. Her tiny round eyes behind her horn-rimmed glasses are not unkind. "How old are you,

Sally?" she says, then glances down at my application again. "Twenty-two. Do you always wear your hair like that?"

I nod. My hair is parted in the middle, framing my face in an upside-down *V*, hanging straight past my shoulder blades.

"When you go to visit the nursing homes, wear your hair up like mine or tie it back, will you, Sally? You look like a young girl. Mrs. Bobbie Sue Drummond and Mrs. Caroline Morris, they are the same age as you, but they don't look so young as you do."

I follow Mrs. Cardwell out to the waiting room. Her girdled buttocks and thighs underneath a tight straight skirt barely move. She seems to be walking only from the knees down. Her nylons swish swish as her upper thighs rub together. A too-sweet smell of powder and perspiration reminds me of my grandmother. I guess I'll never see my grandmother again.

There are two waiting rooms, one on the right and one on the left of the center hallway. Both are filled with people sitting on the straight rows of chairs and leaning up against the walls. In the room on the right, they are all white. In the room on the left, they are all Negro.

"A United States government court order told us to integrate our waiting rooms," Mrs. Cardwell says. "We took down the signs that said *Colored* and *White*, but the people go to their rooms just the same as they always did. Must be the natural thing, don't you think, but just try to tell the United States government that."

"It might be habit," I say. I'm surprised there are just as many whites as Negroes on welfare.

"I beg your pardon?"

"Both rooms are filled."

"Oh, surely poverty doesn't discriminate against anybody in Alabama. I don't know how things sit up North."

I follow Mrs. Cardwell down the long, low-ceilinged center hall. She stops in every office and introduces me. The caseworkers are two or three in each small office crammed with oversized wood desks and swivel chairs. In a big room at the end of the hall there are the typists and file clerks, who are fatter and not so nicely dressed as the caseworkers. They are all women except the director, who isn't in today, and Wicker Tully, a round, red-faced young man in a white sport jacket who is in the hall, leaning over the switchboard, talking to the girl who answers the phones. As Mrs. Cardwell and I go by, he grabs a ringing phone and answers it, "Public Dole."

Mrs. Cardwell hides her smile behind a tsk tsk. "Why, Wicker Tully, you surely are the devil's incarnation."

An old colored woman with her hair done up in something that looks like a worn-out slip or nightie is coming up the hall, bent over a misshapen bucket that's sloshing water onto the floor as she moves.

"Careful you mop up after you, now, Mattie," Mrs. Cardwell says.

"Mattie's not all there, poor thing. Why, she was working here when I came, and that's near thirty years ago. She was a pretty little thing then, couldn't have been more than seventeen years old."

I try to imagine Mattie as a pretty little thing. I try to imagine Jeannetta Cardwell on her first day at the Department of Relief and Security thirty years ago. She was probably about my age then, her dry, dull brown hair shining, maybe done up in two braids on either side of her head as she suggested I wear mine. I try to imagine walking up and down this hall for thirty years. I try to imagine doing anything for thirty years.

We stop in an office, and Mrs. Cardwell introduces me to Mrs. Bobbie Sue Drummond and Mrs. Caroline Morris. After the four of us smile at each other, Mrs. Cardwell says, "I expect you three girls must have very much in common. Mrs. Sally Feldman's husband is in the law school out at Appalachia, and," she turns to me, "Bobbie Sue and Caroline both have their husbands in medical school over at the University of Alabama."

"You'll come to lunch with us today," Bobbie Sue says. "We're going to drive out to Li'l Bo Pig. It's Caroline's favorite restaurant. The pork barbecues are right good there."

"They have other things, Sally," Mrs. Cardwell says to me. She looks a little worried. "They have beef barbecues and fried chicken, don't they, Caroline?"

"Surely they do, Mrs. Caldwell," Caroline says. "But the pork is the best."

"I'm not Jewish," I say. "My husband is."

"Oh, my land," Mrs. Cardwell says, and we all smile again. "Now I don't know for certain, but I hear the Jews don't eat pork. Is that so? Because if it is, they are surely missing out on something good."

In the office next door, there is a good-looking Negro woman in a red dress. The only Negro who worked at the Mutual Protection Life Insurance Company was a messenger. He wore a white shirt and a dark tie every day. I always smiled at him in the elevator.

Mrs. Cardwell leans her head into the office. "This is our

new worker in the nursing homes, Mrs. Tompkins. Mrs. Sally Feldman, Mrs. Melba Tompkins." I smile at Melba a little harder than usual.

"A United States government court order, in case you're wondering," Mrs. Cardwell says when we leave. "We got so many United States government court orders we could set fire to them and have our own barbecue right out back in the parking lot.

"I don't know why Melba wants to be working here. She had a job with Social Security down the road at the federal building. Paid more, too. We reckon the N double A C P sent her."

"She seems nice," I say. I'm thinking maybe I should try to get a job with Social Security.

"They get paid four hundred dollars a month over yonder at Social Security. I don't know why she wants to work here."

Mrs. Cardwell takes me into a room so small that the two oversized desks are pushed up against each other, facing each other, with the swivel chairs behind, scraping against the walls. "This will be your office, Sally," Mrs. Cardwell says, "and this is Mrs. Polly Purvis, the other nursing home worker. I'll leave you here with her, and she can tell you everything pertinent."

Polly Purvis is a small woman about thirty years old with a cute little piggy face and a big smile with dimples. I can only see her from the collarbones up behind the piles of papers on her desk.

As Mrs. Cardwell goes out the door, she says, "I told Sally she ought to tie up her hair when she goes out into the nursing homes. She looks like a young girl." Then she smiles at me. "Don't know what we can do about that accent of yours, though."

Polly leans over her desk towards me, narrows her eyes and screws up her mouth. "You ain't been here ten minutes and they're trying to change the way you look and talk," she says.

"It don't matter no how. Half of them old toads can't hear a word you're saying, and if they can, they think they're talking to their daughter or some old cousin who passed on twenty years ago. You just make them sign on the dotted line, so's they can keep getting their checks for another year. I've got one ninety-one-year-old lady, been in a coma for two years. I march right in, put my face down to her lips to see if she's still breathing, mark an X on her application, and that's it until next year."

Polly looks at her watch. "Hey, come on, Sally. Let's go get us some coffee."

The lounge across the hall is a large square room with chairs lined up against three walls. There is a table with a piece of oilcloth on it, and on top of that, a coffeepot, a flesh-colored melamine bowl with sugar in it, and an open can of Magnolia Condensed Milk.

"Coffee here tastes like tar," Polly says. "Ain't nobody died of it yet, though."

The *V* in the top of the can of condensed milk has light yellow congealed milk around its edges. It runs thick and gluey into my coffee, turning it the color of rust.

I notice Melba Tompkins come up behind me in the coffee line. I turn to her and say, "I hate condensed milk."

"So do I," she says.

"Coffee-mate is better."

"I like it better, too."

It's nice to have something in common with somebody. "Would you like to chip in and buy a jar?" I say. "It doesn't have to be refrigerated. I could pick it up at the Piggly Wiggly tonight."

Melba reaches into her pocketbook and gives me some change.

I see how the chairs have filled up around the room without a break. I go and sit down next to Polly and wait for Melba to sit down next to me. But when Melba gets her coffee, she turns around and leaves the lounge.

Each woman who comes in sits down in the first empty seat and pulls down her skirt, tucking it neatly under her thighs. In a few minutes, all the caseworkers except Melba Tompkins are sitting in the lounge, holding their coffee cups on their laps. They all have their skirts pulled down to cover their knees. My skirt doesn't reach that far, so I just sit there, my knees exposed.

I am in the bathroom, leaning over forwards, my hair hanging down past my knees. I'm brushing my hair. Barry comes in and says, "Why are you brushing your hair upside down?"

"I can't talk. I'm counting strokes."

Barry sits down on the bathroom floor, looks up at me, and smiles. "You're beautiful upside down, baby. You're the only chick I've ever seen upside down." He pauses for a minute. "I think."

I keep brushing my hair into his face.

Barry crosses his legs and leans back on his elbow. He makes the cold tile floor look comfortable. He looks over at the toilet. "You know, I've never seen you shit, baby. You don't shit, do you?" He laughs his high, reckless giggle. "No, it's impossible. Baby, if you shit, don't tell me. I would be crushed."

He puts his hand on my ankle. "You have such beautiful ankles, baby. They're aristocratic. They're the ankles of a Spanish courtesan." He runs his hand up and down my nylon between my ankle and my knee. "Come on, baby," he says. "Let's go to bed."

"Seventy-three, seventy-four, seventy-five."

"How many strokes do you do, a quadrillion?" Barry is tugging my skirt.

"One hundred."

The front door of the apartment opens and slams shut. "Hey, Feldmans!" Mel calls out. "Get out the cards."

"Where are you guys?" Patsy yells. She sounds scared.

"In the bathroom," I yell back. "We'll be right out." I close the door, lock it, and turn on the switch for the bathroom fan. Its dull roar fills the room, shutting us off from the rest of the apartment, as if we were in a lavatory in an airplane. I turn to Barry. "Let's make love here. Right now."

"Baby, you're too much." He pulls me down on the floor and pushes my skirt up over my hips. We don't look at each other. I unbuckle his belt, careful not to let the buckle clang against the tile floor. Barry pulls down my panties, slides on top of me, and fucks me with my head wedged in between the toilet and the bathtub. When we get up, we still don't look at each other. He zips up his pants, and I pull up my panties. I look at myself in the mirror. There is no sign that anything has happened.

Mel has dealt out four hands of Bridge on the coffee table.

He and Patsy are sitting across from each other, waiting.

"Move over, Pasty," Mel says. "Feldman and I will be partners against you and Sally."

Patsy looks at me and then at Mel. "But we always play that way, Mel. Sally doesn't want to be my partner every time."

"Well," I say.

"Okay," Mel says. "Sally and I will be partners against you and Feldman."

"That means I have to play with Patsy," Barry says.

"Let me be your partner, Mel," Patsy says. "If I get the bid, you can play my hand."

"That isn't fair," Barry says.

"Then you play with Patsy," Mel says. "I'll play with your wife."

"I'll play with Patsy," I say.

I get a hand with twenty-two points. It's a beautiful hand, the aces and the red and gold kings and queens and jacks staring out at me, all together as if they were at a royal wedding. I open the bidding with two clubs. Mel passes. I flex my foot with tension, waiting to hear what suit Patsy bids.

"Pass," Patsy says.

Mel claps his hands. "Feldman passes! It's your bid, Mrs. Feldman: two clubs."

"Patsy, you can't pass a two clubs opening bid," I say.

"I can't?"

"No coaching!" Mel says. He throws out the two of hearts. "Lay your hand down, Patsy. The bid is two clubs."

"Come on, Mel," Barry says. "Patsy doesn't know what two clubs means. Let her take her bid back."

"I can't do anything but pass," Patsy says. "I don't have seven points."

"You don't have to," I say. "If I bid two clubs, it means I have enough points for both of us."

"Lay your hand down, Patsy," Mel says.

"Let Patsy bid," Barry says. "Bid your longest suit, Patsy."

"Patsy can't bid now," Mel yells. "Pass, pass, pass," he says, pointing to himself, Patsy, and Barry. "The bidding is closed."

Patsy looks like she is going to cry. She throws her hand down on the table, face up. "See! I don't have enough points to bid."

I look at Patsy's hand. I pick the five of diamonds out of the section of hearts and put it with her other six diamonds. I spread my hand out on the table. "If Patsy had bid her diamonds, I would have bid seven diamonds. I could have taken every trick."

Mel and Barry lay their hands face-up on the table.

"I may never get a hand like this again," I say.

"I'm sorry," Patsy says.

"Do you want to play the hand out now, baby?" Barry says.

"It isn't fair," I say to Barry when we're in bed. "I always have to play with Patsy."

"You don't have to, baby. You volunteered."

"No one else would play with her."

"She's terrible, baby. She can't count her points. She can't remember what trump is." Barry laughs his reckless giggle. "How could Mel do it? How could he marry a chick who can't count her points?" Barry's head is thrown back, and

I can see down his throat. He's laughing so hard his whole body is shaking. "How could he do it? His whole life is cards, and he marries a chick who can't count her points."

I'm laughing, too, but then I stop. "It isn't any fun having Patsy as a partner. We never win."

Barry wipes his eyes with the backs of his hands.

"I see what you mean, baby." Barry says. "But, look, we shouldn't be talking about Patsy this way. She is a really nice chick, a generous chick, and she loves the hell out of Mel. That's what really counts."

"Then why doesn't Mel play with her?"

Barry smiles. "I don't know. I'll have to think about that."

"I'm sick of Bridge."

"We switched from Hearts to Bridge because of you, baby. I thought you loved Bridge."

"I did."

Polly Purvis and I are standing at the back door of the Department of Relief and Security, waiting for Barry. He pulls up to the door in the Supersport, leans across the front seat, and swings open the door on my side. "Barry," I say, "I'd like you to meet Polly Purvis."

Barry says, "Hi, Polly." He smiles his very charming smile.

"What was that all about?" Barry says when I get into the car.

"She told me she had never met a Jew before."

"Groovy," Barry says. He starts tapping on the steering wheel along with the tune on the car radio. He raises an eyebrow and turns up the volume.

I start humming along with the tune. "Sssh!" Barry says.

He reaches over and puts his hand on my mouth to stop me from humming. In a few seconds, he takes his hand away. "Did you hear that, baby? The bass player is doing something really interesting. Can you tell which the bass is? It's the one going dum dum dum dum in the background. Hear it, baby?"

After dinner, I'm washing the dishes. Barry comes up behind me and puts his arms around my waist. I can feel his breath on my neck.

I whirl around. "Leave me alone!" I scream. Soapy water from my hands sprays to the floor as I turn. I am huge and monstrous with my wet hands and my screaming voice. I can see my reflection in Barry's eyes.

"Jesus Christ," he says, clipped. He turns and goes out of the kitchen. He flips on the Muzak and sits down at the dining-room table and lays his head on his crossed arms.

The Muzak is my fault. Before Barry married me, he only listened to jazz.

Bobbie Sue and Caroline and I are having lunch at the Li'l Bo Pig Bar B Q restaurant. I am hungry and order the pork barbecue special with fried potatoes and cole slaw. I look down at the slab of meat, its hot sauce staining the paper plate an orangey red. I sip on my Coke. I'm hungry, but I don't feel like eating. Bobbie Sue is talking about the new material she has bought to make herself a long dress for the spring formal at the medical school. "What are you going to wear, Caroline?" she asks.

Caroline has just taken a bite of her barbecue. She smiles with her mouth closed as she chews and swallows. "I have a bridesmaid's dress from Rebecca Plimpton's wedding, you know, the girl I told you about who married the West Point cadet down in Dothan? I believe if I take the flower off the bodice and put a brooch in its place — I have a pretty diamond brooch from my grandmama Tyler — it will look right fine."

Caroline smiles and turns to me. "Do they have a spring formal up at the law school, Sally? I believe Melanie Cox and her husband went to dances when he was at Appalachia, didn't they, Bobbie Sue?"

"I do believe so," Bobbie Sue says, and they both turn to me.

"I don't know," I say. "I wasn't here last spring."

"My, you have been married such a short time," Caroline says. "Tell me, Sally, how long have you and your husband been married?"

"Almost three months," I say.

Bobbie Sue throws her hands up in the air. "But you're still a bride, Sally. Oh, Caroline, Sally is just a bride." They both smile at me. "Here I am talking about sewing dresses, and Sally is still a bride. I remember so well when I was a bride. There were so many parties, so many presents, so many friends and family coming in and out. It was such fun."

Bobbie Sue and Caroline are both looking at me and smiling, waiting for me to say something. There is nothing I can think of to say right now. I was never a bride. I try to smile back at them.

"Now we are old married ladies," Caroline says. "Do you know I was twenty-three last month, Sally? I wish James would hurry up and get through that old medical school, so I could start having babies."

"How much longer does your husband have in law school?" Bobbie Sue asks me.

"A year, if he passes."

"Oh! I envy you, Sally," Caroline says. "You won't have to wait but a year to have your babies."

"Caroline!" Bobbie Sue says. "Sally is just a bride. She is not thinking about babies yet. She wants to keep her husband all to herself for a little while." Bobbie Sue smiles a small, slow smile and runs her hand over the surface of her belly. I realize she is pregnant.

There is nothing for me to say. I try to swallow. I look down at my plate. The gristle from my barbecue is lying in the orangey red sauce in the largest section of the divided paper plate.

Mel and Patsy must have been waiting at the door with their coats on, because when we pull up in front of their apartment, they come right out.

"How are we supposed to fit in the back seat with all those law books, Feldman?" Mel says. He pushes two of them to one side of the seat and brushes a pile of parking tickets off the seat onto the floor. "What if some B-ham cop looked into the back seat while he was writing out a ticket, Feldman?" Mel says. "What do you think he'd do to a Jew-boy with Florida plates and a back seat full of Alabama parking tickets?"

Barry thinks a minute, pulls away from the curb. "Lynch me. Maybe just beat the shit out of me. Break all my bones. Sink his stick into the top of my head."

"What's this movie you're taking us to, Sally?" Patsy asks.

"*The Pawnbroker.* I saw it in New York."

"And you want to see it again?" Patsy says.

"Don't you ever go to see a movie twice?"

"We never even go the first time," Patsy says. "We haven't been to a movie since we've been married. Mel is only going because you want to go."

"I like movies, Patsy," Mel says.

"How come we never go?"

Barry pulls up in front of the theater and parks in a No Parking zone.

After the movie begins, Barry does not hold my hand. He is slumped in his seat, staring straight ahead at the screen. When Patsy passes him the popcorn, he just shakes his head without looking at her. Towards the end of the movie, he gets up and I figure he's going to the bathroom. He doesn't come back, and when the movie is over, he's standing in the lobby, leaning against a wall. He looks pale.

"Great movie!" Mel says. "By the way, what happened to you, Feldman?"

Barry looks like he didn't hear him.

Patsy shivers and smiles at the same time. "I thought I'd die when the pawnbroker put his hand through that sharp thing he kept his bills on. I almost couldn't look."

Mel is walking with his arm around Patsy. He pulls her a little closer to him. "Oh, yeah," he calls out into the night. "That was too much. A terrific story! A terrific performance by Steiger! Feldman, your wife sure knows how to pick movies."

Barry is walking a little off to the side, as if he weren't with us.

"So what did you think of the movie, Feldman?" Mel says.

We're at the car now. Barry leans back against the front door, slumped there with his stomach hollowed out as if someone had pushed him against the car and punched him in the gut.

"Feldman didn't like it," Mel says. "Hey, aren't we going to get into the car?"

People from the theater are filing out and going off down the street one way or the other.

"I don't think I can drive," Barry says.

Mel shakes his head as though he didn't hear Barry quite right. "What?" He's smiling, but then he looks at Barry, and he stops smiling. "Hey, what's wrong? Are you sick?"

"I don't know." Barry looks down at the sidewalk and shakes his head. "I don't know how I feel."

"Give me the keys, Feldman," Mel says. "I'll drive."

"I'll drive," I say. "I'll have to drive after I drop you off anyway."

Barry takes the keys from his pants pocket and lets them hang at his side in his hand. I take them and open the car door. Mel and Patsy get into the back seat, and Barry gets into the front. "Are you all right?" I ask Barry.

"I just want to go home," he says.

"Well, I guess you don't want to go out for pizza or anything," Patsy says.

"I'm starving," I say and start the car.

"Drop Feldman off, and we'll go out for pizza. Okay if your wife goes out for pizza with us, Feldman? She'll bring you back a slice."

Barry is slumped so far down his head only reaches the middle of the back of the seat.

"I think I'd better go home with Barry," I say.

He is bracing himself, holding both sides of his seat with his hands. "You make it sound like you *have* to," he says.

"Well."

I think about how Patsy would feel if Mel got sick. She would bring him soda and sandwiches in bed. She would deal out his cards for him. But I can't imagine Mel getting sick.

I drive through the dark countryside. For about a mile there is nothing but a shack here and there, and then, suddenly, Mel and Patsy's white brick apartment building with its kidney-shaped swimming pool looms up out of nowhere. In a minute, Mel and Patsy will get out of the car, and Barry and I will be alone in the car, and then we'll be alone in the apartment. I turn around and say to Mel and Patsy, "When I saw *The Pawnbroker* in New York, I thought that the cattle cars going to the concentration camps looked like the subway cars at rush hour, that the concentration camp might be a symbol for modern life."

"Gee, do you always think about stuff like that?" Patsy says. "I'm usually thinking about how much garlic powder to put in my stuffed cabbage."

"Well, your stuffed cabbage *is* good," I say.

Barry and I go inside the apartment, and, without turning around to face the door, he slams it with the back of his hand. Then he falls back against it, his arms spread, as if there were a band of wild Indians on the other side, their pursuit stopped short by the slammed door, the way it happens in cartoons.

I go into the kitchen and get a beer. I imagine being out for pizza with Mel and Patsy, all of us talking about the movie. I look into the refrigerator for something to eat, but I'm not hungry anymore. I go back and sit down across from Barry on the couch. The beer tastes good. Maybe I am hungry after all. I go back into the kitchen and get a bag of potato chips. "I wish I had some dip," I say.

"How can you eat?" Barry says.

The next Saturday night, Mel sticks his head inside the front door. Barry is lying in the corner of the couch with his Torts book. "Sure you don't want to come, Feldman?"

Barry shakes his head.

"We'll take good care of your wife."

I go out to the car with Mel. Patsy waves hi from the front seat. "We can all fit in the front," Mel says. "Right, Patsy?"

"I don't know, Mel." Patsy looks worried.

I get in the back. Patsy turns around. "What movie are we seeing tonight?"

"*Darling.*"

"Who's in it?"

"Julie Christie. It's an English film."

"Mel, I can't believe we're going to a foreign film."

"I like foreign films," Mel says.

"You do? You never told me that."

"Look, Patsy," Mel says in the theater. "Hot buttered popcorn."

"Oh, Mel. I really shouldn't eat it. But I will." Mel buys her a jumbo cone of hot buttered popcorn.

"Do you want some, Sally?" Mel says. "I'll get another jumbo, and you can eat from mine."

Besides Mel, Patsy, and me, there are about six people in the movie theater.

"Do you think this is going to be any good?" Patsy whispers.

"In New York, you had to wait in line to see it," I say.

Mel sits between Patsy and me in the theater. The darkness and the quiet feel good. I reach into the cone of popcorn that Mel is holding between his legs. I sink back into my chair and wait for the movie to start. Mel is so big and good-natured, he'll like the movie no matter what it is. Even if he doesn't, he won't blame it on me.

In the movie, Julie Christie is a model. Every time she changes clothes, I think about the three things I wear to work week after week. In the movie, everyone calls Julie Christie "darling." She is beautiful, of course, and rich, and famous, and she marries a prince at the end. But she's miserable. I believe she's miserable, but I envy her anyway. At least she is rich and famous and married to a prince.

In the car on the way home, Mel says, "You look a lot like Julie Christie. Doesn't she, Patsy?"

"Huh?"

"Doesn't Sally look like Julie Christie?"

Patsy twists her head around and looks at me as if she'd never seen me before. "Yeah," she says. "You do. I think Julie Christie is kind of odd looking. I mean, she's different looking. She doesn't look like anyone in Birmingham."

"She's gorgeous," Mel says. "What are we seeing next week, Sally?"

"I don't know. I have to check the paper."

"I wish Barry had come with us," Patsy says. "Don't you think you could get him to come next time? I feel sorry for him, sitting home alone in the apartment while we're out having a good time."

"He doesn't want to come," I say. "He says he has to study."

"But Mel has to study, and he comes."

"Feldman doesn't like the movies, Patsy," Mel says. "Forget it."

"But he's your friend, Mel."

Mel laughs. "He doesn't like the movies, that's all. Leave him alone."

"It's really nice of you two to let me come along tonight," I say. "I really appreciate it."

Mel smiles his big, wide smile. "Hey, let's go for pizza. We don't have Feldman this time to get sick on us."

"I'm starving," I say. "But I don't know if I should stay out any later."

"You can call your husband from the restaurant. How about it, Patsy? Picture a nice big thick pizza pie dripping with cheese and hot bubbling tomato sauce, mushrooms, sausage, anchovies —"

"I hate anchovies," I say.

"Scratch the anchovies."

"Mel! I was just starting to taste the anchovies," Patsy says.

"You can have them on your half," Mel says.

When we get back to the apartment, it's after midnight. Mel jumps out of the car. "Be right back," he says to Patsy. "I just want to see how much studying Feldman is getting done."

Mel and I go up the stairs to the apartment. "Ten to one Feldman is asleep," Mel says.

The drapes are drawn, but there's a light on in the living room. I start to put Barry's key in the door, and Mel takes the key from me and opens the door. He peeks around the corner into the living room, turns to me, and smiles. "What did I tell you?"

Barry is asleep in the corner of the couch with his Torts book open and on his chest. His glasses are hanging from one ear. Mel goes over to him and shakes him by the shoulders. "Feldman. It's nine o'clock. You are in Torts. Professor Edwards is looking at his roll book. Who is he going to call on next? 'Mr. Feldman, will you be so kind as to explain Blank vee Blank to us this morning? Mr. Feldman? Mr. Feldman?' "

Barry opens his eyes. "Where am I? Hi, Mel. Hi, baby. Did you have a nice time?"

Mel takes a matchbook from his rear pocket. "Look at this, Feldman. I've been working on it at the law library. It's foolproof. Spring vacation, we'll use it at the dog track." Mel bends over the matchbook. "Look: we bet one-tenth of our stake on the first race, and if we lose, we double our money on the second —"

Barry looks around the room. "Where's Patsy?"

"In the car. Now this is where my system is different. On the third race —"

Barry sits up, lights a cigarette, and looks at the matchbook. "If your system is foolproof, why didn't anyone think of it before? Why didn't Einstein think of it?"

Mel throws his head back and raises his eyes to the ceiling. "Say we bet a hundred dollars on the first race, and we lose. We bet two hundred on the second race. Now if we lose that one —"

94

Barry looks up at no one. "Where are we getting the money?"

"Those bonds you carry around in your glove compartment, Feldman. Listen, on the third race —"

"I'll go get Patsy," I say. "She must be freezing in the car."

When Patsy and I come back upstairs, Mel is hunched over Barry in the corner of the couch. They are both smoking and looking at the matchbook. Barry points to something and says something to Mel. Mel jumps up and throws the matchbook across the living room. "I'm ruined! Why didn't I see that? Feldman, you've ruined me."

"I almost lost all my bonds," Barry says.

Mel goes across the living room and picks up the matchbook. "The system just needs a little refinement. I'll work on it tonight. Let's go, Patsy."

Patsy looks around the room. "Okay. I thought I just got here."

"What time is it, baby?" Barry says.

I go into the kitchen and look at the clock on the stove, then see Barry is wearing his watch. "One-thirty."

"One-thirty. Shit. I have a Torts quiz at nine tomorrow."

"I go to work at eight tomorrow. I go to work at eight every day."

"I know, baby. I drive you there, don't I?"

Polly Purvis is driving me to the Rosy Hillside Nursing Home in her Dodge sedan. On the radio, a man is singing about leaving roses on his mama's grave. I ask Polly if she wants to change the station.

Polly turns up the sound. "Listen to the words," she says. "This song is real sweet."

"I think it's real depressing."

"You do? It's about a man who loves his mama so much he puts flowers on her grave every morning. I don't expect my kids will do that. If I up and die on them, they'll probably forget my name in two weeks."

A commercial for pork sausage comes on, then a mooing voice singing "Hillbilly Heaven."

"This must be the death hour," I say.

"I like this one," Polly says. "I want to meet all of them country singers up in Heaven. Beats meeting all these darned old folks every day. I can't hardly remember how to talk to a normal person, I'm screaming at the old ones all day and at my kids all night. Any kind of heaven sounds good to me."

A car driven by a Negro passes us on the left. "Wouldn't you just know it? You give 'em civil rights, and they think they can run you right off the road."

"Do you really believe that?" I ask her.

"You bet I do. Did you see the way that nigger tried to run us off the road? Nearly took half the car with him."

"I mean, do you really believe you'll go to Heaven?"

"Sure. Unless I poison my husband's grits or drown my kids in the river, and I ain't done neither of them things yet. It is not like I haven't been provoked, either."

"I'd like to believe I'm going to Heaven, but I don't."

"Lord! You don't think you're going to the other place, do you?"

"I don't know where I'm going. But I don't think it's anyplace special."

Polly laughs. "Don't you tell my husband that. We eat oleo, and he gives one-quarter of his salary to the All World

Bible Church out in California. He drags me and the kids out there every summer so's we can sit around in the desert praying and near pass out from the heat. Can't eat meat for the two weeks we're there. If Jess hears tell there's no Heaven, he is sure going to be mad at somebody."

Polly turns down the radio. "But you talk funny, Sally. Weren't you raised up in any church?"

I look out the window. The grass is starting to come up on the hills, and the trees are starting to grow leaves again. I never expect the seasons to change. "My family was Methodist," I tell Polly. "When I was late for school, I used to pray to Jesus for a ride. I usually got a ride, so I believed in him. I was afraid to test him with anything harder, though. I liked having him around to talk to, but I wished he would answer me sometimes."

"You bet," Polly says. "I could pray for a new washing machine till I was blue in the face, and I'd still be washing clothes in the bathtub." Polly scrunches up her mouth and eyes, and her voice gets serious. "But I figure Heaven will be my reward for all this sweatin' and slavin'. Heck, Sally, if I didn't believe I was going to Heaven, I would be tempted not to get out of bed in the morning."

"I know," I say. I don't want to tell Polly there is no Heaven. She might believe me. "I wouldn't go, anyway," I say. "They told us in Sunday School that anybody who didn't believe in Jesus would go to Hell. Like Heaven is some kind of eternal country club. I had one Jewish friend, and I asked if she would go to Hell. They said yes. I said that didn't make any sense because if I had been born to her parents instead of to my parents, I would be going to Hell. They said, But you weren't, you're lucky. But what about my friend? I said. They said, Too bad, that's the way it goes. I figured if God is that stupid, I didn't want to have anything to do with Him."

"Ya hoo!" Polly cries. "If Mrs. Cardwell heard you talk, her hair bun would stand up and fly away. She has been the organist at the First Baptist Church for twenty-five years.

"But you know what, Sally? Every Sunday I iron my kids' dresses and hair ribbons, and I take them to church. It's the only day of the week they look decent. But I don't think much about God and Heaven. What I'm thinking about is how I'm going to get my husband to fix my darned washing machine. I've been doing the laundry in the bathtub for three weeks."

Polly slows down and points to a billboard that is standing in the middle of the open fields. It says, "Impeach Earl Warren." "You can always tell where to turn for Colonel Hamley's nursing home since they put that sign up," she says.

We pull into the driveway of a pink brick building that kind of reminds me of the apartment building Barry and I live in. A sign on the lawn says "Rosy Hillside Nursing Home." I pull my hair back and fasten it at my neck with a barrette.

"I like to come here on the first of the month, so's I can check on the colonel to see if he's stealing those twelve-dollar checks. You know, the ones they get for buying candy bars and cigarettes. Course, he gets it one way or another. Last month he was charging them for Kleenex and Chux."

"Morning, Mrs. Purvis," says a blond woman with her hair teased up in a beehive, who is wearing a red Governor Wallace button on her blouse over her heart. "They're all inside." She points to a door on the left. Inside, a few weak voices are singing "Happy Birthday." It's a big room. There are about forty old people sitting in a circle in wheelchairs. In the middle is a short man with a mustache, who is wearing a tuxedo and white gloves. He is holding a long knife over a white cake that says *Happy Birthday* in pink script.

"I hoped to miss the damn-fool birthday party," Polly whispers. "First of the month, the colonel jacks them all up in their chairs and wheels them in here whether they want to come or not. They all get tummyaches from the cake."

Most of the old people aren't singing. They're just sitting there. The voice of the man in the tuxedo is strong and dramatic, ringing out over the pink bald heads and permanented hair.

"The colonel used to be in vaudeville," Polly says. "And he can't never forget it."

"He looks like a magician," I say.

"Yes siree, he sure makes them checks disappear fast enough."

The colonel's arm sweeps out from his chest as he holds the last note of "Happy Birthday." He cuts a piece of cake and then with a flourish passes the knife to a nurse. He crosses the room towards Polly and me and sweeps his gloved hand to the floor in a bow. "What a delightful surprise, Mrs. Purvis," he says. "I am so glad you could come to our little party, and brought your daughter with you, too." The colonel smiles at me.

"Oh, beans, Colonel Hamley," Polly says. "My oldest girl ain't but eleven. This here is Mrs. Feldman, the new caseworker in the department."

The colonel pumps my hand. "Pleased to meet you, Mrs. Feldman. If you are even half as nice as our Mrs. Purvis here, you and I will get along right fine."

"If she isn't half as nice, you'd better shut down and go back to dancin'," Polly says when we're down the hall. "That thieving old fake gives me a pain."

Negro orderlies in green shirts and pants and white nurses in white uniforms are wheeling chairs past us and into the rooms off the hall. "Can't you report the colonel or something?" I say.

"Sure I could. But where would all these old people go? Folks ain't taking care of their mamas and daddies anymore. They just stick them in a nursing home and trot on down to the Welfare. They think they're entitled."

Polly walks fast, tilted forward in her three-inch heels. I follow her to a room at the end of the hall. The room is small, clean, and quiet. There is a bed with bars on the sides like a crib. Inside, lying on her back, dressed in a white cotton lace nightie is a woman who would not be more than four and a half feet tall if she were standing up. Her hands lie crossed on her chest, as though they had been arranged there by someone else. The bones in her hands are incredibly small. Her tiny head is covered with a little lace cap.

Polly digs into her bag and takes out her clipboard. She leans over into the crib and says, "Mrs. Sifton, this here is Mrs. Feldman. She is a caseworker for the department."

"How do you do?" Mrs. Sifton says. Her voice is a breath.

"How are you feeling, Mrs. Sifton?" Polly asks. "You look real nice." While she is talking, she is making checks on Mrs. Sifton's eligibility form. "You don't get anything from your grandson over in Talladega, do you?" Polly doesn't wait for an answer. "Say, I see you were one hundred years old last month."

"One hundred years old," I say. "You don't look that old." I smile down into the crib at Mrs. Sifton.

She stares straight up at me. "Well, I sure do feel it."

Polly reaches into the crib and takes Mrs. Sifton's hand in hers. Their two hands pencil an X on the eligibility form. The X is light and wavering, as if it had been drawn by a moth.

"Don't you have to ask her all the questions on the form?" I ask Polly out in the hall.

"I don't reckon Mrs. Sifton's circumstances are bound to change much. Now we got to see Mr. Perkins. You can take him, Sally. You got to start somewhere."

Mr. Perkins is a short, stocky baldheaded man, wearing a sleeveless undershirt and chinos. His penis is hanging out of his fly. It looks dry and flaky. "You would have to see that right off," Polly says in a normal tone, then in a scream, "Zip up, Mr. Perkins. You got company."

Mr. Perkins cups his hand to his ear.

"You got company."

"Eh?"

"Oh, never you mind." Polly goes out into the hall and grabs an orderly. "Would you please zip up Mr. Perkins so we can get him to make his X and get out of here before rush hour?"

Polly leans over Mr. Perkins and puts her mouth up close to his ear. "This here's Mrs. Feldman, your new case-worker." Polly hands me the clipboard and steps out into the hall.

"How are you feeling, Mr. Perkins?" I say, but he looks right past me. I lean over and yell into his ear. "How are you feeling?" He doesn't say anything. "I hope you're feeling all right." He just sits there, staring straight ahead, so I figure I would be better off standing right in front of him. "Is your Social Security still fifty-three dollars and seventeen cents per month?" I scream. I poise my pencil above Mr. Perkin's eligibility form. He doesn't say anything.

"Do you receive any other pensions?"

He doesn't say anything again.

"Do you have any money in the bank or any bonds?"

Mr. Perkins looks up at me, and his eyes shift into focus. "What's that about a bank?"

I smile at him. "Do you have any money in the bank?"

"You ain't taking my money. I can spot a gold digger a mile away."

"I don't want your money, Mr. Perkins."

"That's what all you young dames say." He is looking straight at me. I wonder if he knows what he's talking about.

"I'm your caseworker, Mr. Perkins. I want to give you money."

"That's a new one. I ain't signing."

I sit down on the edge of Mr. Perkins' bed and light a cigarette. My feet hurt. I take off one of my shoes and rub my foot with my free hand.

"You got a cigarette for me?"

I look out into the hall. I don't know if I am supposed to be giving out cigarettes. I give Mr. Perkins a Marlboro. I hold up his eligibility form in front of his face. "If you don't sign, you won't get your twelve-dollar check for cigarettes."

"What twelve-dollar check are you talking about?"

I smoke and rub my foot and stare at Mr. Perkins. The outline of muscle is still there in his bare arms. He has only a couple of teeth, but his jawbone is strong. Probably he was a handsome man before his hair fell out and his penis turned flaky.

"I got twenty-seven thousand dollars in the First National Bank of Bessemer, Alabama," he says. "I won't tell you which bank it's in. I'm not signing anything just so's you can go over to Bessemer, take out my money, and buy yourself some fancy clothes."

"I could use a pair of shoes," I say.

"What's wrong? Your husband a bum?"

"He's a law student."

"Any man can't buy his wife a decent pair of shoes is a bum."

"I don't know. Look, would you sign this for me?" I put the form on Mr. Perkins' lap and put the pencil in his hand. "Right here in the corner, see?"

"How much does a pair of shoes cost?"

"I don't know. Twenty dollars."

"Too much. I'm giving you fifteen and not a penny more." He marks an X in one corner of the form. "You take this on down to the First National Bank. They know me there. Why would a pretty young girl like you marry a bum?"

I put my shoes back on. They always hurt more after I've taken them off. I look over to Mr. Perkins to say something nice, but he is staring down at the space between his two feet. When I say good-bye, he doesn't look up.

"The last one we got to see is Mrs. Driscoll," Polly says. "She got voted Shut-in of the Year by the radio station. We got to check if she got any prize money, because if she did, we can deduct it from her check."

Mrs. Driscoll is lying in a dim room with the shades down, her blanket pulled up to her armpits and stretched across her chest like a band. Her thin arms lie unmoving on either side. Her short white hair is curled in neat little doughnuts all over her head.

"Hey there, Mrs. Driscoll," Polly says. "How you feeling today?" The old lady opens her mouth to answer, but Polly cuts her off. "This here's Mrs. Feldman. We hear you were voted Shut-in of the Year at the radio station."

"I just lie here all day," Mrs. Driscoll says. "I don't know why I got a prize for it."

Polly leans forward. "You got a prize, did you? What kind of prize was that now, Mrs. Driscoll?"

She inclines her head towards her right arm. There is a small gold watch on her inert wrist. "I don't know what they think I need a watch for."

"Well, that's real nice, Mrs. Driscoll. We got to go now." Polly is out the door with her clipboard. "Weren't even any little diamond chips in it," she says.

Barry pulls the Supersport up to the back door of the Department of Relief and Security, leans across the front seat, and pushes open the door for me. "Hi, baby," he says and kisses me on the cheek.

I kick off my shoes and feel my feet swell. "I interviewed my first client today. Polly took me to the Rosy Hillside Nursing Home."

"Yeah, baby?" Barry turns up the radio. "How was it?"

"Clean."

We don't say anything for a while.

"I'll have to take the car to work on the days I go to visit the nursing homes."

"You'll have to drive me to school," Barry says. "I guess I'll have to stay on campus and study at the law library."

"I guess so," I say.

When we walk into apartment, Barry picks the mail up from the living-room floor. "Here's something for you. It's from New York."

I get that lurching feeling in my stomach. I don't want to hear from anyone in New York. New York doesn't have anything to do with me. I go into the kitchen and get a beer.

"Don't you think you're drinking too much beer?" Barry says. Without looking up from the letter he's reading, he slides a six-inch square card across the coffee table to me. "What is it?"

It's a black and white photograph of a pile of automobile parts standing in an open field. The card says, *Sculpture, J. D. Nugent, April 1–10.* The gallery is on Prince Street.

"An announcement for an art show," I say.

"Why would they send it to you?"

"I know the sculptor." My voice sounds funny. What I'm saying is true, but I feel like I'm lying. I feel like a traitor, not to Barry and not to J.D. either.

"Who's that, baby?"

"J.D. I told you about J.D."

"Yeah? What does he say?"

I turn the card over. My name is written there in J.D.'s neat squared handwriting with his black felt-tip pen. Salina Jane Feldman. J.D. liked to call me by my full name, Salina Jane. I liked it because it sounded like the heroine in a southern novel. Across the line from my name and address is a message:

> I leave Sisyphus at the foot of the mountain! One always finds one's burden again. But Sisyphus teaches the higher fidelity that negates the gods

and raises rocks. He too concludes that all is well. This universe henceforth without a master seems to him neither sterile nor futile. Each atom of that stone, each mineral flake of that night-filled mountain, in itself forms a world. The struggle itself toward the heights is enough to fill a man's heart. One must imagine Sisyphus happy.

— Camus

"He doesn't say anything," I say to Barry.

"There's some writing on the card," Barry says.

"It's a quote," I say. "J.D. didn't write it. J.D. didn't even sign his name." I don't know what makes me feel worse: that he didn't sign his name or that he sent the card at all.

I can tell the letter Barry is reading is from his father because of the three crisp folds in the white typing paper. Barry tosses it onto the coffee table. "My dad is coming to visit the weekend after next."

"Oh."

Barry leans towards me with his elbows on his knees. "Baby, come on. My dad has really turned his feelings around about you now that you're family. Listen to this." He shakes the letter open. " 'Congratulate Sally for me on her new job. She is making a very good salary by Birmingham standards. She must be a smart girl to find such remunerative employment. I had feared that her new last name would give her problems. I know from my work in the A.D.L.' blah blah blah."

"Read that part, Barry."

" 'I know from my work in the A.D.L. that Birmingham

is not the finest place for a Jew. Even the Jews there I have found to be more Southerners than they are Jews.

"'I would like to bring Sally something from the store when I visit. What would she like? Please advise.'"

Barry puts the letter down. "See, baby?"

"It sounds like he likes my job."

Barry doesn't say anything. He just looks at me. He looks at me the way J.D. used to look at his sculpture when there was some part of it that didn't turn out the way he had intended.

"Let me read the rest of the letter," I say to Barry, and he slides it across the table to me.

"Dear Barry, Am distressed to learn that Sally is not doing well health-wise. What seems to be wrong? And I hope it's not what I think it is."

"What does he mean by this: 'I hope it's not what I think it is'?"

I slide the letter back to Barry.

"I wrote him about those stomachaches you were having. I guess he thinks you're pregnant. I had better write him and tell him you're better."

"I'm not."

Barry looks at me that way again. "I mean, I'll write and tell him you're not pregnant."

"That's different." I pour the rest of the beer down the side of my glass, watching the head carefully so it doesn't foam up over the top. "Your father knows I'm taking the pill. He got you the prescription for me."

"But the pill doesn't take effect right away. Or you could forget to take it."

I stare at the pale foam in the bottom of my glass. "I am

not going to get pregnant. You and your father can be sure of that."

"How do you know?"

"I don't want to have Jewish grandchildren!" my mother screams. Her nails are digging into the flesh of my inner arm just above the wrist. Barry is pulling me by the other arm. "Let's get out of here," he says.

We are standing in the hallway near the elevator on the fifteenth floor of the hotel, just down the hall from my mother's room. It is two in the morning.

I yank my arm away from my mother, and Barry and I are swallowed into the elevator. As we descend, I see my mother standing alone in the hall, her eyes flying, her mouth working its way into words that no one will hear. I wonder if she has a key to her room, if she has let the door slam locked behind her. I don't want her to wobble down to the lobby and ask for a key. I don't want her to hear what they will say about her as she is leaving.

Barry drives fast through the empty streets, as if my mother were in pursuit.

"I'm sorry," I say.

I look at my wrist. The skin is broken in three places and bleeding slightly, just above where you'd slash it in a suicide.

J.D.'s card is lying on the coffee table. I stuff it into the bottom of my purse and go into the kitchen to make dinner. At least when Barry's father comes to visit, he'll take us out to dinner.

Barry sticks his nose into the pot where I'm stirring the Betty Crocker Noodles Romanoff. "Ummn. I love your noodles, baby. I want you to make those noodles for dinner when my dad comes."

While I'm cutting the frozen Sara Lee pound cake the telephone rings. "I wonder what Mel wants," Barry says and goes to the bedroom to answer the phone. He drags the telephone out into the hallway and stands there, legs wide apart, watching me at the dining-room table, sawing through the pound cake. "The law library? Nope. I don't like to leave Sally alone."

"You can go. I don't mind."

Barry squats and puts the phone down on the carpet. He leans forward on the balls of his feet and looks up at me. "Mel wants me to study with him for the International Law exam at the law library. I told him no."

"Why don't you go? It would be easier studying with someone else."

Barry picks up the receiver. "Hold on a minute, Mel." Now he turns back to me. "Do you want to go with us, baby?"

"What would I do in the law library?"

"You could read. That's what you do here."

"I have to wash my hair."

"Do you want me to drop you off over at Mel's? You could spend the evening with Patsy."

"Doing what?"

"I don't know, baby. You could wash your hair there." Barry picks up the receiver again. "Hold on, Mel. I'm discussing it with my wife." He puts the phone back on the carpet. Mel's voice bellows out from the receiver, "The law library closes at ten, Feldman."

"You had better hurry," I say.

Barry picks up the receiver. "Okay, Mel. I'll meet you there." He hangs up and turns to me. "Are you sure you'll be all right here without me, baby? I can call Mel back and and tell him I'm not coming."

Barry picks up a matchbook from the dining-room table and writes a number on it. "If anything happens, call me at the law library. I'll come right home."

From the picture window, I watch Barry go out into the parking lot. His bony frame leans slightly to the right towards his briefcase that's heavy with law books. He gets into the Supersport, and the white car climbs the hill out of the parking lot, levels at the road, and turns. I go into the kitchen and get another beer. I dig into my purse and take out J.D.'s card. I stare at the card, its square white outline solid against the dark wood of the coffee table.

The photograph of the sculpture is too dark, but I recognize the piece. Printed underneath it, in J.D.'s neat black handwriting, is "Industrial Nightmare III." I watched him work on it with his acetylene torch, a little god in goggles beside his ten-foot monster. I slept in his bed, and he kept his shorts on. Before we went to sleep, he said, "Marry me?" and I shook my head no. In the morning he said, "Are you sure?" J.D. came up to my chin. I couldn't sleep with him. He said I didn't have to, he would marry me anyway.

I wanted to marry him, but I didn't love him the way I was supposed to. He was too short, and he looked like Alfred E. Newman, a goofy little boy with black horn-rimmed glasses, hunched into his army jacket, scowling. I liked to kiss him on the front seat of his Ford. We were fine as long as we had our clothes on. But he didn't have any muscles, his skin was soft, and he didn't have a beard. It had something to do with hormones. So I could have married him anyway and I would have slept with some tall good-looking guy in cowboy boots roaming around the Village. I couldn't have done that to J.D. and to me.

I don't want to look at the card anymore, but I don't want to throw it out either. I stuff it down into the bottom of my purse again.

The phone rings, and I go to pick it up from the hall carpet where Barry left it.

"May I speak to Mrs. Feldman, please?" Barry says.

"Hi, Barry."

"How did you know it was me, baby?" Barry laughs. "Are you okay?"

"Sure."

"What are you doing?"

"Talking to you on the phone."

"Before that, baby."

"Nothing."

"Sounds groovy, baby. I'll be home about ten-thirty."

"Okay."

"I miss you."

"You'll be home in an hour."

"Baby, you can be so deflationary sometimes. Why are you like that?"

Something is tickling my neck. I turn my head over and wrap my arms around the pillow. It's Saturday, and I don't have to wake up. I feel the same tickle on my neck, and then Barry's voice, close to my ear. "Baby, get up and make me some pancakes and bacon."

"You woke me up," I say into the pillow. I can't open my eyes and look at him. If I do, I'm sunk.

"It's ten o'clock."

"So what? It's Saturday." I lie still. I don't want to encourage Barry about the possibility of my moving.

"I'm dying for pancakes and bacon."

I don't say anything, and I don't move. Finally, I feel the mattress rise slightly, which means Barry has gotten off the bed. I go back to sleep and wake up two hours later, feeling tired. In the kitchen, Barry is leaning on the counter, drinking a Carnation Instant Breakfast. I take a glass of orange juice, lean against the counter next to him, and as I raise my glass, directly in my line of vision, propped up against the living-room wall, is a five-foot-square canvas, mainly green. It looks like two tables leaning against each other at forty-five-degree angles.

"What's that?"

Barry looks at the painting as though he hadn't noticed it before. It takes up one whole wall. "It's a wedding present. Susie dropped it off. I wanted to wake you up, so you could thank her, but she said she didn't want to bother you."

I look at the painting. I like all shades of green except avocado, which I hate. The painting is mostly avocado.

"It's nudes," Barry says. He goes over to the painting and points to part of one of the tables. "Ummn, this is the head of the first nude, see? And here's an elbow." He steps back and considers the painting. "Oh, here are the legs of the figure that's sitting down."

"Let's get it out of here."

"Why?"

"Because it stinks."

"I think it's kind of hip."

"I think it's lousy."

"Maybe you'll get used to it."

"Why do I have to get used to something I hate?"

"It's my present, too."

I stare at Barry.

"You'll have to write Susie a thank-you note." He hands me half of a matchbook cover with a New York City address on it. "She's leaving for New York tomorrow. She asked me to say good-bye to you."

I take the matchbook cover and put it in the pocket of my jeans. My fingers touch something soft and wadded up, and I realize it's the matchbook cover with Bruce's address in Miami.

The night before Barry's father is coming to visit, I'm on my hands and knees on the bathroom floor. In the corner where the white tiles meet the wall, I scrub out a few black, wiry hairs of Barry's. The bathroom door is open, and I can see into the bedroom. Barry is lying on the blue sheets, propped up on his elbow, smoking a cigarette and talking on the telephone. "Yeah, Mom," he says. "Sure, I love her. She worked her ass off today."

I finish the floor, but I still have the toilet to do. I go into the bedroom to have a cigarette. Lying down at the foot of the bed, propped up on my elbow, smoking a cigarette, I am the mirror image of Barry. I stare at the squared-off angles his shoulder forms the way he's lying sideways. I think about something his mother said. When Barry told her about me, how beautiful I was, how smart I was, etc., she said, "But Barry, you haven't mentioned one quality that would make her a good wife. You haven't said anything about warmth, sympathy, generosity."

With his whole hand Barry rips through a notebook that's lying next to him until he finds a blank page. He starts writing something down.

"Well?" I say when he hangs up.

"Yeah, baby?"

"What did your mother want?"

He tears out the piece of notebook paper and spreads it on the sheet like a napkin. "She checked herself into the spa again, and she thinks the doctor there is lying to her. She wants me to call him."

"What does the doctor say is wrong with her?"

Barry starts tapping the tip of his ball-point pen on the piece of notebook paper. It makes little hollow thuds on the sheet. "Nothing." The ball-point breaks through the paper with a crisp pop.

"What does she think is wrong with her?"

Barry shrugs. "Everything. Ulcers. Gallstones. Cancer. She put herself on a diet of carrot juice and vitamin capsules."

Now Barry is clicking the top of the ball-point up and down. Barry's mother won't eat and my mother won't stop drinking. They both expect us to do something about it. Barry's father wants him to be a lawyer and my father wants me to marry into the country club. Or else. I wonder what it's like to have a father who wants what you want. I wonder what it's like to have a mother who knows how to eat and drink.

Barry's father gets off the plane wearing a nicely tailored gray suit and a dark tie with a small diamond tie pin. He is a short, compactly built man. His hair is combed straight down from the perimeter of his balding head. No one feature stands out in his face. He is the kind of man nobody could suspect of anything.

He kisses me politely on the cheek. "Call him Dad," Barry has told me. But I can't even call my own father Dad. I can't call Barry's father Mr. Feldman. I can't call him Myron. I can't call him anything, so I just say hi.

He hugs Barry. I look at the two of them: the small, neat older man, and the taller, skinny son, his hair too long over his collar, his unshaven face, his shirttails hanging out of his pants. ("What are the two of you going to do with your lives?" he asked us before we got married. "Sit around and watch each other's hair grow?")

We get into the Supersport, Barry's father in the front seat and me in the back. He tells Barry to drive straight to Pizitz. He wants to buy Barry a suit.

"I don't need a suit," Barry says. "I thought we could go back to the apartment and watch football. Alabama is playing LSU. Baby, do we have anything to nosh on during the game?"

"Sally wouldn't know what *nosh* means," Barry's father says. "I do want to see the game, Barry, but I insist on buying you a suit first. That suit you wore when you got married was disgraceful."

"Maybe that's because I got it for high-school graduation," Barry says.

Barry's father gives off an almost imperceptible shudder. "In your profession, it's mandatory that you look well."

"My profession?" Barry laughs his short, unfunny laugh.

His father smiles at him. "You will be a lawyer before you know it. In a year, you'll be back in Florida taking the bar. You'll set up practice, and, after you get your feet wet, I still hope you'll decide to go into politics."

I look at Barry slouched behind the wheel of the Supersport. I wait for him to say he doesn't want to go into politics. I don't want Barry to go into politics. I have never even seen Barry read a newspaper.

"I have to pass the bar first," Barry says.

"We'll take care of that. Just get through school. I'm aware that the Florida bar is one of the most difficult in the country and that you are at a disadvantage going to a law school out of state. But we can enroll you in a preparatory course. You might give some thought to taking the New York bar exam as well. There is a great deal of business being transacted between Florida and New York."

"I think we have some potato chips and pretzels at home," I say. "I could make some dip."

Barry's father turns around. "Oh, you know what *nosh* means already, Sally? Barry, you are making a real Jewish wife out of her."

"She loves lox and bagels," Barry says.

"Except we can't afford lox."

"Baby!"

"It's true."

"On our way back from Pizitz, stop at a deli, Barry. We'll pick up some nosherai. We'll buy Sally some nova."

At Pizitz in the men's department, I sit down on a stool outside the dressing room between a rack of overcoats and winter jackets, one-half off. I'm holding my coat on my lap. Barry shuffles after his father and the salesman who are walking beside a row of suits. The heater is right behind me. The heat and the wool are making me sleepy. I can see across the floor into the women's department where a manikin is wearing a lavender sweater and skirt set. Lavender is my favorite color. The lavender clothes shimmer, the manikin sways, and I realize my eyes are starting to close. I slap my cheeks.

Barry's father has him standing in front of a full-length mirror in a midnight blue pin-striped suit. The tailor is standing to one side with a hunk of chalk, and Barry's father is standing behind, shifting the shoulders of the jacket as if Barry weren't in it at all. He runs his palm down the spine of the jacket, then with both hands claps Barry on the biceps. "Mark it up," he says to the tailor.

At the deli I wait in the car. Barry and his father come out and Barry hands me a white paper bag. I can smell the pickles, the herring, the lox, and the chopped liver.

"We're already on our way out to the law school, aren't we?" Barry's father says. "Why don't we drive out there. I would like to take a look at it."

"You saw it the last time you were here, Dad," Barry says. "It's the same."

"I would enjoy seeing it again. I have never been inside the law library. Do you find that the law library is extensive enough for your needs?"

Barry laughs his short, unfunny laugh. "It's too extensive for my needs."

I follow Barry and his father into the law library. It has a cathedral ceiling and mahogany-paneled walls. Long dark wood reading tables gleam under hanging lamps. Barry and his father look small in the large important room, Barry with his shirttails hanging out of his pants and his father in his neat suit. His father stops at the card catalogue and opens one small drawer, then another. He lays his hand on the smooth wood top of the cabinet.

Barry claps his hands, then spreads them wide apart. "Well, that's it, Dad. The law library."

It's a warm day for the middle of March. Barry has all the windows up in the car and the heat on. The smells of the pickles, the herring, the lox, the chopped liver, rise from the bag on my lap. The smells in the too-warm car are making my head spin. If I open a window, someone might notice I'm here. Someone might ask me what I'm doing here. My eyes start to close, I think about what Barry's mother said about sympathy, warmth, and generosity. I wonder why I don't have any. My eyes start to close, and I feel the deli bag slipping off my lap. I open my eyes, and the bag is still there, clutched in my hand.

"We're home, baby," Barry says.

I put the pickles, the herring, the lox, and the chopped liver on plates on the coffee table. Barry wheels the TV into the middle of the living room. He and his father sit down on the couch and start watching. I sit in one of the chairs with my book, but when I look at the words, they shimmer and slide on the page. I look from Barry to his father to the TV screen, at the little men running around in the mud, falling all over each other. My mother and my father and my brother used to sit around the family room and watch football. Sometimes I would sit there with a book just to be in the same room with them.

"Aren't you going to have any lox, Sally?" Barry's father says. "The Nova Scotia is the best lox you can buy."

I spread some cream cheese on a bagel and pick up a piece of lox. The orange fish is slippery in my fingers. I lay it across the bed of white cream cheese, then put the top of the bagel over it. Now all I have to do is eat it.

By halftime I have finished most of the lox and bagel. A marching band comes on TV, and Barry gets up and turns down the sound.

"I brought you kids something from the store," Barry's father says. He gives Barry a small white cardboard box and me a larger box.

"Open yours first, baby," Barry says.

Inside the box, pink tissue paper is folded over and held with the gold seal of Barry's father's store in Miami Beach. I tear the paper without breaking the seal and lift out a glass dish in the shape of a shell. "Oh," I say. "This is very nice."

"You put nuts or candy in it when you have company," Barry's father says.

Barry opens his present and holds the box away from him in his hand. He doesn't say anything for a moment. Then he takes the gold tie pin out of the box. It is in the shape of the scales of justice. "Thanks, Dad," he says. His voice is high and hollow.

I get up to make dinner, and Barry's father says, "I wish you two kids would let me take you out. I don't want you to go to any trouble."

I take the roast out of its cellophane wrapping. The green price sticker says $3.65. The red hunk of meat is pushing itself out of its string ties. When I pick it up, it leaves blood in the indentations of the cardboard tray. *The Better Homes and Gardens Cookbook* says to roast the meat for thirty minutes a pound. The day I bought the cookbook with its red-and-white-checked cover, the sun was brilliant and the Alabama sky a thick, deep blue, like Barry's sheets. "I love you, Feldman!" I yelled through the open windows of the Supersport.

I crumble pieces of real bleu cheese into the Good Seasons Italian Dressing. The white porous cheese swims around in the oil and vinegar. It smells funny to me, but I don't trust my senses. I ask Barry to taste it. "It's the same as always," he says.

I never noticed how yellow the sauce is for the Noodles Romanoff. I'm stirring it on the stove, and Barry leans into the kitchen doorway. "Is dinner ready? I'm getting hungry, baby."

I cut into the roast, but dark red blood spurts out of its center. I look at the cookbook to be sure I read the directions right, but I know I did because I read them three times. I take the salad off the table and put it in the refrigerator. I turn the heat off under the noodles.

In fifteen minutes, I cut into the roast, and its blood gushes into the bottom of the pan. Barry has followed me into the kitchen and is standing on the other side of the open oven door. He stares down at the meat. "What's the matter, baby?"

"I don't know. It was supposed to be done fifteen minutes ago."

Barry looks at his watch. "It's getting late. My dad must be hungry."

I stand in front of Barry with the pot holders in my hands. Barry's father comes up behind Barry and stands in the kitchen doorway, blocking it. He looks over Barry's shoulder at the roast.

Barry looks back at his father. "I'm sorry, Dad," he says.

I serve the salad and the three of us sit down at the table. I pick up my fork, but I don't like the way the oily dressing with its whitish lumps of bleu cheese is lying in the folds of the lettuce.

"It's a great salad, baby," Barry says.

"Yes, Sally, it is very good," his father says.

"Aren't you eating any, baby? It's your favorite salad."

In the kitchen I slice the knife into the cut I've made two times before. The blood comes out a thin light pink.

I lean over Barry's shoulder to set the roast on the table. The smell of the steaming meat rises into my face. "Excuse me," I say.

In the bathroom, I turn on the fan. The whir blocks out the sounds of Barry's and his father's voices. I put both my hands on the countertop. In front of me, my face shimmers and slides in the mirror. "You don't shit, do you?" I hear Barry saying. "Baby, if you shit, don't tell me. I would be crushed."

I drop down onto the toilet. I double over, clutching my thighs, which are shaking from the force of the stomach cramps.

When I get up, my legs are weak, and my face is pale but steady in the mirror. My stomach feels as though I've been beaten there.

Polly and I are having lunch at a restaurant where you can watch TV while you eat. There are three small rooms, each with rows of one-armed school desks and at the front of the room, a twenty-five-inch television hanging from a steel arm. Polly and I get hamburgers and french fries and take them on our trays into the room where a *Ben Casey* rerun is on. A beautiful young woman lies in a hospital bed, her thick black hair swirling out from her pale face onto the white pillow.

"What's wrong with her?" We have come in late, but Polly knows all of the plots.

"Stomach cancer, if I'm remembering right."

"Can you get stomach cancer when you're that young?"

"Nobody'd watch the show if it was old people who got sick."

I pick up one of the limp, white french fries, then drop it back onto my tray.

"I got sick this weekend. I had diarrhea. I had to stay in bed all day yesterday. Barry's father was visiting from Florida."

"If Barry's daddy is anything like Jess's ma, you were lucky," Polly says. "I'd like to get sick every time she visits. Especially if I could get into the hospital with Ben Casey. I haven't seen Jess in bed for two weeks. He's been doing inventory nights at the store."

Ben Casey is leaning over the hospital bed, taking the young woman's pulse. Now he's probably going to sit down and listen to her life story while the rest of his patients die of neglect.

"Where does your husband work?" I ask Polly.

Polly turns from Ben Casey to me. "He is the manager of the shoe department at Pizitz." There is real pride in her voice. I run through some trial phrases in my head: *He is an assistant district attorney in Dade County. He is on the Supreme Court of the State of Florida. He has his own firm in Miami.*

I look down at my feet, at the brown shoes with the little spool heels I wore when I got married. They still hurt. "Is he working all afternoon?" I ask Polly.

"Did you ever see Ben Casey leave the hospital?"

"I mean your husband. I need some shoes."

"I would like you to meet Sally Feldman, Jess," Polly says to her husband. "She is the girl I have been talking about all the time."

122

Polly's husband is tall, thin, and wan with limp blond hair.

"Can you get one of the men to fit Sally up with some shoes, Jess? Her feet are killing her."

"I'll help her myself," Jess says quietly.

I look past Jess to the small gatherings of shoes posed here and there on countertops, on tables, on shelves underneath a soft pink light. There are so many shoes, and I have been wearing a pair that pinches my feet. I walk through the room on the soft carpet, around the couches, looking at the shoes. I want to see every pair before I make my choice. Polly is right behind me.

Polly picks up a pair of pumps with three-inch heels, the kind she and the other women at the department wear. "How about these, Sally? These would look real good on you."

I shake my head no. I am in kind of a trance, looking at the shoes. "Hey, look at these." Polly is holding up another pump with three-inch heels. "Try these on. I have a pair just like them. I like this bone color for spring. It would look right nice with your bag."

I shake my head again.

"What's wrong with this pair, Sally? They go with your bag. Bone is good with everything."

I turn to Polly. "I don't want high heels."

Polly takes a long look at me. "You don't? That's what all the ladies wear, except Betty Anne Markland and she's six feet tall."

"I don't care. I'm tired of being uncomfortable."

"You get used to high heels," Polly says. "After you wear them long enough you don't even notice they hurt."

"That's what I'm afraid of," I say. I show Jess the shoes

I want to try on. One pair is soft black leather with flat heels and two straps across the arch. The other pair is sand-colored, with low heels, and looks like a child's sandal, little holes in the toe of the shoe, two straps with buckles.

"Are you going to wear these to the playground, Sally?"

"We just got those two pairs in from New York," Jess says. "I am curious about how they will sell."

Jess brings out two shoe boxes and takes one of the black shoes in my hand. On the inside of the soft black leather there is a bright red cushiony lining. I put the shoes on and walk around the carpeting. They feel light on my feet, almost as if I am walking barefoot. "I'll take them," I say.

Polly picks up the empty shoe box and looks at the end. "Jumpin' Jehoshaphat. Aren't you even going to look at the price? This pair is twenty-seven dollars."

I feel a little thrill at the bottom of my spine. "Let me try on the other pair."

"You are not going to buy two pairs of shoes, are you, Sally? I get a twenty percent discount, and I still wait until the end of the season so I can get them on sale." Polly rummages through her bag, takes out a pack of Juicy Fruit and puts a stick in her mouth. "Why, I wouldn't pay twenty-seven dollars for a pair of shoes if I had to wear my bedroom slippers to work. The Pizitzes have a nerve to charge anyone twenty-seven dollars for something to cover their feet."

"These shoes are imported from Italy," Jess says.

Polly whistles, "Do you mean we have two hundred million people in this dang country, and not one of them can make a pair of shoes that costs less than twenty-seven dollars?"

I walk around the soft smooth carpet in the second pair

of shoes, the ones that look like a child's sandals. It feels good to have my feet on the ground.

While I'm walking I see another pair of shoes, one I didn't notice before, a dress pump with a high heel and one sleek strap across the instep. "I'll take the ones I'm wearing," I say to Jess and hold up the dress pump. "And I want to try this one on, too."

"I thought you didn't want a high heel," Polly says.

I hold out the shoe in my palm and stare at it. "I don't. But this is the most beautiful shoe I have ever seen. Look at the curve of the strap and the gold buckle."

"This is a shoe store, Sally. The Birmingham Museum of Art is over on Eighth Avenue North."

I slip the pumps onto my feet. They feel a little tight across the toes, but they're beautiful and I love them, and they'll probably stretch. I look at my feet in the low mirror. The strap snakes across my instep to just below my ankle.

"I didn't know Birmingham had an art museum. Have you ever been there?"

"Sure. I went with my daughter and twenty-three fourth-graders on their class trip. My head was like to split by the time I got home."

"I'll take this pair, too," I say to Jess.

Polly looks at me sharp. "Are you going to walk up and down the corridors in the nursing homes in those, Sally? Any of your clients look at your feet, they'll think Elizabeth Taylor quit the movies and come to work for Welfare."

"I won't wear them to work."

"Where are you going to wear them? You already told me you don't go to church." Polly picks up the shoe box and brings it close to her eyes to look at the price.

"I don't know," I say. "Maybe someday I'll go some-place."

Polly gathers up her bag and her sweater, and we follow Jess up to the register.

I take out the one check from Barry's and my joint checking account that he gave me to keep in my wallet, in case of emergency. The edges are worn where the check is folded in two. Jess rings up the total on the register: seventy-three dollars.

Walking through the parking lot to the car, Polly grabs my arm, and talks to me, her face leaning into mine, her mouth an inch from my cheek. "Heck, Sally, if I spent that kind of money on shoes, my husband would either kill me or divorce me, I don't know which. What are you smiling for, Sally? I ain't joking."

When Barry comes to pick me up, I am wearing the new pair of black shoes and carrying three shoeboxes tied together with string. One of the boxes has my old shoes inside.

"You didn't buy all those shoes, did you?" Barry says.

"No. One box has my old shoes in it."

"But that means you bought three pairs of shoes."

"Uh huh."

"That's a lot of shoes, baby. Do you need three pairs of shoes?"

"I needed two."

"What did you buy the third one for?"

"Because they were pretty."

"That doesn't seem to be a very good reason to buy a pair of shoes."

"It doesn't?"

"Can you take them back?"

126

"I don't want to take them back."

"Why not, baby? You said you don't need them."

"Maybe I want something I don't need."

I go in the front door of the apartment, untie the shoe boxes, take the box with my old brown shoes that pinch, go through the apartment, and out the back door to the trash bin. I throw the box over the top and into the bin.

Even though it's 5:30, it's still light outside. The trees behind the parking lot are full and green along the hill, their tops merging in a wavy green line below the blue sky. In the black dirt at the side of the trash bin, three crocuses have pushed out of the ground. I squat down to look more closely at their purple petals. The ground smells of fresh rich dirt. The leaves of the crocuses are dark green against my new black shoes. I breathe in the dirt, look up again at the tree-tops, green against blue sky. I'm glad I don't have anything to do with the seasons. If it had been left up to me, I would have forgotten and spring would never have come.

In the apartment, Barry is sitting at the dining-room table, slicing through a tomato with a serrated knife. He says, "While you were at work, a chick came by selling maga-zines. A pretty chick. Blond. She started coming on to me. I told her I was married, but she didn't believe me. She said, 'I can tell you're not married because of the way your apart-ment looks. It doesn't have a woman's touch.' "

Barry's knife is poised midair. He is leaning his head on his hand, looking up at me. I look for some sign of nastiness in his face, but I can't find any. He looks innocent, as though he is simply relating an anecdote to me, not accusing me of being a bad wife, not warning me that while I'm gone, a perfect stranger can come in and offer to do a better job of it. The only thing in the apartment that was not already here when we moved in is the bookcase I made of wood planks laid across cinder blocks. Barry's law books are on the bottom shelf, and my paperbacks, with their shiny covers, are on the top shelf. Sartre and Camus and Gide. But I guess a bookcase is not what the girl selling magazines considers "a woman's touch." What would she put in Barry's apartment that I haven't? A vase? A tablecloth? Doilies? I don't know. I don't know what a woman's touch is. I don't know what a woman is.

I watch Barry's long, quick bony fingers dance in the juice of the cherry tomatoes, picking up the floating seeds and putting them into his mouth. Barry is not a man, either. That's why I like him.

I throw my hand out into the air. My wedding band flies off. It hits the wall, bounces, and rolls across the living-room rug.

I follow it and pick it up. It is a wide gold band with a delicate filigree pattern between the borders. The ring's width reaches to my knuckle. The night before the wedding, Barry had to jam it on my finger, and my finger turned white above the knuckle. I had to soap the ring off in the bathroom sink while all of Barry's relatives sat in the living room. In the morning, we had the ring stretched. Now it's too loose.

I set the ring on the table between Barry and me and stare at it. I think about Barry and me going to a motel the first night we met. I was wearing a cameo ring, and I turned the woman's face around to my palm, so it looked like I was wearing a wedding band. I liked being married to Barry before we got married. I stayed with him in Birmingham for a weekend, for a week, for three weeks. One night he was lying on the couch studying, and I was reading an article in *Mademoiselle*. When I'm not reading Sartre and Camus and Gide, I read *Mademoiselle* to tell me how to live. The article said that being married was like living with your best friend, only better because there was sex. I liked that part. I read it out loud to Barry. The article also said something about always being honest with each other. I liked that part, too, and I read it out loud to Barry. "So if that's what marriage is like, let's get married," I said. "But just in case, maybe I should put a sign up on the wall that says, 'BE HONEST.'"

I look away from the wedding ring. There is no sign about honesty on the wall. The only thing on our wall is Susie's painting.

"Did you go to bed with her?" I say.

Barry looks up from his plate of tomato seeds.

"Did you go to bed with the blonde who was selling magazines?"

Barry looks at me, his eyes wide and his mouth twisted. "Are you kidding?"

"I'm sorry," I say.

"Jesus Christ."

"I'm sorry." I look at my hands on the dining-room table, my ten naked fingers stretched out before me.

Didn't I ever tell you what Barry looks like? I write my friend Miranda in Taos. *He is 5'7", skinny, and Jewish. He has long, bony fingers that fly in the air when he eats. He plays the piano, like you do. Only not "Moonlight Sonata," but tunes you can't recognize. He is a Gemini, like you. He has black hair and blue blue eyes. His two front teeth overlap in front. His hair is long (of course) and he is sloppy but elegant. He talks funny. He says "wild bananas." He has this smile. Um, he had this smile. . . .*
I look up from my typewriter. I look at Barry lying on the

couch with his Torts book. I should have written Miranda before, when I believed in what Barry looked like. I tear the sheet out of the typewriter and crumple it up.

I put a new sheet in. *Dear Miranda.* What am I supposed to say now? I tear the sheet out and put a new sheet in and write fast.

Dear Daphne. Since I have been sold into the white slave trade, I have found a peacefulness in my soul that I never dreamed possible in this life. Here in Ankara, surrounded by muscular half-dressed Turks who, putting their money where their muscles are, have bid massive sums for me on the auction block, I have found bliss, a sense of transcendent mirth. I must say, however, the food stinks. I am given every material pleasure — fine silks, combs of rare gems for my hair (mousy brown, so exotic in this culture where raven black abounds), perfume so costly the whole of India could eat steak or maybe lobster on one ounce of the oil I employ in my daily bath. But there are no books. It's hard to get a decent conversation going around here, especially as no one speaks English.

How I miss you, dear Daphne! Our games of Cribbage! Our intimate midnight talks about logical positivism! Leave Taos, leave your motorbike (dangerous, my dear, without a helmet), your bohemian lovers with their dirty hair and hand-tooled sandals.

I must go! Raul calls! (It's odd how many Turkish men have Spanish names.) Much love and squalor. Zou Zou.

I type an envelope with Miranda's address in Taos and stuff the letter inside. Then I unfold it and stick it back in the typewriter. *P.S. I am miserable, but it's not the kind of miserable we were at school where we were all miserable together, getting drunk and laughing and being clever and excited about it all the time. I'm miserable alone.*

I stuff the letter back into the envelope and seal it. Barry looks up from his law book and smiles. "What were you writing, baby?"

"A letter to Miranda."

"That's nice."

I leave the letter on the dining-room table and start to go into the bedroom. "I might steam it open and read it," Barry teases me.

"It doesn't matter. None of it is true."

"What do you mean?"

"I made it up. Miranda and I have imaginary identities."

"You and your friends are pretty weird, baby."

"I thought you were weird, too, Barry. You talked weird. I thought we would move to the Village, and you would play piano. I thought we'd fly to Rio and blow your bonds at Mardi Gras. I don't know. I didn't think we would stay here."

"You didn't?"

"Not really."

"It's only a year, baby. Then we'll be in Miami. We'll get a place with a swimming pool."

"We have a place with a swimming pool," I say.

In the bedroom I put on my salmon-colored babydoll pajamas. I packed the pajamas the last time I came to visit Barry after he called me long distance from a pay phone in the Boom Boom Room. "The go-go girls don't get me hot anymore, baby. I must be in love. Come down here and marry me." A month later the telephone company called and asked me if I knew anyone who might have called from a phone booth in Miami: he owed them six dollars. I said no. The salmon pajamas smelled of Barry's sweat and my perfume. They smelled of bourbon and Kool-Aid. Of Larks.

Salmon silk against blue sheets against tan skin, our bodies dusky blue in the morning, the sunshine diffused through blue drapes.

I look at myself in the salmon pajamas in the bedroom mirror, at the ruffles like cotton candy around the straps and neck. I pull the top off over my head and stuff it back into my drawer. I rummage through Barry's bottom drawer and take out the pajamas his mother bought him in case he has to go to the hospital. They are gray and red plaid cotton, Sanforized. I put the top on and get into bed. I pull the blanket up to my cheeks. I have to be at work at 8:00 in the morning. Miranda is probably sleeping in the back of some guy's van tonight. She'll ride her motorbike to work in the morning.

I am in a deep, dreamless sleep. I feel Barry's hand on my ass, feel his bony knees press into my thighs, his penis into my belly, every bone separate and prodding. It is like the first night, when he put his penis inside me, I felt as though I were giving in not to a man — I'd done that before, I knew what that felt like — but to a snake, to a beautiful, cold, wet, undulating snake, exotic and deadly. Now I feel a scream from in my belly, a wave of nausea. "No," I say and move away from Barry towards the edge of the bed.

"But, baby."

"I can't."

"It's been a long time."

"I'm sorry."

I lie stiff at the end of the bed. The mattress shifts under me as Barry changes positions, then it jumps a little, the pounding of a foot or a fist. His side of the mattress rises, and I hear his footsteps into the bathroom, the click of the light, the whir of the fan. Then he is back, throwing himself on his side of the bed, like a staggering man at the edge of a pool.

I lie still and wait.

"I masturbated," Barry says. "I haven't had to do that since I was fourteen."

I feel my body recoil, my breath suck in. My fists clutch the pillow. I lie still and wait for Barry's soft sleep breathing to release me into sleep again.

When Barry picks me up at work, the sun is still bright. The air is warm and so thick you can feel it on your hands. I get in the car, throw my head back, and sigh. I don't want to go home.

"Let's go out for dinner," I say to Barry. "We don't have to go anyplace expensive. I'll go anywhere."

"We can't afford it, baby," Barry says.

"It's a couple of dollars. We can eat hamburgers at a drive-in."

Barry doesn't say anything for a minute. "We should be saving money now, baby."

"Why?"

"Next year, I'll just be starting out. I won't be making that much right off."

Spring hangs in the air. The trees are heavy with leaves. The Supersport moves smoothly along the hilly roads, under the blue sky. The windows are down and the car fills with the warm breeze and smells of new leaves and flowers, of fresh tar on the road. I close my eyes and become Salina Jane Adams, heroine of a southern novel.

When I open my eyes, we're passing a drive-in hamburger restaurant. "Let's stop here," I say to Barry.

We're sitting in the car eating our hamburgers and french

fries. Last spring in Ohio, J.D. and I ate at Frish's Big Boy every night. "The problem with you, Salina Jane," he said, "is that you're a cynic. I'm a skeptic, and that's healthy." J.D. was too short to reach the microphone that hung on a pole outside the car window. He had to get out of the car and order dinner standing up.

I look over at Barry. He is wearing a crisp white shirt. I look at him in his white shirt, leaning against the red leather upholstery, chewing a french fry. Until last spring, he did not exist. I had never seen him. I met him in Florida on Good Friday. The next day I flew back to Ohio. How did I get here from there?

I feel I have to say something. I don't know what to say. I say, "In Ohio, the winters were so cold, and women couldn't wear slacks to class unless it was below twenty degrees. Everyone stayed inside. In early spring there was the monsoon season. It rained for weeks. We slipped through mud on the way to class. When spring came, everyone went crazy. All day we would lie out on the grass in the sun. All night we would lie on the grass at the riverbank. The air was thick, just like it is today."

"I don't know, baby," Barry says. "In Florida the weather is the same all the time. Nothing changes."

"I would hate that," I say. "I hate winter, but I would miss it. You can't have spring without winter."

"Sure you can, baby. In Florida, it's like spring and summer all the time."

Barry crumples up the wrapper from his hamburger and starts the car. The wind blows my hair off my neck. The Supersport glides through the hills. We descend Red Mountain and pass the fifty-foot iron statue of Vulcan, God of the Forge. He looks down at us, unmoved and unmoving.

On my first visit to Birmingham, Barry brought me to the Vulcan. At the entrance to the innards of the statue, hanging on to Barry, kissing and giggling, I signed the guest book: *Salina Jane Adams, Greenwich Village, New York.* Under *Comments,* I wrote: *Excruciatingly Southern.*

Now we don't say anything. I look up at the massive iron figure on its pedestal on top of Red Mountain. We shouldn't have laughed at the Vulcan. The Vulcan will endure.

It is Saturday afternoon and Patsy and I are sitting on the grass on a hill on the college campus, the sky stretched out over us like a deep blue sheet. Little clumps of students are sitting and lying on the grass, reading and talking. Patsy and I are waiting for Barry and Mel to come out of the gym. They are playing in the finals of the university handball tournament.

Barry and Mel come running towards us up the hill. They are wearing dirty white gym shorts and T-shirts. Mel raises both his arms in the air, throws his head back, and cries, "We won! Steingut and Feldman, Champions!"

As they reach the top of the hill, I can smell their sweat. Mel grabs Patsy in a bear hug, and Patsy giggles. "Mel!" she cries.

Barry's T-shirt is hanging out from his shorts, stretched out and drenched in sweat. His sweat socks are sagging down around his ankles. A goofy, happy smile on his face, he is coming towards me, his arms outstretched, stiff, ready to take me in all his triumphant nakedness. I smell his sweat, see it on his glistening face, and I turn away from the kiss.

We sit down next to Mel and Patsy on the hill. Mel is talking fast about the game and Patsy is looking up at him and smiling. The sky is so blue, I have never seen it so blue, like Barry's blue sheets, only the sky goes on forever. I don't want to look at the sky. I don't want to look at the grass. I don't want to look at Barry.

I take out my nail file and start filing my nails. Barry stares ahead and says, "I've never been so lonely in my whole life." I sit still at his side, and stare out into the blue sky, filing my nails into perfect arcs.

I am driving alone in the Supersport through the countryside to Ruby Postum's Nursing Home. The Alabama country is hilly and green, not like country where I grew up, the Illinois prairie stretched out flat and unchanging as far as I could see. The seasons are changing fast now. I can see that. A field that was green last week today is blue with cornflowers. The air blowing through the open windows is warm now, almost hot some days, and it's getting hotter.

I turn off the highway onto a one-lane paved road, and, from there, onto a dirt road. At the end of the dirt road, rising from the dirt and the weeds and the grass is a dark red brick building that suffers from the same neglect as the ground around it. I pull the Supersport up in front and park in the dirt.

A big meaty black man, one of Ruby Postum's sons, stands in the door of the building smoking a cigarette. I take a deep breath and follow him inside. As soon as I go through the door, the stench, heavier now in the warm air, stuns me. Ruby Postum's Nursing Home smells like the lion house at the zoo.

The light inside is dim. As my eyes adjust from the brilliant sunlight, the room appears as if in shadows. At first I see only a low large dark shape, with two tall dark shapes, but as my eyes focus, I see the first shape is Ruby Postum's big desk with Ruby behind it, not much taller than the desk itself and almost as wide. Behind her are her two other sons. A framed photograph of President Kennedy's face on a background of royal blue velvet hangs over Ruby's desk.

"Afternoon, Miz Feldman," Ruby says. "Who you got to see today?"

I put my folder on the edge of her desk and run through the eligibility forms, saying the names: *Willie Harper, Hattie Mae Turner, Earline Lloyd.*

Ruby shuffles through some of the dusty papers on her desk. "Hattie Mae, she passed."

"I beg your pardon?"

Ruby looks up at me. "She passed."

"Oh." I take Hattie Mae Turner's form out from the pile. "We didn't get any notification of her death."

Ruby looks up at me, a long blank gaze, her eyes dull and mudlike, eyes that have seen a thousand bodies come to her half-dead in an ambulance and leave all-dead in a hearse. Some all-dead ones come in an ambulance and stay awhile, Polly says.

Ruby picks up a flattened pack of Camels and holds it out to me. I take a limp Camel. Ruby turns her head to one of her sons and he comes over and lights my cigarette. His hand is the size of a ham.

"The others is still here," Ruby says. "Luke, take Miz Feldman to see Willie and Earline."

Luke is the biggest of the three sons, the one who met me outside at the door. I follow him down the dark hall. The back of his neck is as thick as a telephone pole. Towards the center of a large dark room the stench gets stronger. There are two rows of cots. Some of the bodies lie still. Some are coughing. Some are mumbling to themselves. A woman, her gray frizzy hair growing straight up from her head, lifts herself up with her long bare arms, leans over the side of the cot, and spits a long, brown stream into a rusty coffee can.

Next to the woman a man lies on his back on a bare mattress, one leg bent at the knee, his pant leg rolled halfway up his calf. Luke inclines his head towards the man. "This one's Willie," he says, and stands smoking at the foot of the bed. I make a note that there are no sheets.

Willie's eyes are closed. "Willie," I say. "I'm Miz Feldman from the Welfare. I want to talk to you for a minute."

The top of Willie Harper's head is a skull, the black skin stretched tight across it. His face looks like the rippled mud of a riverbed. He opens his eyes. The whites are red and watery. He tries to pull himself up to his elbow.

He has no teeth. His gums look hard. His shoulders are a scarecrow for the unbuttoned shirt that hangs on them.

I look down at his eligibility form. He has no Social Security, no veteran's pension, no income. Ruby Postum is keeping him for his $200-a-month welfare check, the same as she's keeping most of the others.

I look closer at Willie's calf where the pant leg is rolled up. There is a growth on it the size of a half a grapefruit.

"Have you been to the hospital with that, Willie?"

Willie smiles at me. "Ma'am?" he says.

"What's this on Willie's leg?" I ask Luke.

Luke doesn't look at me. "You ask Velma," he says.

"Who's Velma?"

"My sister."

"Why would I ask her?"

"Velma, she's the nurse."

"Would you get her, please? I would like to ask her about Willie's leg."

Luke looks at me and doesn't say anything.

"Could you please tell Velma I'd like to talk to her a minute?"

"Velma's boy took sick." Luke is looking down at the floor.

"Do you mean she isn't here?"

He looks up at me. He doesn't say anything, so I figure I got it right. "Well, bring over one of the other nurses, then."

Luke doesn't move. He drops his cigarette on the floor and stamps on it. He's not going anywhere.

"Is Velma the only nurse?"

Luke's big head drops forward.

I put Willie Harper's form back in my folder. I lean over his bed and talk close to his face.

"Does the nurse give you medicine when you have pain in your leg?"

"Ma'am?"

"Does the nurse give you a pill or needle when your leg hurts?"

"It always feel the same, ma'am."

"Do you get enough to eat here, Willie?"

"Yessum."

"Is there anything you want to tell me?"

"No, ma'am."

I take Willie's hand in mine, and we make the X on the eligibility form. "Remember, you get a twelve-dollar check every month so you can buy cigarettes or candy."

He just looks at me.

"You get a twelve-dollar check every month that's just for you — not for the nursing home, not for Ruby."

"I don't know, ma'am. You ask Ruby about that, ma'am."

I follow Luke up a narrow staircase into a kind of tower. The brick walls are unpainted. Up here in the tower, the stench is stronger than it is downstairs. I try to disguise the revulsion I feel here, inundated by the smell of unbathed human flesh, of spittle, of urine, of shit, all existing here together for so long the smell has gone into the walls, into the floors, into the dirt ground the building is sitting on.

In a small room, alone, sitting on the edge of a cot, is a tall, thin woman in a worn silk dress. Her hands are on her knees, her back and neck arched in profile. She is in the pose of waiting. I go up behind Earline Lloyd and put my hand lightly on her shoulder to let her know I'm here. "Miz Feldman from the Welfare," I say.

Luke slumps in the doorway.

The woman whirls around and faces me. "I been waitin' for you. You got to get me out of here, Miz Feldman. They forgets to bring my dinner up here. If I gets to the bathroom I got to feel all the way along the wall with my hands." Earline Lloyd stands up, her tall body in sharp angles against the dark brick wall. Her hands move like lovers along the brick wall as she moves towards me, and I see her eyes are unfocused, glazed over with a thin white film.

"Just let me feel your face, please, ma'am." Earline Lloyd's bony black fingers move over my eyes, mouth, nose. Her fingers are dry but move quickly. "I sees you is a nice lady, ma'am. Please, ma'am, get me out of here. My niece, please, ma'am, she take me in."

Luke is hulking outside the doorway. Earline leans close to my ear. "The men, they beats me. They lock me in the room." Her chest sinks in and she doubles over herself, then she straightens her body and throws her arms wide. "Don't leave me here, ma'am," she cries, and her long, bony arms envelop me, her wet cheek presses into mine.

I pat her hand. "I'll try to get in touch with your niece," I say.

"Ma'am?"

"Do you know her address?" Earline lets go of me, and the tautness of her body gives way to a gentle shaking. She looks down at her hands in her lap.

"If you want me to call your niece, I have to know her name and where she lives," I say.

Earline speaks slowly, her words plodding. "I calls her Ollie, but Tessie call her Leola, Tessie, she my sister, been dead thirty years now. Ollie, she marry Cleophelus, but he no good, so Ollie she live out yonder with Jimmie. He gone now."

"Earline Lloyd says you locked her in a room."

Ruby lifts one of her hands with a ring on her finger like a string on a sausage, and takes a drag on her Camel. Her mound of flesh sits in the dark behind the big dark desk, silent, enduring, a mound of earth. She shakes her head and makes a soft rumbling sound.

"I done keep Earline two months before the Welfare sent a check."

"She says she has a niece she could live with."

Ruby's immobile face, a mountain, a swamp, sits before me. Smoke drifts out of her nostrils, out of her mouth.

All the way to the law school library and all the way home I think about Earline Lloyd and the graceful arch of her back against the dark red brick wall. In the apartment I go into the kitchen and take the bottle of bourbon, Charred Oak, and pour some in a glass. There's about three inches of bourbon in the bottom of the bottle. "I haven't had any of that bourbon," Barry says. "The bottle is almost finished, and I haven't had any of it."

I sip the bourbon and take down a can of Heinz Vegetarian Beans from the shelf. I wonder why everything is my fault. I dump the beans into a saucepan and put it on the stove. I spent the day with Earline Lloyd and Ruby Postum, with human stench, with disease, with poverty, with open sores, blindness, madness, and death. Barry has spent his day with the cool, white pages, the logic of his law books in the rich luster of mahogany at the law library. I stir the beans halfway around the pan, lean against the stove, and take another sip of bourbon. Barry is sitting at the dining-room table, hunched over on his elbows, smoking a Lark, waiting for his hot dogs and beans.

After dinner, Barry lies down on the couch, his law books and notebooks and legal pads stacked up on the coffee table in front of him, his cigarettes and ashtray balanced on the edge of the couch cushion. I clear the table, scrape my dinner off my plate into the garbage, wash the dishes, pour myself another glass of bourbon. I go into the bedroom and lie down with a paperback book. The words lurch to one side, lift up off the page, then recede. I put the book down.

My eyes close, and I see Earline Lloyd sitting in her tower room, waiting, her arched back, her long black arms. She turns towards me, and she has my face.

I pick up the glass of bourbon and take another sip, but there's no bourbon left, just yellowish melted ice. I look at the clock. It's 9:30. I look around the room at the blue drapes, the dresser, the messy blue sheets. I haven't seen anything else today but Ruby Postum's Nursing Home and Barry Feldman's apartment. I get out of bed and go into the bathroom. Barry is still lying on the couch. In the bathroom, I squeeze toothpaste onto my toothbrush, then I put it down. I go into the kitchen and pour the last inch of bourbon into my glass. I drop the bottle into the garbage.

I wait after the bottle has crashed to the bottom, but Barry doesn't say anything. I take the glass into the bedroom, and wait for the bourbon to make the room look fuzzy, different. When I've finished the bourbon, I get up and turn off the light. The glowing numbers on the alarm clock say 9:35. In New York, J.D. and I would be out standing on some street corner, trying to decide where to eat. Greasy hamburgers on paper plates at the White Horse, chili at the Corner Bistro where we'd play the jukebox, spaghetti and wine at La Marionetta. I haven't had dinner, and I'm hungry, drunk-hungry. Maybe J.D. is already home.

I drag the phone off the night table and pull it down into bed with me. I pull the blankets over my head and dial "0" and give the operator J.D.'s number.

His voice comes on the phone, and in the background, I can hear a car horn honking, and I am back in New York, on the corner of West 4th Street and Bleecker, a little drunk, J.D.'s arm around me, running across Bleecker past the honking taxi.

"This is a collect call from Salina Feldman. Do you accept?"

The operator's voice is pure Alabama, the words coming out as if through a mouthful of oatmeal, *this* and *is* two syllables, *Feldman* emerging as *Fieldman,* and I'm back in

Birmingham again, a little drunk hiding under the blankets with the phone.

J.D. laughs. It's not a particularly good-natured laugh.

"Do you accept?" the operator says.

"What are the alternatives?" J.D. says.

"Pardon me?"

"I accept," J.D. says. Then to me, "I thought you got married."

"I did," I say.

"I can't hear you."

"I did."

"We must have a bad connection. Want me to call you back?"

"It's not the connection. I'm not talking very loud."

"What?"

"My husband is in the living room."

"Jesus."

"J.D.?"

"Yeah."

"How are you?"

"Me? Oh, you know, okay. A little stoned. We've got some hash and there's the daily Dexedrine. Salina Jane, why did you get married? No, don't tell me."

"I don't know."

"What?"

"I don't know why I got married."

We don't say anything for a moment.

"J.D.?"

"Right."

"I missed your show."

"I noticed."

I hear the door to the bedroom open, and I put the receiver

back in the cradle. I feel my body go stiff as the light clicks on and Barry's footsteps come closer to the bed. He lifts the blanket up and throws it back. "What are you doing in bed with your clothes on, baby?" he says.

I just look at him.

He drums his fingertips on the night table where the phone usually sits. He presses down the button on the traveling alarm clock. He sits down on the edge of the bed. His hand lands on the phone cord.

He throws the blanket all the way down to the foot of the bed and stares at the black phone on the blue sheets.

"Who were you calling?" he says.

"Miranda."

"Why were you calling her from under the covers?"

"I didn't think you'd want me to make a long-distance call."

"Baby, you don't have to hide things from me." He comes closer and puts his hand on my shoulder. He leans towards me to kiss me on the cheek. Then he pulls away. "Wait a minute. You said Miranda doesn't have a phone. You read me a letter she wrote, and she said she didn't have a phone." Barry's eyes are wide, and his voice is loud and hollow.

I throw my legs over the side of the bed and stand up. I feel wobbly from the bourbon, so I brace myself on the night table. If Barry says anything about my being drunk, it's all over. "She got a phone," I say. "She sent her number in the last letter."

I take a few steps back until I am standing in the doorway between the bedroom and the bathroom. I am poised, waiting the appropriate number of seconds until I can either go into the bathroom and shut the door without looking like

I'm running away — or until Barry asks me to show him Miranda's letter. Barry is leaning against the dresser, staring at me, chewing gum in slow, deliberate rotations of his jaw. "If I asked you to show me the letter, it would mean I don't trust you, and if I can't trust you, it wouldn't matter what the letter said because we wouldn't have anything together anyway."

"Ummn," I say. I wait a few seconds, step back into the bathroom and close the door.

" 'Enclosed is a check for $20. I insist that you use it to take yourself and Sally out for dinner on your birthday. You two kids deserve a good time.' " Barry reads me the excerpt from his father's letter and tosses the check onto the coffee table. "Where do you want to go, baby?"

I shrug.

Barry and I stare at each other over the coffee table. "I'll look up someplace in the Yellow Pages," Barry says. He goes and gets the Birmingham phone book and brings it over to the coffee table. His long, bony fingers fly through the tissue-thin pages. He clears his throat and reads: "Al's Pig Tail, Big Daddy's Restaurant and Lounge, Catfish Cabin, Cliff's Pit Stop Barbeque, Gus's Hot Dogs, Jesus Christ, baby. Oh, here's something classy. Pierre's Rotisserie at the Hamilton House Hotel. How's that sound?"

"All right," I say.

Barry and I take the elevator to the top floor of the hotel. There is a small cocktail lounge with a baby grand piano, and beyond, a large dining room surrounded by windows overlooking downtown Birmingham, its small-scale skyline, its clear black starry sky.

From a table next to the maître d's post, Barry picks up a color postcard of the dining room of Pierre's Rotisserie, its empty tables set with white cloths and silver, and puts the card in the breast pocket of the dark blue pin-striped suit his father bought him. "We'll send a card to my dad, so he'll know we used the twenty dollars the way he wanted."

"We could have just come up here, taken a card, and left without eating dinner," I say.

We follow the maître d' across the plush red carpet to a table in the middle of the room. I am wearing my new pumps that I bought with Polly, and they pinch my toes. The restaurant reminds me of the places I used to go with my father, with my dates after big high-school dances. At the table, I look across at Barry, at the shoulders and the arms of his pin-striped suit on either side of the tall slick red menu.

"What are you going to have, baby?" Barry says.

"A whiskey sour."

"I mean to eat."

"Oh." I pick up the menu and glance down the center column. "Duck, I guess."

The waiter brings my whiskey sour. Barry takes out his ball point pen and writes something on the postcard. He gets up to ask the maître d' to mail it. Then I see him turn and go into the cocktail lounge. I look at my whiskey sour in its stemmed glass, the light orangey liquid, and the white froth on top, the orange slice impaled on the side of the glass, the red cherry lying on its side at the bottom. I take a sip. I look around at the windows overlooking the city and the sky. There is no moon, but there are stars like rhinestones on black velvet. It is Barry's twenty-fourth birthday we are supposed to be celebrating in this high, starry place.

When I met Barry, he told me his birthday was the same day as mine, and I believed him. I sent him a card on my birthday, which was supposed to be his birthday too. He sent me a letter back. "Thanks a lot for the birthday card. It is the hippest card I ever got, not only on August 30, but also on June 5th which is my birthday, so you are either three months too late or 9 months too early."

I stare down at my new shoe, the sleek strap snaking up from my instep to my ankle. I stare at my leg in its nylon. It's the same leg I had then, thinner now, more graceful, but I don't need it. I need a practical leg, one to hold me up when I stand or walk, a thicker ankle, a more muscular calf, a sturdier foot.

Piano music comes in from the cocktail lounge, "Tenderly" played slow. It doesn't sound like the waterfall rippling of the keys in cocktail music. It slips into something really pretty, like something on one of Barry's Bill Evans records.

I finish my whiskey sour and pick out the foam-covered cherry from the bottom of the glass, suck it away from its stem, squeezing out all the sweet liquor before I swallow it. I decide to get one of the postcards to send to Miranda with some fictional message. The piano music has taken a turn now, something disjointed and jumpy.

In the cocktail lounge, Barry is sitting at the piano, knees wide apart, shoulders hunched over the keyboard. When he sees me, he looks at me with a blank stare, moves both hands to the low end of the keyboard and holds them there for a few seconds, lifting his fingers slowly until the sound stops. Then he gets up. "This box is out of tune," he says.

We sit down at the table again. The salad and the rolls have already been served. I look at Barry chewing his lettuce. I want to say something about the music, about how beautiful it was, but I don't. "Do we have enough money for wine?" I say.

The piano music comes on, "Stardust" this time, and it sounds as though the piano player is being paid by the note. I could say that to Barry, and he would like it, but I don't say that, either.

"It's for you, baby," Barry says when the waiter brings the bottle of wine. "I don't want any."

The duck comes smothered in a thick sauce. I drink another glass of wine. The windows all around the dining room start to spin, and I feel as though I am on a Ferris wheel gone wild, the glittery stars in the black sky whirling all around me.

"We'll have to write my dad and thank him for dinner," Barry says when we get back to the apartment.

I get out of my clothes, drop them on the carpet, and get into bed. Through the blue drapes in the light of the balcony, I can see the silhouettes of the trees behind the parking lot. I close my eyes, and the trees dance in a black fantasia on my eyelids. I feel Barry pressing up against my belly.

"I can't," I say and flop over on my stomach.

"Baby," Barry says.

I clutch the pillow with my fists.

Barry sits up in bed. "I can't take this, baby. We haven't fucked in two weeks. I never had to hassle with a chick just to get laid."

I let go of the pillow and sit up in bed. The walls fall

away from the ceiling and spread out as in a fun house mirror. Half of Barry's face moves to the left as if he had taken off a mask and were holding it beside his face.

"You make me sick," I say.

Barry looks at me. "How can you say that, baby? You're my wife."

"You make me sick."

"You're drunk."

"I know."

Barry leans back on his pillows. "Do you know what you're saying, baby? Do you know what you sound like?"

"I don't care."

"Baby —"

"All Feldmans make me sick. Birmingham makes me sick. The Department of Relief and Security makes me sick. The Appalachia School of Law makes me sick. The apartment makes me sick. The Supersport makes me sick. Miami makes me sick. Bill Evans makes me sick. Ray Whiteman makes me sick. These blue sheets make me sick."

"Baby, are you crazy? Do you know what you're saying?"

"Your toes make me sick. Your knees make me sick. Your chest makes me sick. Your lips make me sick."

"I refuse to stay here and listen to you," Barry says. He starts to get out of bed, but I grab him by the arm.

"I'm not finished. Your eyes make me sick. Your glasses make me sick. Your teeth make me sick."

"Let go, baby."

I dig my nails into Barry's forearm.

"Your ears make me sick."

"Let go." Barry wrenches his arm free, but I throw myself across the bed and grab him again.

"Your father makes me sick."

"Don't bring my dad into this."

"Your prick makes me sick — especially your prick."

Barry's free hand reaches out and slaps me on the side of my face. I fall back onto the bed, letting go of his arm. He stares at me. "You wanted me to do that. You wanted me to do that so that I would lose respect for myself. I have never hit a woman before in my life."

He goes to the closet, pulls on some pants, goes out of the bedroom. I hear the front door slam and then the sound of a car engine.

The next morning I'm drinking a glass of orange juice at the dining-room table. Barry comes in, wearing the pants of his blue pin-striped suit, rumpled now, and a sweat shirt. He hasn't shaved, of course, and his cheeks are dark shadows.

"I stayed in a motel," he says. "It cost fifteen dollars. I have an apartment and a wife, and I have to stay in a motel by myself."

"I'm sorry," I say.

"You are?"

I nod.

Barry sinks down onto the couch and puts his head in his hands. "This is terrible, baby."

"I know."

"Are you all right?"

"Yes."

"I shouldn't have left you alone."

"I'm all right."

"What's happening, baby? Tell me."

"I don't know."

"In a year we'll be in Miami."

I don't say anything.

"You didn't mean those things you said, did you?"

"No."

"You shouldn't drink so much, baby."

"I know."

"I'm sorry I hit you. I'll never forgive myself for that."

"It's all right. I deserved it."

"I love you, baby. I never want to hurt you. I love you more than anyone or anything else in the world."

"You do?"

"Oh, baby, are you kidding?"

The front door opens, and Mel and Patsy come in. "Hey, Feldmans!" Mel says.

"We were just on our way back from the K mart," Patsy says. "I told Mel we shouldn't just drop in without calling first."

"What's that you're wearing, Feldman?" Mel says. "Your suit pants and a sweat shirt?"

Barry looks down at his clothes. "It's the latest," he says.

"Hi, Edwina," Mel says to me.

"What?" Patsy says. "Why did you call Sally Edwina?"

"I like it," Mel says. "All right if I call your wife Edwina, Feldman?"

Barry spreads his hands in the air. "Sure," he says.

"I saw an old Marilyn Monroe movie on TV last night. Her name was Edwina. I thought I would call Sally Edwina from now on."

"Okay," I say.

"Do we have anything in the refrigerator for lunch, baby?" Barry says.

"Are you hungry?" I ask Mel and Patsy.

"Oh, we couldn't eat a thing," Mel says. "What have you got?"

I go to the refrigerator. "I can make peanut butter and jelly on English muffins."

"Great, Edwina," Mel says. "Have you got any soda?"

"I'll have Tab," Patsy says.

Mel and Patsy and Barry and I are eating our peanut butter and jelly sandwiches at the dining-room table when the doorbell rings. Barry looks up at me. I shrug my shoulders. He puts both hands on the dining-room table and lifts himself up to standing, then goes to answer the door. A man wearing a cap stands in the door, and Barry signs something. Barry comes into the living room carrying in front of him a cardboard carton that's about four feet tall and four feet wide.

"Hey!" Patsy says. "You guys didn't tell us you had ordered some new furniture."

"Come on," I say and go up to the box. Barry and I stand in the middle of the living-room floor and stare at the box between us.

Barry looks at the label. "It's addressed to you," he says. "It's from your hometown."

"Oh."

"Open it!" Patsy says. "How can you just stand there? I'm dying to know what's inside."

"Okay."

Barry goes into the kitchen to get a knife. He cuts through the masking tape at the top of the carton. Every time I see masking tape, I remember sitting in my parents' living room and listening to the news on the radio, and the announcer saying that the three missing boys have been found in the Forest Preserves, not far from our house, their bodies stabbed, naked, and frozen, tied to trees with masking tape.

I spread the flaps of the carton where the tape is cut and reach inside. On top of a lot of crumpled newspaper is an envelope. It says "For the bride." I open the envelope and inside is a card with a pair of white wedding bells and silver script saying, "Congratulations on your wedding." Inside, there is a handwritten message. "Dear Sally, Since you got married without letting any of us know, we decided to have a bridal shower for you in absentia. Your mother was planning to come but she became ill and couldn't make it. Her gift is enclosed with the rest. We all wish you the best of luck." The names of twenty of my mother's friends in the neighborhood are written there, mothers of friends of mine I had known since I was six years old.

I hand Barry the card.

"Some of my mother's friends had a shower for me," I say to Mel and Patsy.

Patsy jumps up from the table. "Wow, the whole town must have gone," she says. "Start opening the stuff."

"Maybe your mother is starting to come around," Barry says.

"She didn't go," I say. "Read the card."

I toss out some crumpled pages of the *Chicago Tribune* and take out a box wrapped in tissue paper. "From all of us," the gift card says. I take out a dishwashing brush with dish towels tied around the handle like a skirt, wooden spoons sticking out like arms, and a Tuffy for a head.

"Look!" Patsy says. "It looks like a doll."

I hand it to Barry.

"What's this, baby?" he says.

The next box is large and heavy. There's a little piece of notepaper attached to it. "This is the present your mother sent over," it says.

I open the box. There is no card inside. It is a sterling silver water pitcher, simple, expensive, elegant, its neck curling up like an egret's.

"Oh, Mel!" Patsy says. "I wish we had something like that."

I put the pitcher back into the box. "She gives the same pitcher to everyone," I say.

"What?" Patsy says.

"Whenever my mother has to go to a bridal shower, she goes to the jewelry store in town and buys a sterling silver water pitcher. The same one."

"She does?" Patsy says, her eyes wide.

"Yes." I look down at the carpet.

"What are we supposed to do with it?" Barry says, looking at the pitcher.

"Come on, Feldman," Mel says. "Edwina can use it for Kool-Aid."

I open bath towels and mixing bowls and casserole dishes and Corning Ware and a recipe box of file cards with a recipe from each woman at the shower. The living-room carpet is covered with newspapers and tissue paper and wrapping paper and ribbons. Patsy is on her hands and knees, crawling around the floor, looking at the gifts. The big empty carton sits in the middle of the floor. I don't know why, but I feel as if something huge has just been taken away from me.

I light a cigarette and stand in the middle of the living-room floor, wondering what to do. Barry is sitting on the couch, and Mel is sitting at the dining-room table drinking soda. The doorbell rings again.

"Maybe these are the wedding gifts," Patsy says.

I open the door, and my eyes are at chest level of a familiar-looking madras shirt. I look up about a foot into a face that looks just like mine, only a couple of years younger. It's my brother, Rod. He is supposed to be in college in Oregon. "Hi," I say. "What are you doing here?"

"I was on my way back to Chicago from Oregon. Just thought I'd stop by."

"Oh." I stare at my brother for a minute, then step back into the apartment. "This is my husband, Barry, and our friends, Mel and Patsy Steingut. My brother, Rod."

My brother stands in the middle of the living room. No one says anything. He kicks a piece of tissue paper. "What's this crap?"

"Some of Mother's friends had a shower for me."

"I hope they didn't invite Mother," Rod says.

Barry is sitting slumped on the couch, looking at the floor. Patsy has jumped up from the floor. "How long are you staying?" she says.

"I'm leaving tonight."

"You're not even staying overnight?"

"Nope."

Mel gets up and stretches. "Well, Feldmans, we've got to go. See you guys tomorrow."

"Nice apartment," my brother says after they leave.

"Thanks," I say. Barry is still looking at his shoes. "It was furnished."

"I got the impression from Mother you were living in a real dive."

Barry lifts his head and stares at my brother.

My brother says, "I didn't eat all day. Do you know where there's a good, cheap restaurant?"

"We could go to the Pancake House," I say.

"Okay."

"Do you want to go?" I say to Barry.

"Nope."

I stand between my brother and Barry. "Well. I'll be right back."

I walk out into the parking lot with my brother. I have been with Barry for so long that my brother seems unnaturally tall next to me, like a giant or some kind of freak.

"Your husband looks like a nice guy."

"He is very nice," I say.

"I came down here to punch him in the face. But when I saw him I didn't want to anymore."

"Oh."

"From what Mother said I thought you were living in a hole with some kind of freak or something. But that guy looks all right. He looks like a lot of Jewish guys. He's a little short."

"Barry is five seven."

My brother laughs an unfunny laugh that sounds like a cough.

At the Pancake House, my brother orders pancakes and sausages. I order a Coke.

"So what do you do around here?" he says.

"Not much," I say. "Barry has to study a lot. I work. That's about it."

"Yeah?"

"Uh huh."

I look at my brother, bending over his plate of pancakes.

He's my younger brother by three years, but he is a whole foot taller than I am. Right now I feel as if he is my older brother.

"How's school?" I say.

"All right," he says.

"Did you just finish finals?"

"Uh huh."

"How did you do?"

"Passed."

"Is that all?" I am asking because my brother has an IQ that shoots off the charts, but he can't do anything right.

"Don't know," he says.

"What are you majoring in now?"

"Poli Sci."

"How come?"

"Why not?"

I watch my brother eat his pancakes and sausage. I want to ask him about our mother and father, but I can't think of a good question.

"How are Mother and Father?" I say.

"How would I know? I'm away at school."

"Oh."

"Mother told me to write to you and tell you not to marry Barry." My brother snorts.

"She did?"

"Yeah."

"But you didn't?"

My brother snaps his fingers over his plate. A few ragged pieces of pancake are lying in the sticky brown syrup. "Aw, shucks," he says. "I guess my letter must've gotten lost in the mail." His smile is crooked.

"What about Father?"

"What about him?"

"Has he said anything about me?"

"Haven't seen him. Haven't talked to him."

I can't think of anything else to say. My brother has driven over a thousand miles out of his way to come to punch Barry in the face, but now he doesn't want to punch Barry in the face.

My brother drives me back to the apartment, and in the parking lot, I say, "Don't you want to stay over? It's a long drive to Chicago."

"Only twelve hours."

"Do you want to come in for a while?"

"Nope."

"Well." I look at my brother, at his long body draped over the steering wheel, at his madras shirt, at his chinos and loafers without socks, at his sandy hair falling into a face that looks just like mine.

"Well, good-bye," he says. "See you around."

"Drive carefully."

My brother backs up the car, turns, and pulls up the hill out of the parking lot.

I'm standing in the middle of the parking lot. Inside the chain-link fence, some bodies in bathing suits are lying on chaises around the swimming pool. Someone is playing a transistor radio. I wonder if my brother came all the way to Birmingham to punch Barry in the face because he cares about me.

"Hey, there!" Lucinda Ann yells from inside the fence. I walk over to the swimming pool. Lucinda Ann and Bobby Lloyd and Aubrey and some others are drinking Big Cat and listening to the radio. "How are you doing, Sally? Get your swimsuit on and come on in."

I go inside the fence and sit down on the edge of one of the empty chaises.

"Ain't gonna get much of a tan in your jeans," Lucinda Ann says.

"I didn't know it was summer already," I say. "I don't have a bathing suit."

Aubrey hands me a Big Cat, and I take a swallow. Aubrey and Bobby Lloyd are talking about Bear Bryant. I drink my Big Cat and listen — not to their words but to the slow low rumble of their southern voices. The sun feels good on my face, and I stretch my legs out on the chaise.

I was lying on a chaise at a pool when I met Barry. It was the last day of my vacation in Miami. I had beach towels covering my sunburned legs and arms, a scarf covering my hair, Noxema on my nose, and I was wearing sunglasses. I had moved a pair of sunglasses and taken the chaise they were lying on. Barry came out of the pool, his tan body dripping, his black hair slicked back. He looked different from any man I had known before, slighter, slicker.

"I moved your glasses," I said to him.

He sat down in the chair where I had put his glasses and closed his eyes, threw his head back full to the sun.

"I took your chair," I said.

"That's cool," he said. He opened his eyes and looked at me, squinting into the sun. Then he put on his sunglasses. They were the black plastic kind you see on Italian movie actors.

"Are you a girl under all that stuff?"

I shrugged. "That depends on your definition of a girl."

"I know they're not cute plump guys."

"What?"

"Mel Brooks. The two-thousand-year-old man. The

cavemen thought girls were just cute plump guys." Barry started to giggle.

"Who's Mel Brooks?"

Barry threw his head back and spoke to the sky. "She doesn't know who Mel Brooks is."

The sun was setting when Barry and I got up to go. I took the beach towels off my legs, the scarf off my head and let my hair tumble down my shoulders. I stood up.

Barry looked at me. "Wel-l-l-l," he said. Then he smiled. His teeth were very white in his tan face.

What would my life be like now if I hadn't moved Barry's sunglasses?

"Blocked pass," Aubrey says.

I open my eyes. "What?"

"Hey, Sally, I didn't know you were interested in football." Aubrey's voice is thick with beer, his face is flushed, and he's smiling down at me.

"I'm not," I say.

Barry comes out on the balcony in front of the apartment, stands there with both hands on the railing, and rocks back and forth on his heels. I wave, but he doesn't look towards the pool. The sun is setting behind the apartment building. It must be almost dinner time.

"Where's your brother?" Barry says when I come into the apartment.

"He left."

Barry doesn't say anything.

"You could have made him feel more welcome."

"Are you kidding? He thinks I'm a freak."

"But he's my brother."

Barry sits down at the dining-room table and shifts the salt and pepper shakers around each other.

I take some hamburger meat out of the refrigerator and start chopping onions to mix in with it. "I stopped by to talk to Lucinda Ann down at the pool this afternoon. I want to buy a bathing suit this week."

"In Miami the pools are right on the ocean, not in the middle of a parking lot."

"But we're not in Miami."

"How can you sit around that pool with those grits? What were they talking about, lynching niggers?"

"Bear Bryant."

Barry lets out a low whistle. "Of course, man. It bothers me that you can talk to those grits. You're so much above them, baby."

"They're just people."

"But you're not just people, baby. You're special, we're special. You know that."

"We are? I'm not so sure."

Barry gets up and comes into the kitchen. He takes my face in his hands and looks at it as if it were something static. "Baby, come on." He gently shakes my shoulders and kisses me on the forehead. "You're being silly. A silly goose, baby. Of course you're special. You're my wife."

You haven't mentioned one thing that would make her a good wife. You haven't said anything about warmth, sympathy, generosity.

You can't kick 5,000 years of history in the face.

I don't want to have Jewish grandchildren.

My father's wedding check, for $500 instead of $5,000, screams in his silence.

Barry is on top of me, fucking me, his eyes wide open, staring ahead into a void. When he comes, his head drops and his eyebrows press together in what looks like unbearable pain.

"Oh, baby," he says when he rolls off me.

Underneath the pillow, I am counting on my fingers the number of months we have been married: February, March, April, May. I count again. It's still four. I feel Barry's breath on my shoulder. His eyes are closed, and a strand of damp black hair is falling onto his forehead. I listen to his breathing to see if he's asleep, and when I know that he is, I brush the hair off his forehead with my palm. Barry is my husband, but I want to kill him, just temporarily, until I feel better, until I figure out what's wrong.

In eight more months we will have been married a year. But eight months is twice as long as four months, and I have been married four months already.

I look at Barry again. He moans and twitches in bed, turns over violently. We used to lie in bed together and twitch, waking each other up all night, making love, smoking cigarettes, talking, chewing sticks of Doublemint gum so we could kiss again. Barry won't just go away. I know what I'm like. I can leave Barry, I can leave Birmingham, but Barry won't go away. He is my husband. I can get divorced, and six months later, I will wake up in the morning and I won't be able to get out of bed. I know what I'm like.

Barry is my husband now. He is my family. People stay with me. They don't leave. Even if I leave them, they follow. My mother and my father are still with me. My brother is still with me. J.D. is still with me. I am not free of any of them. And this is much worse. I married Barry. But that's not that worst part. The worst part is the part I don't understand. One day I will wake up, and I will want to kill myself for something then, and I won't know what it is. I don't know what it is now.

In the morning, Barry is awake before me. He is kneeling on the bed, lightly slapping my cheeks with my own hands and shaking me.

"You have to get up and take your wares into the marketplace," he says.

I put out my hands to push Barry away, but he grabs my hands with his. Then he starts slapping my face with my own hands. "Hey, why are you hitting yourself, baby?" He's smiling.

"Stop it!" I'm screaming. He isn't hitting me hard. It doesn't hurt. "Stop it."

Barry stops smiling and lets go of my hands. "I was just kidding around, baby."

I hold my palms to my cheeks. Barry gets up and goes into the bathroom. "You used to have the best sense of humor of any chick I ever met."

It's the beginning of June. I wait at the back of the Department of Relief and Security, and when Barry pulls up, I run from the air-conditioned office to the air-conditioned car. In the parking lot my body goes damp and my blouse is sucked to my breasts, my skirt to my legs. My hair goes limp and rests heavy on my back and shoulders, the hot air trapped underneath. I can't breathe.

I get in the car and throw my head back, wait for the air conditioning to make my body livable again. "It is impossible that any place can be this hot," I say.

"It's the South, baby. It'll get hotter."

Walking from the parking lot to the apartment, my nylons

feel like hot, melted butter on my legs. My skirt sticks to my thighs. My eyelashes are heavy with dampness.

Inside, Barry turns on the air conditioning. Outside, it is one hundred degrees with no breeze, the hot air trapped and unmoving in Birmingham's valley. In the apartment, it's hotter. The air is more still. It hangs there in the heat. "I can't stand it," I say.

"It'll get cool, baby," Barry says.

"I can't stand it." I peel off my nylons and drop them on the floor, pin my hair up on top of my head, anticipate the coolness at the back of my neck. But it doesn't come. "I can't stand it. Leave the air conditioning on tomorrow morning. I can't stand coming home to a place like this."

"You want me to leave the air conditioning on all day, baby? We can't do that. We're paying for electricity."

"I don't care. This is too much. Barry, I work all day. I see horrible things. I can't come home to a place where I can't breathe."

"We can't afford to leave the air conditioning on all day, baby."

He scoops the mail up from the floor. "You got a letter from Miranda," he says and tosses it over to me. "Hey. Wild bananas. A letter from Phil. Remember, baby? The cat I played with in Miami. Dropped out of law school to blow jazz in the Village?"

Miranda says she's leaving Taos and going back to New York. She's traveling via Pine Mountain, Georgia, where her grandmother lives, and that just happens to be less than two hundred miles from Birmingham. She'll fly straight to Birmingham to visit Barry and me and go on to Georgia from here. I let the letter fall into my lap. I try to see Miranda sitting at the dining-room table with Barry and me. Miranda sitting on the couch flicking ashes into the ashtray on the coffee table. I can't see it. It's as though I had known Miranda in another life, and now she's writing that she's coming to visit this one.

Miranda and I telling our fraternity boys we're going to the bathroom and sneaking out the back door of a bar, running across the parking lot to have a drink in another bar with the townies. Miranda and I getting up at eight Saturday mornings to play our running Cribbage tournament. Miranda and I during the Ohio heatwave, sitting on the edge of the bathtub in our un-air-conditioned apartment, drinking screwdrivers with our bare legs stuck in ice water. I look at Barry, at his law books, at the apartment. What will Miranda think of all this?

"Miranda's coming to visit," I say.

"Hey, that's great, baby."

I get up, light a cigarette, and start pacing around the living room. Miranda sitting at the dining-room table? I can't imagine anyone I've ever known being here, except me.

"Listen to this," Barry says. "Phil sat in on a set at the Village Gate. He's really doing it. Living in a roach-infested apartment on the Lower East Side and playing his ass off."

"Oh, yeah?"

"Yeah. He says I would really dig his music now." Barry looks past me. "I'd really love to hear him play."

"Why don't you visit him?"

"In New York?"

"Uh huh."

"I can't do that, baby. The plane fare is ninety dollars round trip."

"I know what the plane fare is. But you could go. It might be good."

"Nah."

Barry whistles. "Phil is a beautiful man. He's following his music wherever it takes him. He isn't falling into this whole middle-class number. And he's doing all right."

"Can he play better than you?"

"Yeah, technically he can. But I can still play some things he can't play, won't ever play. I mean, nobody else *could* play them."

"But before. When both of you were in Miami."

"I don't know, baby." Barry laughs his unfunny laugh. "We were great! What can I say, man. *We* thought we were *great*."

"Do you think he's doing the right thing?"

"I don't know. What if it never breaks for him? What happens to him when he's forty and nothing's happening? He's playing 'Stardust' in some cocktail lounge with the bartender looking over his shoulder making sure he puts enough ripples into his notes?"

"What happens to us when we're forty?"

Barry looks at me for a moment. "The same as what happens to everybody else."

"What's that?"

"Baby." Barry leans all the way across the coffee table and tousles my hair.

It's Saturday morning. I get up and put on my new bikini. Polly and Jess are coming over to sit around our pool in the parking lot.

Barry is already at the dining-room table, drinking a glass

of V-8. "They aren't going to stay long, are they?" he says. "I've got to study."

"Polly has been really nice to me."

"Yeah?" Barry is staring at me over his V-8. "You have got an almost perfect figure, baby. If you did a few sit-ups, it would be perfect."

"I don't want to do sit-ups," I say.

"Why not, baby?"

The doorbell rings, and Polly and Jess come in.

"Is that your bathing suit, Sally?" Polly says. "Heck, I'm embarrassed to take off my clothes and show you the old one-piece thing I've got on underneath."

"It doesn't matter," I say. "You can change in the bedroom."

Polly comes out of the bedroom wearing a suit with a little ruffled skirt. Jess is wearing swimming trunks that come down almost to his knees. They're elasticized at the waist and balloon out over his narrow hips. He has the whitest skin I have ever seen. Barry's eyebrows go up and he smiles. I know what he's thinking; he's thinking what I'm thinking, but it isn't a nasty smile.

Lucinda Ann and Aubrey and Bobby Lloyd and their friends are sitting around the deep end.

"Hey, Sally," Lucinda Ann calls out.

Barry and I sit at the shallow end with Polly and Jess.

"Heck, look at them two," Polly says to Jess, looking over to Barry and me. "I mean, have you ever seen such a perfect couple? Sally, I have never seen such a perfect couple as you and Barry. You just look like you two belong together."

Barry leans towards me and puts his hand on my leg. Polly is staring at us, beaming. "And I just love your apartment. It's so sophisticated, isn't it, Jess? Not like our old hand-me-down furniture, not one piece matching another."

"It's furnished," I say. "That's why everything matches. It matches all the other apartments in the building."

"I envy all of them matching appliances in your kitchen. All my appliances is matching, all white, and all chipped. But I do love the color you have — harvest gold. And a swimming pool right here in your parking lot. This is really the life, ain't it, Jess?"

Jess doesn't say anything.

"I said ain't it the life, Jess?" Polly yells, her voice sounding the way it does when she's talking to the old people in the nursing homes.

Jess nods.

"I swear, Jess says he's getting hard of hearing, but he won't go to no doctor. I'm thinking he just don't want to listen to me."

I smile as if to say, Isn't that silly, but when I ask Jess if he wants a cigarette, he answers right away, and I'm sitting twice as far away from him as Polly.

"No, thanks," he says. "I quit near five years ago."

"You did?" I say. "How did you do it?" I want to know how he quit smoking. I want to know how anyone quits anything.

Jess leans forward, his concave chest over his skinny white legs. "I quit the same day as I pledged myself to the All World Bible Church out in California. I bought myself three packs of Camels and locked myself in my room with all the windows closed. I smoked one cigarette after another, all three packs but for two cigarettes in the last one, then I went into the toilet and puked. I never touched a cigarette again."

Barry is laughing his reckless giggle, but Jess isn't smiling.

"Smokin' ain't the only thing the All World Bible Church would have you quit on," Polly says. "They'd have you quit eatin' if you'd send them the money you saved on groceries."

"You really did that?" I say to Jess.

"My face was green as that Chevy over yonder," Jess says. "I ain't never been that sick before or since. I emptied the last two cigarettes into the toilet with my vomit. Watched it all flush down."

Polly gets up and pulls at Jess's arm. "Hey, this is like to be the last time all summer I'll get to go swimmin'. Come on, Jess, let's go in." Polly pulls on a white bathing cap with bow-shaped indentations on it.

Jess doesn't get up. "Heck, come on, Sally. Let's go in the water and leave the boys up here to shoot the breeze."

"Okay," I say. I sit on the side of the pool and swing my legs over into the water. The swimming pool is only about twenty feet long and twelve feet wide, but I'm afraid to swim in front of Barry, anyway. The first time we went swimming he said, "Your sidestroke is pathetic, baby." He jackknifed into the deep end and told me he was the number one diver in the state of Florida. I wrote that to my mother to impress her. I didn't know Barry was kidding.

Polly lowers herself inch by inch down the ladder at the side of the pool into the water. We stand in the shallow end in water up to our midriffs. "Barry is so handsome," Polly whispers. "I just love the way he smiles. And he is so smart, too. I can just tell he will be a very successful lawyer, Sally. You two is sure lucky, but, shucks, a girl as pretty and bright as you would just have to marry someone like Barry.

Tell me, Sally, how did you two meet? I just know it'll be all romantic, not like Jess lookin' for a mother to his two little girls after his first wife got carted off to the insane asylum. Come on, tell me."

Polly is talking too close to my ear. I keep moving away from her down towards the deep end, and now we're both standing in water up to our shoulders. I'm a few inches taller than Polly, though, so I figure I'll be able to get far enough away so that I can't feel her breath on my ear while she's talking. But when the water reaches Polly's chin, she starts doing a dog paddle alongside me.

"What did he say when he first saw you?" Polly is saying.

"He didn't see me," I say. "He didn't say anything."

"Oh, come on, Sally. Don't be so secretive. It must really be good if you won't even tell."

Barry coming into me like a black snake that night in the motel, the next morning carrying me, barefoot, across the lawn. Then the letters. Then the weekend, and then a week, and then three weeks. I was immersed in him, in his tanned skin, in his sweat and Jade East, in his jazz, in his smile that came on his face slow as a sunrise, in his jagged bones silhouetted against the white bedroom wall, his black hair against the blue, blue sheets.

I turn back and say to Polly. "There's not that much to tell."

I sidestroke ahead of her and my head bumps into someone's stomach at the deep end of the pool. Aubrey's body is hanging into the pool, his bent elbows braced up on the side of the pool, keeping his head above water.

"Sorry," I say, and tread water around him.

"How about a purple passion?" Aubrey says. He's holding a plastic cup with some purple liquid in it. "Grape Kool-Aid and sodium pentothal. Bobby Lloyd stole it from the lab at the dental school."

"No, thanks," I say.

Polly is right behind me. I head for the ladder in the corner of the deep end and climb up. Barry is lying on a chaise with his face up to the sun, eyes closed. Jess is sitting at the edge of his chair, elbows on his knees, kind of looking out into the parking lot. A pink sunburn is already spreading across his shoulders. I sit on the edge of Barry's chaise, and put a wet hand on his stomach.

"Ummmn," he says and sits up. He pulls me down on his lap. His hand rests on my thigh and his palm is hot, burning through the cool water on my skin. It feels as though it will leave an imprint, but when he takes it away, there is none. The skin is not even drier where he had touched me, because the sun has dried my legs all over.

"Oh, Jess," Polly says. "I have never seen anything like it. Have you ever seen two people more in love than Barry and Sally?"

"It's impossible," Barry says in his soft, offhand voice.

I try to keep from smiling too much. But I do smile. I can't help it.

Marbury v. Madison. "Barry, do you want your footnotes single-spaced?" I am hunched over Barry's typewriter at the dining-room table, squinting at the loose unnumbered notebook pages with Barry's stunted scribble, words crossed out in black circle after circle, arrows moving phrases up and down, numbered and lettered inserts from one page to another.

172

"Let me take a look at it, baby." Barry moves his Torts book off his chest and gets off the couch. He comes up behind me and stares over my shoulder. He gives a little wince. "Baby, I wanted the quotes indented and single-spaced."

"You didn't tell me."

Barry taps the end of his ball-point pen on the table next to the typewriter. "The professor will probably take off for it," Barry says.

"He will?"

"Yep."

I lean back in my chair and turn around to look up at Barry. "You could tell him your wife typed it and made a mistake."

"Ummmn." Barry is thinking. "I don't know if I can take the chance."

"I'll type it over," I am supposed to say.

I open my mouth to say it, but the words stick in my throat. I don't say anything. Barry just stands there, waiting for me to say, "I'll type it over." Patsy would type it over for Mel. I am probably the only law school wife who won't type her husband's paper over. It would be so easy to say, "I'll type it over," and everything would be okay. But then I would have to type it over, and I do not want to type it over. I don't know why. I don't know what's wrong with me.

Barry is tapping his pen on the table top, slower now, and slower, slower to the last tap. Then he flips the pen in the air and turns away. "Okay," he says in his high clipped voice.

I take a deep breath. Barry is back on the couch, lying under his Torts book.

"What about the footnotes?" I say. "I asked you about the footnotes."

Barry doesn't look up. "It doesn't matter. Do them any way you want."

I sit and stare at Barry's Swiss typewriter. I wonder why he has such a good typewriter if he doesn't know how to type. I think about the papers I wrote in college. They were good. I think about how I did the footnotes. I suppose you do the footnotes the same way in law school. I could call Patsy and ask her how she's doing the footnotes for Mel, but that's crazy. Barry is right here. It's his paper. It's 1:00 in the morning, and I have to get up for work at 6:30. I type the footnotes the only way I know how.

On Saturday, I get out of bed and put on my bikini. The air-conditioned air is cool and dry on my skin. Down the hall, the living room is dark with the drapes drawn against the morning sun. Barry is lying on the couch with his law books, studying for finals. As I am going out of the bedroom, in the mirror over the dresser I see someone with a deep ochre tan and long sunbleached hair, wearing a blue bikini. Young, carefree, unaffected. I put my palms on the dresser and lean into the mirror to look more closely, to see if I show through somewhere. My palms feel clammy on the glass top of the dresser.

In the living room, Barry doesn't look up at me. I know how I look. Why doesn't he look at me? "Good morning," I say.

"Morning, baby," Barry says. He doesn't look up. He's chewing on a pencil.

I go into the kitchen and get a glass of orange juice. I sit at the dining-room table and put my feet up on the table. My bare legs are long and slim, tan.

"What are you doing today?" Barry asks through bites on the pencil. He still doesn't look up.

"Playing tennis."

Barry taps his pencil in short jabs on his notebook, then looks up.

"What do you think I'm doing today?" I say.

Barry lays his pen down on the table. "I don't know how you can spend time drinking beer at the pool with those grits."

"What else am I supposed to do?"

He looks at me over his glasses, then pushes his glasses up his nose with his pencil. He doesn't say anything.

I take a towel and a paperback book and go out into the parking lot. Two friends of Lucinda's are playing Frisbee in the parking lot, but no one is at the pool. I lie down on a chaise and close my eyes. The sun, already hot, presses into my skin. I wait for it to get hotter and hotter until I can't move.

A Frisbee glides past, grazing my shoulder, then waffles to a landing at my feet.

"Hey there, sorry about that," one of the players calls out. I pick up the Frisbee and toss it back over the fence. Then I turn over on my stomach. The plastic strips on the chaise press into my skin on my stomach and thighs, the hot sun on my back. My hair is wet around my temples, and my eyelids are damp. I fall asleep.

When I wake up, my hair is thick and heavy with moisture on my neck. The skin on the back of my legs is stretched tight and hot. Voices combine in a steady noise of words I can't recognize. I pull myself up on my elbow and lift my head, open my eyes to a yellow glare, punctuated with shadows. Then I feel something icy on my palm.

Aubrey is pressing a Big Cat into my hand. I bring the can to my lips and take a swallow. The malt liquor is thick and cold down my throat.

"Afternoon," he says. "We were just about to baste you and turn you over."

"I don't burn," I say.

I press into my shoulder with my finger, and as I release my finger a white spot appears, then turns pink.

I hand Aubrey back his Big Cat, but he's already cracking open another one.

"Plenty more where that came from," he says.

Lucinda Ann is sitting on the other side of Aubrey, along with about ten of their crowd, drinking beers and Big Cat. Bobby Lloyd has a portable radio playing some country guitars and a low male voice singing something I can't make out, except the words *love* and *die*.

"Where's your husband?" Lucinda Ann says.

I turn around and look up towards the balcony and our apartment. "Upstairs," I say. "Studying."

Aubrey takes a swig of Big Cat. "I don't let studying get in the way of my rays."

I wince at the word *rays*. "Barry is in finals now," I say.

"You bet," Aubrey says. "I got a pathology final Monday, nine A.M."

"Oh."

"I swear your husband is always studying, seems like, Sally. And you're always walking around with a book. You two must have a very intellectual household," Lucinda says.

"What are you reading?" Aubrey asks.

176

I look over the chaise, down at the cover of my book. "André Gide's *Journals*."

"What's it about?"

I look up at Aubrey to see if he really wants to know. He's lying with his face to the sun, eyes closed, one arm hanging off the chaise, a Big Cat in his hand on the poolside floor. "It's not about anything," I say.

Aubrey groans. "Sounds real interesting."

"I mean, André Gide is a French writer who keeps a journal. He writes down his thoughts about things."

"Why do you want to be reading something like that?"

"I'm interested in reading about people who think about things."

"Do you think about things?"

"Yes."

"And what have you come up with?"

I put my Big Cat down, lean back, and close my eyes. "Not much," I say. The sun is hot on my eyelids.

Lucinda's voice comes screaming through the sun. "Hey, Aubrey, Sally, wake up. We're playing Twenty Questions."

I sit up in my chaise. "What time is it?" I say.

"Two o'clock," Aubrey says.

"Two o'clock?" I turn and look upstairs at the balcony and at our door. "I didn't fix lunch for Barry," I say, but Lucinda has already started Twenty Questions and Aubrey is handing me another Big Cat.

We play Twenty Questions again and drink more Big Cat and beer. About the third time I look up at our apartment, I see Barry standing on the balcony, his hands on the railing, rocking back and forth on his heels. I wave, but he's not looking down at the pool. He's looking into the parking lot. He knows I'm at the pool, but he's not looking down at me. He turns around and goes back into the apartment.

"What time is it?" I say again, and Aubrey looks at his watch. "Five o'clock," he says.

I had better go upstairs and make dinner.

"Sun's still out," Aubrey says. "We got a Big Cat to finish."

I'm turned around in the chaise, looking up at our apartment door. Barry comes outside and, without looking over at the pool, goes down the stairs into the parking lot, gets into the Supersport, and drives off.

I lean back in the chaise, and Aubrey hands me the Big Cat. "You don't have any communicable diseases, do you?" I say.

"Don't know. If I do, I can steal us some penicillin from the hospital."

I take a drink and hand the can back to Aubrey. I wonder where Barry went in the car.

The sun is going down, Lucinda Ann gets up and stuffs her beach towel and her deck of cards into her bag. "You all come on up, and we'll start some real drinking," she says.

Aubrey passes me the can of Big Cat.

I hear a car turning into the parking lot. I look up, and it's the Supersport. Barry gets out and walks upstairs with a bag of groceries. His shirttails are out of his pants, flying in the air as he goes up the stairs.

I pass the can of Big Cat back to Aubrey. "Want to go out tonight?" he says.

"What?"

"You heard me. I don't make a practice of going out with married women, and I probably wouldn't be asking you if I weren't drunk."

I look at him. He just wants to have a good time.

"I can't," I say.

"What are you going to do tonight?"

"I don't know. Maybe go to the K mart with my friend Patsy."

Aubrey laughs. "If you change your mind, I'm in the phone book."

"I've got to go up," I say.

When I get up from the chaise, my body feels soft and easy from sun and Big Cat. With my towel over my shoulder, I walk across the parking lot to the stairway. Inside the apartment, I can't see anything but darkness. When my eyes adjust to the dim light, I see Barry come out of the kitchen, carrying a tin foil tray. He sits down at the dining-room table and starts eating a TV dinner.

I hadn't realized how hungry I am. I go into the kitchen and look into the oven. It's empty. I look into the freezer, then, but there's no TV dinner there either.

"Where's mine?" I say to Barry.

He doesn't look up. "I only bought one."

"You didn't buy one for me?"

He shakes his head.

I stand over the dining-room table and watch Barry cut his turkey. The knife makes a shrill whisper on the aluminium foil plate. I go into the bedroom and step out of my bikini. I put on my jeans, a T-shirt, and sandals, take the car keys off the dresser, and throw them in my purse. I walk through the living room past Barry. "I'm going to the K mart with Patsy," I say.

He doesn't stop chewing. I get in the car and drive straight to the K mart. When I get there I remember I am supposed to be going with Patsy. I go inside the K mart and walk alongside a rack of cheap blouses, then circle around the end and walk back along a row of cheap slacks and shorts and back out into the parking lot. I start walking towards the Supersport, but I see a telephone booth, and I walk over to it. I open the phone book and look up Aubrey's number. Then I dial it.

"Hi," I say.

"Are you coming over?"

"Uh huh."

"Okay. You know the street right before you take the turn into the parking lot? Take a left there and go about three blocks. The number is —"

"It's here in the book."

I hang up. I get back in the Supersport and pull out of the parking lot into the highway. I can tell Barry I went to the K mart by myself. I won't even be lying. I see Barry sitting, hunched over the dining-room table, eating a TV dinner. "Where's mine?" I say. "I only bought one." The tines of his fork and the serrated edge of his knife are scraping against the bottom of the aluminum plate as he cuts big slices of turkey and puts them in his mouth. "I only bought one," he says. The mashed potatoes are a little yellow on top, and the peas are crinkly. I don't care. He should have bought me one. "I only bought one," he says. "Where's mine?" I say. "Where's mine?"

I am about to turn into the parking lot at the apartment when I remember I am not going to the apartment. I look up at our front picture window, but the blue draperies are drawn tight across the window. I double back and drive to Aubrey's street. It's only three blocks from the apartment, but I have never been there before. I follow the numbers and pull up in front of a two-story frame house with a swing on the porch. As soon as I take the keys out of the Super-sport, Aubrey is on the porch, waving me in.

"I can only stay for an hour," I say.

"Okay. Make yourself comfortable. Play some records."

He leaves me in the living room. A pale flowered carpet is on the floor, white lace draperies on the windows, the kind of couch my grandmother calls a *davenport:* fat round arms, cushions that spill you down towards the center split when you sit on them. I haven't heard from my grand-mother. I wonder if anyone told her I got married.

I look through Aubrey's records. He has at least a hundred, lots of rock, no jazz. He comes downstairs with a bottle of bourbon and two paper cups.

"You've got Aretha Franklin and the Beatles and the Stones," I say. "How can I decide?"

"Play them all." He pours two glasses of bourbon.

I pick out an armload of records.

"Hey," Aubrey says. "Don't you have any music at home?"

"Just jazz," I say. "And Muzak."

"I Want to Hold Your Hand" is tuned up real loud, and Aubrey and I are drinking our second glass of bourbon. I'm telling Aubrey how Miranda and I used to get money from the oilmen who showed up in the campus bars during a boom in Ohio. Aubrey is laughing so hard, he jerks forward and sloshes bourbon all over my jeans.

"Damn, sorry about that," he says.

I follow him into the kitchen, weaving a little behind him. When I see the kitchen I realize I haven't had anything to eat all day. Aubrey runs some water on a sponge and hands it to me. I start rubbing my jeans, but the wet spot gets bigger and bigger until one leg is wet all the way down the thigh.

"Hey," Aubrey says and points to my leg. I collapse onto the kitchen floor. I can't stop laughing. Aubrey is laughing, too, leaning against the refrigerator. *I once had a girl, or should I say, she once had me.* Soft, slow Beatles wafts in from the living room.

I stop laughing. "Do you have anything to eat?" I say. Aubrey opens the refrigerator door and holds up one egg between his thumb and forefinger.

I start laughing again. Then he starts laughing. He collapses next to me on the floor and puts his arm around me. He pours us more bourbon.

"Can't eat. We might as well dance." He holds out his arms to me. I get up and then I remember my pants. I take a kitchen towel and start dabbing at the wet spot.

"Do you have anything I can wear?" I say.

"Sure. You can wear one of my skirts."

Aubrey goes upstairs and comes down with a pair of gym shorts. "I'll wait in the living room while you change," he says.

I take my jeans off, and all of a sudden I feel scared. I put on the shorts. They're big but they have a drawstring, and I pull it tight. I lay my jeans over a kitchen chair to dry. I take another swallow of bourbon and lean back. The refrigerator door is cool on my back. It is hot tonight, but the heavy, thick air feels good on my bare legs. I look up and there is a clock hanging on the kitchen wall. At first I think it says 11:00. Then I look again, and it does say 11:00. The K mart closes at 9:00.

I go out into the living room where Aubrey is sitting on the couch, leaning back with his eyes closed. "I have to call my husband," I say.

He gives a little start. "Phone's right there," he says. He turns down the stereo.

I dial our number. A low, syrupy voice says, "Hey," and I hang up. "Wrong number," I say to Aubrey. I dial again. "Hello." Barry's voice sounds as though it's coming from very far away, as though I'm calling long distance, not from three blocks away. I hold the receiver tight. "Hi, Barry," I say. "Listen, I'm not coming home tonight. I didn't want you to worry. I'm all right. I'm just not coming home."

"Where are you?" Barry says.

"I'm not coming home, Barry. Please don't worry." And I hang up.

Aretha Franklin is singing *Sock it to me. Sock it to me. Sock it to me.* I take a swallow of bourbon. Aubrey taps his foot on the carpet like a square dance caller. I go up to him and we start to jitterbug.

I wake up when the sun comes through the lace curtains of the upstairs bedroom window. I am ravenously hungry. I look at Aubrey sleeping next to me, the skin of his ass like mashed potatoes on white sheets. "How can you hang around with those grits?" I hear Barry saying, see his elegant body, on blue sheets. I swing my legs over the bed. Aubrey's gym shorts are lying in a flaccid pile on the floor at the side of the bed. I tiptoe downstairs and put on my jeans. Somewhere in the bourbon, Aubrey's landlady came home last night. She was bearing a bikini bathing suit with a nightgown over it. Her husband was wearing a white straw hat and a vest with a watch fob. Someone else was with them, a pale young man who said he was a painter. We all sat around on the porch swing in the heat and drank bourbon.

The swing squeaked, a low long continuous sibilant squeak, but there was no breeze, no breeze at all, just a shift in the strength of the scent of magnolia blossoms from the tree in the yard.

I splash some water on my face at the kitchen sink. I take in the faded checkered curtains on the windows, the pale worn linoleum on the floor where I collapsed last night, laughing before the dancing, before the porch swing, before —

I wish I hadn't slept with Aubrey. I didn't want to sleep with him. I wanted to sink, untouched, soaked in bourbon and heat, into the soft mattress.

I take my purse and go outside. Already the air is hot and wet. The porch swing is still. There is not the slightest movement. There is no squeak. I get into the Supersport. It has sat all night with the windows closed tight. The hot trapped air smells of steaming leather. I put down all the windows, put the key in the ignition, start the motor, and as the engine turns over, I realize I have done something stupid, possibly worse.

My throat is dry and my skin coated with dry sweat. I need a glass of orange juice. I need to take a shower. I don't know what time it is, but there aren't any cars on the road yet. I hope Barry is still asleep.

At the apartment the blue drapes are drawn across the living-room window. I turn the doorknob, but the door is locked, and I don't have a key. I ring the doorbell. Barry opens the door. Without looking at him, I walk into the living room.

The couch and all the chairs are turned over. The turquoise cushions have been thrown all over the room; some landed upright, some on their sides, some at oblique angles to one another. All my books have been dumped from the bookcase and are lying on the carpet, some closed, some spread-eagle, their paperback covers dots of color on the carpet.

I look at Barry. His white shirt is hanging open, unbuttoned. His dark pants are wrinkled. His black hair is trampled, his cheeks dark with growing beard. His blue eyes are dilated, fixed. He takes my forearm and leads me into the bedroom. We pass the bathroom door, and floating in the toilet is the pink dial of my birth control pills, empty.

In the bedroom, the blue drapes are drawn, and the room is a dusky blue from the sun filtering through. The blue sheets are rumpled, and the telephone is sitting on the sheets. Barry pulls me down on the bed next to him.

I start to put my arms around him, but he pushes me away. He turns away from me and picks up the telephone and dials. "This is Barry Feldman," he says. "I reported a missing person last night. . . . My wife is home." Then he hangs up.

"I called you," I say. "I called you, so that you wouldn't worry."

Barry is staring staight at me. The angular lines in his face are set, jagged. "Where were you?"

"I —"

"Did you sleep with him? Did you commit adultery?"

The word *adultery* falls between us, a black iron piling on the blue sheets. *Adultery*. Adultery involves either passion, or revenge. I didn't do anything like that.

"Did you commit adultery?" Barry says.

"No," I say.

"I don't believe you. Where were you?"

"I was at someone's house. I slept there."

"Whose house?"

"Someone I know from work."

Barry raises his head to the ceiling. I can see his Adam's apple. Then he looks down at me again. "Someone you see at work every day?"

"No," I say. "He just came through a couple times last month. He was in training for another office. He lives in Bessemer. I'm sorry. I got drunk, and I couldn't drive home. I didn't think it would matter to you."

Barry's eyes open and stare, all pupils. "What?"

"I didn't think it would matter."

"You're my wife." Barry's head falls in his hands. "You are my wife."

I sink down to the carpet on my knees. "Barry, I'm sorry. I'm really sorry." I want to cry. It would work if I could just cry. I feel awful enough to cry, but I can't cry even one tear. I pull on Barry's arm. I feel foolish on the floor, the unfaithful wife pleading for forgiveness. I don't belong here. I don't know why, but what we are both saying is missing the point. I don't know what the point is, though. "I didn't sleep with him," I say.

"I don't believe you."

I am lying, but he should believe me because I'm telling the truth. I didn't commit adultery. I got drunk and slept with someone I don't even especially like. Who cares?

I look up at Barry. He cares.

I get up from the floor. "Well," I say.

Barry looks at me for a long time.

"I'll have to divorce you now," he says.

"You will?"

"I think so."

I feel dry and empty. I have to get my hands on some birth control pills without letting Barry know, and the only pills I have are from his father's doctor in Miami.

"I didn't mean to hurt you. I know that," I say. "I've been so unhappy. I know I'm a terrible wife. I don't know what to do."

The telephone rings and Barry answers it. "Yeah, she's home. I don't want to talk about it. Ask her." Barry turns to me. "Mel and Patsy and I were out in their car looking for you last night."

"You were?" I was only three blocks away. Why didn't they find me?

Barry hands me the phone. "Is everything all right?" Mel says.

"No," I say.

"Do you want to come over and talk?"

I turn to Barry. "Is it all right if I go over to Mel and Patsy's to talk?"

"Sure," Barry says.

"Okay," I say to Mel. "I'm coming over."

I hang up the phone. I can't look at Barry. I go into the bathroom. I can't take a shower here. I reach into the toilet and fish my birth control dial out of the bowl and throw it into the wastebasket.

Barry is standing behind me in the doorway. "I flushed all your pills down," he says. "You and I haven't had sex yet this month, so you won't need them."

"But I have to keep taking them," I say. "I can't just stop in the middle of a cycle. I have to finish the cycle. Otherwise my system will get all screwed up."

I look out into the living room with all the pillows and

books thrown around and the furniture turned over. "I'll clean up the apartment when I get back from Mel and Patsy's," I say.

When I pull into their parking lot, Patsy is sitting at the swimming pool, reading *Good Housekeeping*. She is wearing a Frederick's of Hollywood type of bathing suit, see-through black lace cut down to her waist in the front and held together by two crisscrossed black laces.

"Hi," I say.

Patsy looks up. "Oh, hi." She smiles. "I just found a great recipe for meatloaf. Listen, everything will be okay. Just let Barry cool down."

"He's not hot," I say.

"Well, you know, just give him a little time. Mel will talk to him. Is there anything we can do?"

"I'm dying of thirst, and I would like to take a shower."

"Oh, sure, go ahead. Mel is inside studying. There are clean towels in the linen closet, you know where it is, next to the bathroom."

"Thanks," I say.

"If you want to wash your hair, you can use my creme rinse. It's on the side of the tub."

"Thanks," I say.

Mel answers the door. "Hey," he says. He is smiling, a smile that's sad but hopeful, and not too serious. He puts his arm around me. "What's wrong, Edwina?" he says.

"Barry says he's going to divorce me."

Mel is quiet for a minute. Then he says, "He won't go through with it. What did you do, anyway?"

We sit down on the bed with Mel's law books and papers. I tell Mel the same story I told Barry. I tell him about the furniture and things thrown all over the living room. "I didn't think he would care," I say. "I didn't think he'd notice I was gone."

Mel laughs. "Yeah, Feldman is like that. Not all there, most of the time. But he loves you."

"He does?"

Mel doesn't answer for a minute. "Yeah. He does."

"I don't feel it."

Mel squeezes my arm. "Hey. Everything is going to be all right."

"I don't know," I say.

"Did you tell him you were sorry?"

"Yes. But he didn't believe me."

"He'll come around."

"I'm not sorry, though. I'm sorry I hurt him, but I'm not sorry about what I did. It was stupid, but Barry makes me feel like I've sinned."

I start crying. Damn. Why couldn't I cry when I was on my knees with Barry? Mel holds me until I stop. "Can I take a shower?" I say.

"Sure." His voice is soft.

In the shower, I use Patsy's shampoo and creme rinse. The hot water feels good running down my body. I love Mel. I love the way he put his arm around me, his soft voice, his sad smile. I throw my head back and let the warm water flow down my hair, down my back, down the inside of my legs, and I think maybe Mel is right, maybe everything will be okay.

I turn off the shower and step out. The clothes I had on last night lie in a pile on the bathroom floor. I have to put on the same clothes I was wearing last night and go home to Barry. Mel can't know that everything will be okay. His wife is out at the pool wearing a Frederick's of Hollywood bathing suit and reading *Good Housekeeping*. I am not like that, and Barry is not like Mel.

I pull on the same panties I had on last night, peach lace panties I bought before I was married. Mel didn't ask me if I loved Barry. All wives love their husbands. The only question is whether the husbands love their wives. I do love Barry, anyway. But I don't know if it matters. Mel wouldn't understand that. I don't understand it, either.

At the apartment, Barry has put the cushions back on the couch and is lying there, studying. He has shaved, and his hair is slicked back, still wet. The bones in his face are sharp and delicate, his eyelashes fine. All the other men I've known, except J.D. of course, looked like my brother and father: big, and, even if they were athletic, awkward in some way, not aesthetically pleasing. I thought that's the way men were made.

"Do you feel like going over to see Mel and Patsy?" I say to Barry. "They invited you to come over and talk, if you want to."

Barry looks up at me. His face is so sad I want to cut off my legs. "I don't have anything to say," he says.

"But maybe you'd feel better if you talked to Mel for a while. He's your friend."

"I have to stay here and study," Barry says. "This is the middle of finals."

I start picking up my books from the carpet and put them back into the bookcase. I do it slowly, smoothing out the covers, and arranging them by size on the shelves, so that they look nice. Then I take out some fish from the freezer for dinner. I want to go into the bedroom and go to sleep, but if I do that it will show Barry how tired I am, and he

190

will remember why I am tired. I wish I could take a shower, but I already took a shower at Mel and Patsy's. I can't go down to the pool anymore, either. I stand in the hall outside the kitchen that connects the living room to the bedroom. I see the blue drapes drawn across the living-room windows in the front and across the bedroom windows in the back. I don't know which way to go, but I have to stay awake. I take André Gide's *Journals* from the bookcase.

"I'm going to sit outside in back," I say to Barry.

I go through the bedroom and out the bedroom door to the balcony that overlooks the back parking lot, the trash container, and a hill that blocks whatever is beyond. I sit down on the cement floor of the balcony and lean back against the brick wall of the apartment building. I stare out between the railing on the balcony at the green hill, splashed with dandelions. I squint my eyes to form a wash of green and yellow, as in Cézanne or a Van Gogh. If I block out the trash container on the left, and the parked cars below, the green and yellow hill is as beautiful as anything I have ever seen.

The next morning the alarm goes off at 6:30. Barry reaches over me and turns it off, then swings his legs over to get out of bed.

"I'm staying home today," I say.

"You're not going to work?"

"No."

"Why not?"

"I don't want to go to work anymore. I've spent too much time at work. I don't have any time to think."

"But you've got to go to work, baby."

"I don't have to go to work today. I haven't missed one

day of work since we've been married." I pause for a minute. "So you can take the car. You can go back to sleep if you want to."

Barry sinks back onto the mattress on his elbows, then pushes himself off the bed. "I might as well get up and study at the law library," he says.

I pretend to go back to sleep. When Barry leaves, he kisses me lightly on the forehead, and then I do go back to sleep.

When I wake up it's 8:30. I call the office and tell Polly I'm not coming in. "I feel sick to my stomach," I say.

Polly lowers her voice and whispers into the phone. I can see just how she does it, her head bent down towards her desk, one hand cupped over her moving mouth and the receiver. She says, "Come on, now, Sally. If you're pregnant, you had better tell me. I'll be darned if you beat me to it. I've been trying for my own kid for four years now. I just bought a new nightgown over at Pizitz so's I can get Jess a little more interested in doing his part. But I can tell you don't have that problem with Barry."

"I'm not pregnant," I say. "I'm taking the pill."

"Oh, darn, I was hopin' we was going to have a little excitement around here. Listen, you got one less client. One of them over at Ruby Postum's passed on."

"Who?"

"Beg your pardon?"

"Who was it? Which client?"

"Oh, you want to know which one it was. Let me take a look — Earline Lloyd."

"Oh."

"You ask me, she's better off. But what do you think Sally? Are you coming in tomorrow, do you know? It's going to be real dull here today without you. I thought we'd splurge and go over to Graham's for a shrimp salad sandwich, if you felt like spendin' ninety cents on lunch. Or we could keep to our diets and split a sandwich. I guess I'll eat lunch at my desk, now, and get some of this damn paperwork done before it reaches my eyebrows. Do you think you want to get a shrimp salad sandwich tomorrow? I have got a real hankering for one."

"Okay," I say. "If I'm better tomorrow."

"What do you think it is you've got wrong with you, Sally? You reckon it's the flu or just something you ate?"

"I don't know," I say.

"I hope Barry doesn't catch it. Oh, rats, Sally, old pruneface is leaning into my doorway — Hey there, Miz Cardwell — I got to hang up."

I put down the phone, get out of bed, go into the kitchen, and pour a glass of orange juice. I am not going to get dressed today. I am not going to wash my face. I am not going to brush my teeth. I am going to think. I drink my orange juice, put the glass down on the dining-room table, and start to cry.

I sit on a chair at the dining-room table and cry. Then I walk around the living room in my shortie pajamas and cry. Then I go into the bedroom and sit on the blue sheets and cry. I go into the bathroom and look into the mirror and cry.

When I'm finished, I drag Barry's typewriter out of the closet and put it on the dining-room table. I put in a sheet of paper and start to write. *Dear Barry.* I don't know what I am going to say, but the words just keep coming out, translated into black letters on white paper. Without thinking what I am writing, I type four pages. I tell Barry how I want to live like Camus and Sartre and Gide, but how I am living like Patsy instead. I tear the last sheet out of the machine. The last sentence is: *You are the only man I ever loved, but I guess I couldn't be what you wanted.*

I stare at the typed page in front of me. The words in black type against the white paper look clean and true. I pick up Barry's ball-point pen to sign my name, then I put the pen down.

I make three crisp folds in the letter and stuff it into the bottom of my purse, unsigned. I will never be able to give it to Barry.

The next day I go back to work. At my desk there is a Styrofoam cup with a tea bag hanging out of it and something wrapped in a napkin. I unwrap the napkin and find two slices of toast, the butter melted into the center so that it's soggy except at the crust. I scrape off as much of the butter as I can with the plastic stirrer that came with the tea.

"Next time I'll tell them to put the butter on the side," Polly says, coming in the door. "I just came from the Dixie Cafe and I thought you might want something to eat. I got tea instead of coffee because of your stomachache. If you drink the coffee here, it might keep you out of work for a month."

I stop scraping the butter off the toast and take a bite of the crust.

"Didn't think there was nothin' nobody could do to toast," Polly says.

"It's all right," I say. "Thanks."

Polly beams. "Hey. Do you still feel like goin' over to Graham's for a shrimp salad sandwich? I still got that hankering."

"Okay," I say. "I have to go over to Ruby Postum's this morning, but I'll be back in time for lunch."

"But what do you want to go this mornin' for, Sally? You're like to lose your appetite."

"I want to get it over with."

"I got to go see Miz Treadle in the file room. I'll pull the file on that one who died over at Ruby's yesterday. What was her name?"

"Earline Lloyd."

"Yep. Earline sure is better off where she is now."

When Polly leaves, I pull out the Birmingham phone book. I'm not going to Ruby Postum's. I look up *Physicians* in the Yellow Pages and follow the listings until I find a gynecologist someplace I know how to get to. There's one on the same street as the doctor as we went to for Barry's ass, downtown near the University of Alabama Medical Center. I write down the name and address on a slip of paper, put it in my purse. As I'm leaving, Polly comes back into the office. "You goin' already, Sally? I'll just wait for lunch till you get back. You reckon you'll be back by twelve?"

"Sure," I say.

"Well, I'll just be waitin' here with these papers and star-vin' to death."

I drive the Supersport past the Dixie Cafe and the sign next door swinging in the slight breeze: *Bail Bonds No Money Down*. After a while the gray flat one-story buildings give way to the white, glistening high-rises of the University Medical Center. The streets are wider here and cleaner. The sun shines brighter.

How am I going to pay for my birth control pills? I keep one check in my wallet for emergencies, but I can't use that check because Barry balances the checkbook and I don't want him to know I went to a gynecologist. He'll think I'm getting the pills because there's a possibility that I'm pregnant, and that there's a possibility that I'm pregnant because I slept with Aubrey, though of course he doesn't know it's Aubrey and probably doesn't know who Aubrey is anyhow. And I'm not supposed to have slept with anyone else except Barry. And I haven't slept with Barry.

I have about five dollars in my wallet. That is enough for a prescription, but not enough to pay a doctor.

I park the Supersport, get out, and look for the address on the slip of paper. I feel exposed on the wide white sidewalk. The street is so wide here that the tall white buildings do not throw a shadow over me. I go inside one of them and look up the doctor's room number on the directory. I take the elevator and follow the numbers to 749, but when I get to the door I stop.

I look down at my wedding ring. I am a married woman, and I am going to get a prescription for birth control pills. There is nothing unusual about that.

I open the door. Inside the waiting room, a nurse is sitting behind a sliding glass window. A pregnant woman sits in a chair, leafing through a magazine. I go up to the nurse. "I would like to see Dr. Mansky," I say.

"Do you have an appointment?"

"No."

"The doctor usually sees his patients by appointment," she says. "Is it an emergency?"

"Yes," I say. "Sort of."

"Oh, I see. Are you in pain?"

"I can wait," I say.

The nurse gives me a card to fill out, and I sit down on the couch and take out my ball-point pen.

Name. Should I put down my real name? I can't let Barry know I'm here. But the doctor might want to see some identification or something, and I have to get the pills. I put down my real name, *Salina Jane Feldman,* and go on to the next line.

Address. If I put down our address the doctor could bill me there and then Barry would know. I put down a phony address, my age plus the street Polly lives on. A phony telephone number. In the box that says *Married* I put an X.

I hand the card back to the nurse. "I don't need an examination. I just want to speak to the doctor."

I sit down and pretend to be looking at a magazine on my lap. I stare at the pregnant woman. She is about my age, a married woman like me. Her hair is perfectly combed and fixed in a short pageboy and she is wearing a neat blue maternity dress, nylons, and low-heeled pumps. Her belly slopes gracefully out from under her breasts. Her face is serene. How did she get that way? I stare at her for clues. I feel my long hair spilling down my shoulders, and I remember what Mrs. Cardwell said about it. From my purse I take out the barrette I wear in the nursing homes. I reach back and twist my hair up into a bun on my head and fasten it with the barrette.

I have been to a gynecologist once before, a year ago, after I had spent the first week in Birmingham with Barry. I had read a magazine article about VD, and I was sure I had it. I didn't, but the doctor found a cut inside my vagina. He was a young doctor, only a year or two older than I was. "What did the guy do?" he said. "Fuck you with a knife?"

"Mrs. Feldman, the doctor will see you now." I jump when I hear the nurse say my name. I had thought I would be able to wait until the pregnant woman had gone inside.

The doctor is sitting behind a large desk. He is a middle-aged man, slightly paunchy, and he doesn't look mean. "What is the problem, Mrs. Feldman?" he says.

"Oh," I say. "I'm sorry I said it was an emergency. It is, in a way — it's an emergency to me, but it's not a medical emergency. The other woman could have gone first. I could have waited." The doctor looks at me, his face impassive. If he thinks I am insane or lying, it doesn't show. I take a breath. "I have been taking Ortho Novum, and I am right in the middle of my cycle — and I lost the dial of pills. My husband is a law student and the doctor who gave me the pills is in Miami. I've missed two days already. Today is the third."

"Could your doctor call in the prescription to your pharmacy here?"

"No," I say. "I can't reach him. He's on vacation this week, and next week would be too late."

The doctor takes a long look at me. I don't care if he believes me. I just have to get the pills.

"It would be inconvenient to become pregnant while your husband is still in law school, wouldn't it?" the doctor says.

"Yes," I say. The doctor writes out a prescription. At the desk, the nurse says, "Would you like to pay now, or shall we bill you?"

"Bill me," I say, "if you don't mind."

I go across the street to a pharmacy and fill my prescription. I take one pill at the water fountain there and shove the pink dial down into the bottom of my purse with the letter I wrote Barry yesterday and the card announcing J.D.'s show.

I get in the Supersport and head back to work. The doctor

gave me the prescription for Barry's convenience, so that Barry's legal career wouldn't be interrupted by the demands of a pregnant wife, a crying baby. I don't care. I have the pills. I'll send the doctor his money before the end of the month.

But I am forgetting something. It's not this simple. If I stop taking the pill in the middle of my cycle, I'll get my period. Barry will expect me to get my period in a few days. I stop the Supersport at an intersection. My period — I have to get my period. I could fake it. Barry wouldn't check. He doesn't make love to me when I have it, anyway. But then when I really did get it, it would be two weeks too soon, and that would be hard to hide. Washing out blood from my underpants behind a locked bathroom door: it's too risky.

But if I tell Barry I got the pills, he will think I was lying about Saturday night. But he thinks I'm lying anyway.

I get back to the office at 11:45. I don't feel like having a shrimp salad sandwich. As I pass Mrs. Cardwell's office, she calls me in.

"Sit down a minute, Sally," she says.

I look at Mrs. Cardwell across her desk, at her makeup that's dried and flaking in her wrinkles, her red lipstick sticking her top lip to her teeth, her dry brown hair in a bun with a little bow in front, her tight skirt, her nylons, her high-heeled shoes. I refuse to be Mrs. Cardwell. I just have to figure out how to avoid it.

"You know, Sally, your hair looks real nice up in the barrette like that, have you ever thought about braiding it and pinning the two braids on the top of your head?"

"No," I say and smile at her. "I never did."

"No, you wouldn't like that, would you? Oh, well, Sally,

I didn't call you in here to talk about your hair. Right along I have been reading the reports you've written on your clients, and, well, I have just found them to be so nicely written, so clear, so — it's funny, Sally, you make them sound like real people.

"Well, now, I thought it would be a good idea to promote you to Intake. You would have a front office and interview folks putting in their applications. You wouldn't have to go out into field anymore, so it is really a nicer job."

"Thank you," I say. Mrs. Cardwell seems to be telling me that I have done something right, and I don't know how that could be. I'm not sure I even want to be doing anything right.

When I walk into our office, Polly is sitting at her desk with her purse in her lap. As soon as she sees me, she jumps up, takes my arm, and starts down the hall. "This place is like to drive me buggy today," she says. "The kids is home sick, and a letter came from their mama in the loony bin. I steam them letters open and read 'em before I give 'em to the kids. This one don't make no sense and is full of words the kids ain't never heard. 'What's she talking about?' Sueann says on the phone. 'Why does our mama write like that?' "

Polly smacks her lips together. "So I call Jess at the store, and I hear him sayin' to one of his salesman, 'Tell her I got a sale on.' Damn. They're his kids. I'm like to die before I have one of my own." Polly leans closer to me, and I can feel her breath on my cheek. She is walking fast, her arm hooked into mine. And she's talking fast, her small lips making little wet sounds when they touch.

"The doctor put me on hormones, same ones other ladies use for birth control, and let me tell you, I just can't wait to get into bed at night. But Jess comes home, wolfs down his dinner, and goes into the living room to read his darn church pamphlets."

Polly slows down and releases my arm. We are halfway across the park between the department and Graham's restaurant. The magnolia trees are past full bloom, their scent too sweet in the hot thick air. The ground is dusty, and the grass is brown and smells burnt. A thin man in shirt-sleeves is sitting alone on a bench.

I wonder what the man is thinking about. I wonder what I would be thinking about, sitting alone on one of those hot, dusty benches.

"Sally, you sure is a lucky one," Polly is saying. "You and Barry ain't got nobody but yourselves to worry about."

"I don't know how lucky that is," I say.

"Take a look see, Sally. 'Less Jess gets another job, I expect I'll be laid to rest in this darned town, ain't never seein' nothin' else but the All World Bible Camp for two weeks every summer. And 'less I get pregnant and it don't look like I will, I'll be trottin' up and down the halls of those darn nursin' homes 'til Jess's kids can stick me in one of 'em, too."

We sit down at the counter at Graham's in front of the fan. I can feel the hot air blowing on the back of my neck, no relief, just more heat. "Let's splurge," Polly says. "Let's us have a whole shrimp salad sandwich each."

"Okay," I say. "If I can't eat the whole thing, I'll take half home for dinner."

"Two shrimp salad sandwiches," Polly calls to the girl behind the counter. "And two iced teas, lots of ice, please."

Polly turns to me. "Heck, I just don't know what I would do without you to talk to, Sally. I'd like to be bored to death by now. I got to live vituperously, ain't that the word?

Tell me, where are you and Barry going to live when he finishes law school?"

"I don't know if he'll finish," I say.

"He's only got but one year left."

The girl sets down two plates with shrimp salad sandwiches on white bread and a few ripple potato chips.

Polly takes a big bite of her sandwich, then pats the corners of her mouth with her napkin. "Come on, Sally. You are right quiet today. Where are you and Barry going to live?"

"We're going to live in Miami," I am supposed to say. I look past the counter and the yellow plastic pitcher of iced tea with three flies buzzing around its top, out the window into the park. I see a white suburban house somewhere in Miami, a swimming pool in the backyard, its blue water stretched tight from end to end. I don't see myself in the picture.

"I don't know," I say to Polly.

"Well, it don't matter none. Anyplace has got to be more excitin' than Birmingham."

"Does it?"

"Sally, if I didn't know you better, I'd like to think you was dumb."

I pick up my sandwich, then put it down again. "I'm sorry. I just get the feeling that no matter where Barry and I live, it will be the same."

"What are you talkin' about, Sally? What will be the same?"

"Everything."

After work I drive to the law school and pick up Barry at the library. He gets in and I ease myself over the empty space between the two bucket seats. "I don't know what we're going to do about the car," Barry says. "I have a job with a lawyer three afternoons a week."

"You do?"

"Yeah. They asked Mel, but he got the job clerking for Judge Harper. So Mel gave it to me. We'll have more bread, baby."

"We? I thought you were going to divorce me."

Barry doesn't say anything.

"Well, are you?"

"You sound like you want me to."

"I didn't say that."

"You brought up the subject of divorce."

"Because you said you were going to divorce me."

"Do you want me to?"

"What do you mean?"

Errol Garner comes on the radio, and Barry turns up the sound. When the commercial comes on, I say, "Well, I don't need the car anymore. Starting next week, I'm not going out into the field."

"Groovy," Barry says.

"I went over to the medical center this morning and got some birth control pills."

"How could you do that?"

"I told Polly I lost them. She said I shouldn't just stop taking them. She gave me the name of her doctor."

Barry doesn't say anything for a few seconds. "Dad's doctor is sending you your pills when you need them."

I light a cigarette and blow the smoke into the windshield.

"Well, now I just won't need them as soon."

I turn away from Barry and look out the window. We are driving up Red Mountain, passing the Vulcan. To and from the law school, we have driven up and down this mountain past this iron giant a hundred times, even more. And every time we pass him, I see Barry and me on my first visit to Birmingham, kissing and giggling, laughing at the Vulcan, laughing at his city as though Birmingham and its god had nothing to do with us.

That was a year ago. I didn't plan things this way, but it's too late now. The Vulcan is part of me. I will be driving through New York City or wherever I go, and I will see something that in size or shape will resemble the Vulcan — or maybe the quality of the air will be as it is today, hot and damp, and I will see the Vulcan on this green hill and remember it all. And it's going to feel bad. It's going to feel terrible. Probably I don't even know yet how terrible.

At the apartment Barry scoops up the mail from the floor. He tosses me a letter from Miranda. "Miranda is arriving at nine Friday night," I say to Barry. "I told her we would pick her up at the airport."

"Okay," Barry says. He dumps his law books on the couch and slumps down with them.

"Are you going to have enough time to study now that you have a job?" I say.

Barry shrugs.

"How did Mel get the job with the judge?"

"He made law review."

"Mel?"

"Yeah."

"Why didn't you make law review?" I want to ask Barry, but I don't have to. Barry didn't make law review because he hates law. He hates law, and it's stupid for him to be in law school, and it's even stupider for him to become a lawyer. And it's even stupider than that for me to be helping him do it. It's all stupid. I wonder if Miranda will notice how stupid it is.

She won't, of course. Miranda doesn't notice things like that. I look around the living room. In seventy-two hours Miranda will be in this room. Except for my brother, who stayed less than five minutes, Miranda will be the only person I knew before I married Barry who will have been in this room.

"You'll love Miranda," I say to Barry.

"I know I will, baby," Barry says.

"You know if you're going to divorce me, you ought to tell me," I say.

Barry sits slumped on the couch and stares at me.

"Well, are you?"

"I don't know. Why do you keep bringing it up?"

"Because I want to know."

"I don't know what to do."

"Well, do you forgive me?"

Barry looks down at the floor. "I can never forgive you for that."

"Oh." I look down at the floor, too.

Friday night the air is hot and so damp water condenses on the windshield. Barry has to turn on the windshield wipers a few times on the way out to the airport. The lights on the landing field are bright in the dark night, high white beacons in the sky, small red lights on the ground on the airstrip. The night Barry and I got married, we flew from Miami and landed here. I held my breath. I am afraid of the sudden power, the ascent until the level-off at cruising altitude. I wanted to grab Barry's hand, but before I could,

I felt his palm pressed on top of mine, and I could feel the cool, stiff fear through his grip.

"You're going to love Miranda," I say to Barry again inside the airport. In a window on the airport corridor, I look at my reflection. I am wearing jeans and a T-shirt, my long hair is pushed behind large hoop earrings. I look the same as I did when Miranda and I were in the Village, the same as I did when Miranda and I were in school in Ohio. I don't know how I can look the same. I don't feel the same. The soles of my sandals make gentle slaps against the floor of the airport corridor.

"You're going to love Miranda," I say to Barry. "She looks just like you. Not her face, but the way she's built. She's skinny and moves the same way you do. She has short, curly dark hair."

"You've told me what she looks like," Barry says. He's smiling. "It's good to see you look happy, baby. I forgot what that was like."

At the gate, people are already coming in from the Santa Fe flight. After the first four or five, a crowd comes in at once. I scan their faces, and when I don't see Miranda, I look past them to the people behind. I'm standing on my toes, leaning forward on the railing that separates the waiting area from the arriving passengers.

"Hi," someone says.

I turn. Miranda is standing right next to me. "I didn't even see you."

Miranda smiles. "You probably didn't recognize me. I gained twenty pounds eating rice and beans."

Miranda is wearing a low-cut T-shirt, the cleavage of what had been her flat chest is pronounced between two full breasts. Her bony hips and thighs are rounded and substantial in tight jeans. Her short hair is long now and pulled back in a band, standing out from her face in a mass of frizz.

"I recognize you now," I say.

"I should hope so," Miranda says. "We saw each other every day for four years."

"This is Barry," I say, and he smiles at Miranda the way he used to smile at me.

"Miranda and I were Ooblicks," I say to Barry.

"Oh, God," Miranda cries. "I haven't heard that word in a whole year."

"That was our club," I say to Barry. "The Ooblicks stood for the opposite of sorority values — you know, virginity, good study habits, girls who made their own clothes and majored in elementary ed. We were notorious."

"You bet," Miranda says. "Don't you miss the Ooblicks? Even in Taos, it's hard to find any girls to be friends with. They're all so much like — like girls, I guess."

"You should join the Law School Wives' Club," I say to Miranda.

Barry picks up Miranda's suitcase and starts down the corridor with it, leaning towards it a little. Miranda and I walk beside him.

"I still can't believe you're married," Miranda says. "When you wrote me that you got married, I thought someone had drugged you or something."

"Did I drug you, baby?" Barry says.

I wonder what Miranda thinks of Barry calling me *baby*. No one in Ohio calls anyone *baby*.

"Sally always did everything first," Miranda says to Barry. Then she turns to me. "But how did you do it? How did you decide to get married?"

"Did we decide?" Barry says.

I look at Miranda. She really wants an answer. "We were sitting in Barry's car at the courthouse in Florida, trying to decide whether or not to get married. It was ten to four and the courthouse closed at four. It was Friday, and Barry was going back to school Sunday night, so if we were going to get married before he went back, we had to get our license in the next ten minutes. We saw a woman walking across the courthouse lawn, and we ran up to her. It was five to four. 'Should we get married?' we asked her.

"She smiled at us and said, 'Yes.' She had been married for fifteen years and they were the happiest years in her life, she said. So we went in and got the license."

"Jesus," Miranda says. "Couldn't you have just lived together?"

I turn to Miranda. The New Mexico sun has turned her cheeks pink and her shoulders are a nutty brown. "Do you remember when we were walking down Bleecker Street and that guy called you a spic? Now you look Mexican." I pause for a minute. "No one lives together in Birmingham, Alabama."

We walk out through the parking lot, and Miranda gets in the back seat of the Supersport. She leans forward between the bucket seats, between Barry and me. "What's it like?" she asks. "What's it like being married?"

"It's different," I say.

Barry doesn't say anything.

"Have you heard from anyone?" I ask Miranda. "I got a card from J.D. announcing his sculpture show."

Miranda squeals. "You heard from J.D.? I love J.D. Has he gotten over you yet? What did he say?"

"He didn't say anything. He quoted Camus."

"That sounds like J.D. God, I miss everyone, don't you?"

I look at Barry. He's staring straight ahead at the road. "Uh huh," I say.

"I love your apartment," Miranda says as soon as we go inside. I fix bourbon and Kool-Aid, and Miranda and Barry and I sit around the dining-room table. Miranda shows us snapshots of her one-room house in Taos with its dirt floor, of herself on her motor scooter, of herself sitting between two Indians, with blue-gray mountains in the background.

I try to decide what it's like having Miranda in this room, but it's not like anything. Because after we drive to Georgia tomorrow, she will stay there and then go on to New York and Barry and I will still be here at the dining-room table. Miranda in this dining room is like a movie. It's not real.

"Gosh," Miranda says. "I mean, do you realize it's been over a year since we graduated?" Miranda giggles. "I still have that Polaroid I took of you and J.D. at graduation."

We're both quiet for a moment.

"Remember the party at Max's the night before graduation?" Miranda says. "Max was blasting Mozart's Jupiter on the stereo and sitting crosslegged on the top of the refrigerator drinking Thunderbird and waiting for the end of the world. You and J.D. and Max and I passed out on the roof of Max's apartment building."

"We woke up in the morning with soot all over us," I say.

"Who's Max?" Barry asks.

Miranda and I are both laughing hard. We both look at Barry.

"He doesn't know who Max is," I say.

We both laugh some more.

"That seems impossible," Miranda says.

"Max is a friend of ours, of Miranda's especially. Or was. He always wore black."

"You knew some weird people, baby," Barry says.

I look at Barry. I look around at the matching plastic furniture and the Muzak speaker in the wall.

"I liked it when things were weird," I say to Miranda.

"Me too," she says.

At about midnight, Barry and I go into the bedroom and drag the mattress out into the middle of the living-room floor.

"You don't have to do that," Miranda says. "I can sleep on the couch."

I bring out one of the pillows from our bed and toss it onto the mattress.

"Good night, Miranda," Barry says and goes back into the bedroom.

Miranda and I sit down next to each other on the edge of the mattress. "I love your blue sheets," Miranda says. "I love Barry. When he smiles, I could melt."

"I thought you would notice that," I say. I take a sip of my Kool-Aid and bourbon. "He doesn't smile too much anymore. I don't melt too much."

"That's sad," Miranda says.

I don't say anything.

"What's wrong?" Miranda says.

"I don't know."

"I'm sorry you two are unhappy."

I jump up from the mattress. "Miranda, I am going to ask you a question, and I want you to tell me the truth. Do I have a southern accent?"

Miranda looks up at me from the mattress. "Yes, you do."

In the morning, Miranda and I are at the front door. "Are you sure you don't want to go with us?" I ask Barry.

"No, baby, I've got to study." He puts his arms around me and kisses me on the lips.

"I'll see you tomorrow night," I say.

Miranda and I walk towards the Supersport. "What kind of car do you have, a Cadillac?" she says.

"It's a Chevy," I say.

"It's a gorgeous car," she says.

"This is the first night I will be away from Barry," I say. "I mean, the second night."

Miranda turns to me and raises her eyebrows. "The second night?"

We get into the Supersport. I take the map out of my purse that Barry and Miranda and I have gone over the night before. Barry has marked the route with red squiggly arrows. It's 170 miles from Birmingham to Pine Mountain, Georgia, but you only have to take two roads: routes 20 and 27. It seems impossible that it's so easy, that in two roads we can go from Barry's and my apartment to Miranda's childhood home.

"Watch for signs that say Pell City," I say to Miranda. "When my father drove us to Florida every winter, Pell City was a speed trap."

I start the Supersport and pull out of the parking lot.

"Oh, you've got a pool," Miranda says. "I didn't see it last night."

I look into the rearview mirror to see if Barry is standing

on the balcony, waving to us. He is standing on the balcony, but he's not waving.

"Remember when we drove Tom's car from Chicago to Ohio?" Miranda says.

"You drove it," I say. "I didn't know how to drive a stick shift. Tom was so scared, he wouldn't come out of his apartment to say good-bye to us. I don't blame him after I found out how you drive."

"What do you mean?"

"Well, you do stop short."

Miranda laughs. "Whatever happened to Tom?"

"I don't know," I say. "I don't know what happened to anyone."

"You were going to marry him."

"I was going to marry everyone."

"Not me."

"No, I wasn't going to marry you."

"I mean, *I* wasn't going to marry anyone.

"We had those great cowboy hats on that trip, remember?" Miranda says. "We were driving eighty miles an hour on the Indiana Turnpike —"

"You were driving."

"I was driving eighty miles an hour on the Indiana Turnpike, and all the truck drivers were honking and yelling at us. We had so much fun. I don't want to grow up, Sally." Miranda pauses. "Do you?"

"I don't know."

Miranda lights a Marlboro and passes it to me, then lights one for herself. "Are you going to stay married?"

"What?"

"Have you gone deaf?"

"I don't know. Barry wants to divorce me. I don't know if he'll do it, though."

"Why does he want to divorce you? He doesn't look like he wants to divorce you. He looks like he's crazy about you."

"He does?"

"Oh, yeah. And I love the way he calls you *baby*. His voice is so delicious when he says it, sort of breathless and soft."

"I wish you wouldn't say things like that, Miranda."

Miranda looks at me. "Why does he want to divorce you?"

"Because I committed adultery."

Miranda laughs. "Is that all?"

"Yes. Even less."

"Who did you go to bed with?"

"Some guy I met at the pool. It was nothing. He was nothing. I got drunk. It was nothing."

"So if it was nothing, then you didn't do anything."

"Barry says I committed adultery."

"Who does he think he is, Moses?"

"Maybe."

"Do you want to get divorced?"

I take a long drag on the Marlboro and feel the hot tobacco smoke burn down into my lungs where I breathe.

"I don't know. I can't imagine being divorced from Barry."

"You've only been *married* to him for five months."

"I know. But how can I divorce someone I've only been married to for five months?"

"Do you love him?"

"I don't know. I don't know anything. I hate being married to him. Miranda, when he shaves in the morning, he stands at the counter in the bathroom —"

"It's a great bathroom," Miranda says. "My bathroom is in the backyard. It's a bitch when you have to piss at night. I try to hold it in."

"And he rests his penis on the counter. It drives me crazy."

Miranda starts laughing.

"I hate him for standing like that. I have no right to hate him for that, do I?"

"Sure," Miranda says. "I don't know why you would hate him, though."

"I don't know, either. Remember when we were all sitting around Buttsy's drinking beer and talking about philosophy, and J.D. said, 'We're all hedonists — except Sally. She's a utilitarian.' I'm not sure what he meant, but he was right."

"Do you like to go to bed with him?"

"I could never go to bed with J.D., you know that." I pause. "He was a virgin."

Miranda smiles. "Not anymore."

"No?"

"No. Max told me. He's sleeping with a couple of his art students."

I think about that for a minute. "I suppose I should be happy for him."

"Well, are you? You're always thinking about how you are supposed to feel and not about how you feel."

"No, I'm not happy for him."

"I just love J.D.," Miranda says.

"Me, too. I wish I could have slept with him."

"But you couldn't."

"But I should have been able to."

"Anyway, I asked you about Barry. I meant, do you like to sleep with Barry?"

"I used to."

"But you don't now?"

"No."

"Then divorce him."

"It's not that simple."

I can't talk to Miranda about Barry. She sleeps with a guy in the back of his van and takes off in the middle of the night. She doesn't know what it's like when you wake up in the morning, and he is still there, and neither of you is going anywhere. And he's there every night, and nothing happens in between. He doesn't drive off in his van or kiss you good-night on the dormitory steps and leave you free. She doesn't know how crowded it is and how empty. And you have to act like a wife, opening cans, folding napkins.

"You were crazy about him before you got married. I mean, Jesus, you moved to Birmingham for him."

"Something happened."

"What?"

"I don't know."

"I love him," Miranda says. "I love him more than your other men, except maybe J.D. and I wouldn't have been able to sleep with him, either. But if you're not happy, you should leave him. You're only twenty-two —"

"You were only twenty-three last month, Miranda."

"I mean, you're only twenty-two. You might live to be eighty. That leaves you — oh, shit, I never could count —"

"It's too many," I say.

"Sixty-eight years with Barry —"

"Fifty-eight —"

"Fifty-eight years with Barry —"

Miranda starts laughing, and I start laughing, too. I'm laughing so hard, I can't see out the windshield. I take a deep breath and try to stop, but I look over at Miranda, and she's looking over at me, and we start laughing again. My cheeks are wet with tears. I rub my eyes, and my vision clears. I see a sign that says *Pell City, Speed Limit, 30 mph.* I put my foot on the brake and slow down fast. When I look in the rearview mirror for a police car, I see my eyes are red and wet, and black mascara is smeared across my cheeks.

After dinner, at Miranda's grandmother's house, Miranda and I are sitting side by side on the front porch swing, sipping iced tea with sprigs of mint. Her grandmother, a great-aunt Tillie, and Uncle Ezra are rocking. The rockers bump the floor boards of the porch. The swing is rusty, and when Miranda or I move, it gives a shrill hiss. Otherwise the night is quiet.

"It surely is nice to have you children staying the night with us," Miranda's grandmother says.

"We're not children, Granny," Miranda says. "Sally is even married."

"You are now?" Ezra says. "What is the young man's name?"

"Barry Feldman," I say. "We live in Birmingham."

Ezra rocks slowly, methodically as he sucks at his pipe. "That is an unusual name for a southern boy," Ezra says.

"It's a Jewish name," I say.

"We don't have Jews in Pine Mountain, do we, Tillie?" he asks Miranda's aunt.

"Why, I don't know for certain, Ezra. I don't know every

soul in town. Maybe there's Jewish folk around here, and we don't know them."

"Sally's husband is so nice," Miranda says. "I might marry a Jewish boy, too."

"I reckon you checked to see if your husband has Burger's disease?" Ezra says.

"I beg your pardon," I say.

"Burger's disease is a disease the Jewish people get."

Miranda kicks my foot under the swing.

"What's it like?" I say. "How can I tell if he has it?"

Ezra just rocks. "Don't know," he says.

"You had better get Barry right on down to a doctor when you get back," Miranda says in her best southern drawl.

"I guess," I say.

A woman comes up the porch steps. She is dressed in a long black cotton dress with a white apron and white cap, like Pilgrim women in a grade-school textbook.

"Evenin', Helen," Ezra says.

"I simply got to put my feet up," the woman says. She sits down in a rocker, and Miranda's grandmother pushes a little stool over in front of her to put her feet on. "Why, it's Miranda," the woman says. "I almost didn't see you two children there, my eyes are getting so bad." She gets up and kisses Miranda on the cheek, and then kisses me on the cheek. "And this must be Miranda's friend, Sally. We have heard so much about you, Sally."

"I've told you about Aunt Helen, haven't I?" Miranda whispers. "She works over at Calloway Gardens in the Pilgrim's cottage."

"No," I say, "you didn't mention it."

★　★　★

"Is there anything to drink around here?" I ask Miranda after everyone has gone to bed.

"I think Aunt Helen takes a nip of brandy every night — for her health, of course."

Miranda and I go into the kitchen and look in the cupboards. Behind a jar of instant Postum, we find a half-full bottle of blackberry brandy. Miranda pours some into two juice glasses, and we sit down at the kitchen table across from each other and sip. The house is quiet. There are no voices, no cars, no garbled music from a faraway radio. The only noise is that of the cicadas, a steady high-pitched hum that seems to enter my head and lodge there in its shrill intensity. There is no breeze, and the thin white curtains hang motionless in the kitchen window. Outside there is nothing but dark.

"Is it always this quiet?" I say.

"Yes," Miranda says.

"I expect Joe Christmas to leap through the window any minute."

Miranda laughs.

"I'm scared," I say.

Miranda opens her eyes wide in mock surprise. "Ezra's daddy got his head blown off by a crazy nigger with a shotgun, but that was forty years back. He probably deserved it, too."

"Maybe I should call Barry," I say.

"Do you want to?"

"I don't know. I guess I don't have anything to say." I run my tongue over the inside of the glass to get the last sweet sticky taste of the brandy. "Can we go out somewhere?" I ask Miranda.

Miranda thinks for a minute. "It's a dry county. But we

could drive over to the next county and look for a bar."

Miranda and I tiptoe outside and get into the Supersport. I put it in neutral and let it roll down the driveway into the street before I start the engine. "Which way?" I say to Miranda.

"I don't know."

"Any way we go will take us out of the county sooner or later," I say.

The air is thick with moisture. There are no street lights, no stars, and no moon. I head the Supersport down one road and then another, going in the same direction as much as I can tell what direction that is, not knowing where we're going, only knowing that we want to go away from where we've been.

The moisture in the air shines in Miranda's curly hair and slicks my straight hair to my neck. We drive and drive, and we do not pass anything. I don't know if we're out of the county or not. There is a faraway rumble, then a burst of thunder and the rain pours down so suddenly, my face and shirt are wet before I can roll up the car window.

I can't see anything through the windshield. I press my foot on the brake and slow the Supersport to a stop. The rain drives against the metal roof of the car. I turn to Miranda. We don't say anything. Then I turn the Supersport around and go back the same way we came.

"The fireworks are going to be ruined if this keeps up tomorrow," Miranda says.

The moisture of the after-rain hangs in the air, and I can hear the sound, like faraway thunder, of early fireworks just as the sun is beginning to go down, descending as behind a heavy screen because it has rained all day, and the rain still hangs in the air. Miranda stands in the dust in her bare feet beside the Supersport. "Maybe we'll meet again in New York, what do you think?" she says.

"Maybe," I say.

"Well, Zou Zou, darling, as soon as you reach Bulgaria, be sure to phone. I will be waiting with my hand on the receiver."

"How will you be able to iron your clothes that way?" I say.

Miranda laughs. "I don't," she says. "Do you?"

"Yep."

I get into the Supersport. I start the engine and pull out of the driveway. I look in the rearview mirror and Miranda is waving wildly, her arm above her head, then her arm reaching around her back and waving from the wrong side, then one leg hiked up and her arm sticking out entangled and waving. Waving like that is one of the things we used to do across a room that would make us laugh, but I can't do it now because I am driving a car, and I don't have to laugh because she would not be able to hear me.

I follow the dirt road out the same way we drove last night trying to get out of the dry county and to a bar, and then I turn onto Route 27. The Supersport is big and empty. I am going to drive 170 miles by myself. I put all the windows down. The moisture fills the air inside the Supersport so that it is too thick to breathe. I hear the sounds of fireworks, but I don't see any lights in the sky. The air is too thick.

As the sun goes down, after I turn onto Route 20, cars are lined up along the road, families waiting to watch the fireworks. People are sitting on the hoods of their cars, drinking beer and waiting. Little kids are running around the road's edge, restless for the fireworks to start. There are so many stopped cars. The road is lined with them. Mine is the only car that is moving. I have to drive 170 miles by myself, and when I get back I will be in Birmingham, Alabama, in the apartment, and Barry will be there. He'll say, "Hi, baby, I missed you," and I won't know why I'm there, just as I don't know why I'm not with a carful of people waiting for the fireworks to begin.

The road is slick with the rain from today and the night before. The tires make a sibilant sound against the concrete. There are no other cars on the road. All the other cars are already where they were going, to the side of the road to wait for the fireworks. I used to sit with my mother and my father and my brother in a car at the side of some road, watching the fireworks. "That one was a dud," we used to say when the rocket shot up into the sky, a promise of falling, dancing, liquid light, and then at its peak, it dissolved, did not spread out into the sky, and was gone. When there was a dud, I felt sad, as if I had lost something, and no matter how many pink and green and white carnivals of fire burst into the sky, I remembered the duds, the disappointments of them, and as each rocket was shot up into the sky, I held my breath.

The night becomes dark, and I hear a loud boom in the distance like a cannon firing, and I know the fireworks have begun. It is the Fourth of July, 1966. The show has begun.

I watch the signs on Route 20 that say *Birmingham, 100 miles, Birmingham, 75 miles,* and it seems impossible that I can drive the whole trip alone. But if I keep my hands on the steering wheel and my foot on the gas pedal, I will because all I have to do is follow the road I am on. And yet it seems as though it should be more complicated. My hands

221

grip the steering wheel tight, and my foot is flexed on the gas pedal. I will not stop until I get home.

But then what? I will go into the apartment and Barry will be lying on the couch, studying. He will look up and say, "Hi, baby," and I won't be home. I will still be on the trip.

If you're not happy, divorce him, Miranda says. *If you don't like to sleep with him, divorce him,* Miranda says. *If it was nothing to you, then it was nothing,* Miranda says. But Miranda doesn't know what she's talking about. I saw Miranda every day for four years. We got drunk a lot and did things and the next morning it didn't matter. Nothing stuck. Things were not serious. There were no consequences. We got up early and played cribbage on my bed until noon. It was a game.

But something has happened. I can't tell Miranda what it is, because I don't know what it is. But I know that what she said does not apply to Barry and me. Other rules apply to us, but I don't know what they are yet. And I'm not going to know what they are any time soon enough to help me. Maybe I won't ever know what they are.

But I do know that what I did was not nothing. And I know it was not committing adultery. I know that it was more painful than committing adultery and that what I am going to do now will be more painful than that. But I'm going to do it anyway. Because if the end of the trip were for me to park the Supersport and go upstairs to the apartment and see Barry lying on the couch, and look up and smile, and say, "Hi, baby," it would be even worse, so much worse that I could not live.

The sun has gone down, and the night is dark, no moon, no stars. The distant sound of fireworks grows louder and louder, and through the thick wet sky I can see a pink splash of fire, not a dud, spreading into the sky like a flower gone wild, like a million champagne bubbles, but because the sky is wet the colored fire is not dry, and when it begins to fall, it looks like a liquid stream, its pink color running into the wet sky. And then the sky is empty and black.

"Are you going to divorce me or not?" I ask Barry.

"You want it, don't you, baby?" Barry says. "That's why you keep saying it."

Barry sits on the couch, and stares at me. "If you want to divorce me, you should do it, that's all. But I refuse to lie. I won't make up anything about you and me. You do it, and I'll sign it. I won't lie."

"Baby," Barry says.

"Look, Barry, I don't like living with someone who won't forgive me."

"If I forgive you, then what? I mean, what if I forgive you?"

"Barry, you can never forgive me. You told me that yourself."

Barry doesn't say anything. He stares down at the coffee table.

"Let's separate for a while, okay? I'll rent an apartment in Birmingham, and we'll try to figure things out."

"No," Barry says. "No. Either we stay together or we get divorced."

"Oh." I try to think for a while. I pace around the living-room carpet smoking a cigarette and drinking a can of beer. Barry hates to see me drinking beer. I stop pacing and sit down in a chair across from Barry.

"Why don't you go and visit Phil in New York for the weekend?"

"We don't have the money for that, baby," Barry says.

"We have over six hundred dollars in the joint checking account. You only have to pay for plane fare. It's ninety dollars."

Barry looks up from the couch. "Why do you want me to go?"

"Well, I think it would be good for us to get away from each other. And you would like to see Phil. He says he's playing some good jazz. I don't know."

Barry stares at me some more. He doesn't say anything.

"Well," I say, "you could go this weekend."

Susie is in New York too, I remember. If Barry goes to New York, will he call Susie? I hope so. Barry slept with Susie, and I will never forgive him for that. And now he might sleep with her again, and I'm sending him there to do it. I don't care. Maybe something will happen. I just want something to happen.

My new office is at the front of the shoe-box-shaped building, all the way up the hall from the office I shared with Polly in the rear. There is a window that looks out onto the square front lawn divided in half by a sidewalk leading to the front door. When I come into the office on Friday morning, a container of coffee and two slices of toast wrapped in a napkin are sitting on my desk.

"Hey," Polly says and comes through my door. "Mind if I sit down?"

She sits down in the chair where the clients sit across from my big oak desk.

"Sure is lonely back in the old office," she says. "I ain't

got nobody to talk to. I hear they are fixing to put old Miz Barstock back there with me. Ain't that something?"

"Jesus," I say.

"Hey, what are you and Barry doing this weekend? Jess and I are having a barbecue tomorrow night. Would you and Barry like to come? It ain't going to be nothing special, but I'd love to see you and Barry. Do you reckon Barry would come to something like that?"

"I don't know," I say. "But Barry might be going to New York this weekend."

"Sally, you didn't hint you two might be doing something exciting like going to New York."

"I'm not going," I say. "Barry has a friend who's a jazz musician and he might go and visit him in New York."

"Would he go without you?"

"I don't know," I say.

"I wouldn't let Jess go no place without me," Polly says. "No, siree. I got enough problems without him fallin' for the first thing in a skirt who sweet-talks him. But I guess you don't have that problem with Barry. I can tell just by looking at him, Barry would never fall for anyone but you."

I take a ragged bite out of the toast. I wish Polly wouldn't bring me toast every morning. Some mornings I would like to eat something else.

"How do you know that?" I say.

"By the way he looks at you, Sally, like you are special. It gives me the shivers just thinking about it. I ain't never had anybody look at me like that."

"You're lucky," I say.

"Oh, beans, Sally. You don't know what you are talking about. Listen, do you want to go watch *Ben Casey* at lunch? I could go for a hamburger and some french fries. Shouldn't eat the fries though." Polly slaps her hands on her hips. "I am still trying to lose that darn eight pounds. How do you do it, Sally? How do you stay so thin?"

I look up at the clock on my wall. It's 8:15. I want to get started with my work. The waiting rooms are full.

"I've been on a diet since I was eleven years old," I say. "But now I've lost my appetite. I just don't like to eat anymore."

"I wish that would happen to me." Polly glances at her watch. "Rats, I got to get back to the salt mines. I got to go out to Ruby Postum's this afternoon. You sure is lucky to get this new job. I been working here seven years, and I still got to stomp up and down the halls of these nursing homes and scream my lungs out at the old folks."

I pick up the first application from the stack on my desk. Rufus Jones receives $82 a month Social Security, so he is not eligible for anything. I hate to tell these people no all the time. I pick up the phone and call Barry.

"Hi, baby," he says. "What are you doing?"

"Talking to you on the phone."

"You always say that."

"I can't help it. Listen, Barry. I just wanted to know if you're going to New York this weekend."

"Why?"

"I just want to know."

There is a silence for several seconds. "I don't want to go to New York, baby."

"You could see Phil. You could go to the Village Gate."

There is another silence.

"It would be good for us to get away from each other."

"Why would that be good for us?"

"I don't know."

226

"You've asked me a thousand times if I'm going to New York."

I don't say anything for a while. "Well, if you go, have a good time," I say and hang up.

"Rufus Jones," I call into the room of colored people.

A slight man with graceful posture wearing clean work pants and a short-sleeved shirt gets up and follows me into my office.

"Good morning," I say. "I'm Mrs. Feldman. I was just looking at your application, and I see that you receive eighty-two dollars a month from the Social Security."

"Yes'm," Rufus says.

"You must have worked a good long time for such a big check, Mr. Jones. But that check makes you ineligible for welfare."

"I don't want help," Rufus Jones says. He fumbles in his pants pocket and pulls out a wrinkled envelope and hands it to me. It's a check from our department made out to Mattie Jones. "My wife Mattie, she gone into the hospital, and she ain't at home no more, so she don't be entitled to this check. I am bringing it back."

I take the check from him. It's for $51. "When did your wife go into the hospital?" I say.

"Last week, ma'am, but the check come yesterday."

I hold the wrinkled check in my hand. It's still warm from being in Rufus Jones' pants pocket. I reach across the desk to hand it back to him. "You can keep the check," I say. "Your wife might get out of the hospital, and she'll need the money."

"No, ma'am. I can't do that. I stay with my Mattie in the hospital every day and she say, 'Rufus, soon as you git my check you bring it down to Miz Cardwell at the Welfare.' We don't want nothing don't belong to us, ma'am."

I look at Rufus Jones. His dark eyes show through red veins. If I were Rufus Jones, I would keep the check. I would like to think he's a fool, but I don't. I think he has character. I don't know why, with all my advantages, Rufus Jones has character, and I don't.

"All right," I say. "You can tell your wife you gave the check back to Mrs. Cardwell herself."

Rufus Jones follows me into Mrs. Cardwell's office. He hands her the check and tells her what he told me. When he leaves, Mrs. Cardwell says, "My land, Sally, did you see how that man cares about his wife? And in all the twenty-three years I have been working here, I have never seen anyone bring back a check." Mrs. Cardwell pauses and smacks her lips together. "And do you know what that makes me think, Sally? It makes me think these coloreds have got feelings for each other — and consciences, too. Just like yours and mine."

"Better than mine," I say.

"I beg your pardon?"

"Nothing," I say.

I call Ocie Yester from the white waiting room. A small woman with a placid face follows me into my office. She looks younger than sixty-one, which is her age on her application.

"I'm Mrs. Feldman," I say. I smile at her. I want my clients to think that if the world were up to me, things wouldn't be this way.

"Is that a Jewish name, Miz Feldman?"

"Yes," I say.

Ocie Yester smiles. So do I. It's so odd to be a Jew in Birmingham, Alabama, especially when you aren't one.

"Are you Jewish?" she says.

"No," I say. "My husband is. People think I'm Jewish because of the name. People always think I'm something I'm not."

"I understand," Ocie Yester says.

"You do?"

She smiles and nods her head. I wonder if she does understand what I said. I'm not sure I understand it. I tell her what I do understand — that because she is not sixty-five years old and does not have any physical disabilities that she is not eligible for welfare.

"I thank you anyway, Miz Feldman," she says. "You are a nice lady."

"I wish I could give you a check," I say. "I know you need it."

"Lord, yes. But I'll get along. Life is hard for poor people." She pauses and then smiles. "But it's hard for rich people, too."

"Yes," I say. "It is."

I wish I could talk to Ocie Yester for a while. I wish my job weren't adding up numbers and telling people whether or not Jefferson County can give them money. I wish I could just talk to them. They know a lot of things I don't know. They are living, and I am not.

"I'm going to New York," Barry says. His voice is tight and hollow. "I'm leaving on Delta at three o'clock. I'm at the airport now."

I squeeze the receiver, but it is hard, of course. It doesn't give. "Have a good time," I say.

"Aren't you going to ask me when I'm coming back?"

"When are you coming back?"

"Shit, baby, shit. You don't give a shit when I'm coming back."

"I just forgot to ask," I say. "When?"

"Tuesday on an eleven A.M. flight."

"Well, have a good time."

I hang up the receiver. I look at the clock. It's 2:45. Barry's flight leaves in fifteen minutes. I try to imagine him at the airport getting on the plane, but I can't. How am I supposed to get home from work? And even if I get home, how am I supposed to get into the apartment? I don't have a key. I look in my wallet. I don't have any money, either.

I never thought Barry would go. I get up and run into Mrs. Cardwell's office.

"Why, Sally, you look all out of breath," she says.

I stand in the doorway. I can't think what I am doing here.

"Come in, child," Mrs. Cardwell says. "Sit down."

I slump into a chair. "My husband just called and said he's going to New York for the weekend, and I don't have any money —"

"Why, I'll loan you some money, Sally, if that's what you are going to ask me."

"No," I say. "I have money. I just wanted to ask you if I could take a half an hour off to go to the bank before it closes."

"Why, surely —" Mrs. Cardwell is looking at me the same way she looked at Rufus Jones, fondly, as though she has just learned something about me she did not expect.

"Thank you," I say. Then I remember I can't get to the bank, because I don't have the car. "But I don't have a car," I say.

Mrs. Cardwell smiles. "Why don't you ask Polly if she'll run you on over? I reckon she'll be glad for the break."

"Thank you," I say and get up. As I'm leaving her office, I turn back to her. "There's something else. I'm locked out of our apartment. I don't have a key."

"Sally Feldman, are you telling me you don't have a key to your own home?"

I just look at her.

"Why don't you call up your landlord, dear? I'm certain he'll have an extra key."

"Thank you, Mrs. Cardwell," I say. "I really appreciate it." As I'm coming back into my office to get my purse, the phone is ringing. Maybe Barry changed his mind and decided not to go.

"This is New York calling Salina Jane Feldman," the operator says.

"This is she," I say. I wonder how Barry got to New York so fast. I look at the clock. It's only 2:50. His plane didn't even take off yet."

"Go ahead, New York."

"Hi, there."

"How did you get my number, J.D.?"

"Miranda told me where you're working. I called long distance information." He starts singing, " 'Long distance information, give me Memphis, Tennessee.' "

"Are you drunk?"

"Let's see. It's Friday. I must be drunk."

He doesn't say anything else for a moment.

"Well, J.D., why did you call?"

"Oh," he says. "There's a rumor you're coming back to New York."

"Barry's in New York now," I say. "I mean, he's getting on a plane in five minutes and flying to New York."

"Barry?"

I look out the window of my office onto the front lawn. An old colored woman turns the corner to the walk and heads towards the front door of the building. She wipes her forehead with her bare arm. It's hot in the sun. But it's 3:00 on Friday afternoon, and nobody will talk to her today.

"You didn't answer my question," J.D. says.

"Oh, Barry — my husband," I say.

"Right answer, wrong question, Salina Jane. I meant about New York. Are you coming back to New York?"

Now I can hear someone yelling J.D.'s name over the traffic noise outside his loft.

"Shit," he says. "I think I'm expecting someone. Maybe more than one. I don't have a buzzer."

"Well, why don't you go let them in?"

"Yeah, that's a good — Salina Jane, that's what I like about you. You always know what to do in a social situation. If you come to New York, call me. I'm in the book. Under Nugent."

"I know."

"N as in narcosis —"

"I know how to spell your name, J.D."

"You do. Well, that's good, Salina Jane."

"J.D.?"

"Yeah?"

"I'm sorry I missed your show."

J.D. doesn't say anything.

"J.D.?"

"I'm here." Then he hangs up.

I leave my office and walk back to Polly's office to ask

her for a ride home. But no one is in the office, and I remember that she said she was going to Ruby Postum's. I thought she could drive me home, but she'll go right home from there. There is probably a bus that goes somewhere near the apartment. I don't know where to catch it, though.

I go back into my office. I sit down and stare at the desk. Why was it I wanted Barry to go to New York? I don't remember. I know it was important, but I don't remember what it was. I pick up the phone and dial Patsy and Mel's number.

"Hi, Edwina," Mel says when he picks up the phone.

"How did you know it would be me?"

"Feldman left for New York, right?"

"How did you know?"

"He left a paper with me to hand in on Monday."

"Oh."

"Now that Feldman's gone we can all go out tonight. Did he take the car? Want me to pick you up from work? I can get you on my way for Patsy. Hey, Edwina, why don't Patsy and I stay at your place for the weekend? We'll keep you company."

"Okay," I say. "Except I can't get into the apartment."

"We're going to stay at Edwina's tonight," Mel says when Patsy gets into the car, "as soon as we get her a key."

"Sally, what are you doing in the back seat?" Patsy says.

"Feldman went to New York and left Edwina alone, so we're staying with her for the weekend," Mel says.

"We are?" Patsy says.

"Yeah. Edwina, where do you want to go tonight?"

"I don't know. Let's go out and get drunk."

"Sally!" Patsy says.

"I heard about a place where there's dancing," Mel says. "How's that sound?"

"You don't like to dance, Mel," Patsy says.

"Yeah, I do," Mel says.

"You never told me that," Patsy says.

"I bet Edwina likes to dance," Mel says.

"Only when I'm drunk," I say.

"So you can get drunk first."

"But I don't like to get drunk," Patsy says.

"You don't have to," Mel says. "They have pizza there, too."

Monday after work, Mel and Patsy and I are coming into the apartment. Mel is carrying a six-pack of beer, a large bottle of Coke, and a jumbo bag of potato chips. The mattress from our bed is lying in the middle of the living-room floor. Patsy and Mel have been sleeping on it since Friday night.

Mel grabs the TV page from the top of the TV. "Hey, there's a great Cagney movie on tonight, Edwina," he says. He throws the bag of potato chips on the dining-room table, then he stops. He turns and looks at me, and then looks at the bedroom door, which is slightly ajar. Barry's suitcase is in the doorway. "I thought Feldman was coming back tomorrow," Mel says.

I go to the bedroom door, and Mel follows me. Barry is asleep, sprawled on the box springs with all of his clothes on, even his shoes. The draperies in the bedroom are drawn, and the room is dark. I turn around and look at Mel. He shrugs and raises his eyebrows, and we go back into the living room.

Mel picks up the potato chips and rips the top off, takes a handful and passes them to me. Then he turns to Patsy and gives her the potato chips to take home with her.

The dining-room table is full of empty beer cans and Coke bottles, crumpled Marlboro packs, and potato chip crumbs. The blue sheets on the mattress where Mel and Patsy were sleeping are rumpled and stained with spilled Coke.

Barry comes out from the bedroom and stands in the hall. His hair is mussed, and his pants are wrinkled from his lying on the box springs. The two ends of his belt hang unconnected from the loops of his pants.

"Did you have a good time?" I say.

He doesn't answer. He goes into the kitchen and takes a can of V-8 out of the refrigerator. Then he stands in front of me and drinks it from the can, throwing his head back. I can see his Adam's apple move as he swallows. "What's the mattress doing on the living-room floor?" he says.

"Patsy and Mel stayed here all weekend."

"Oh yeah?"

"Yeah. I didn't have a car or anything. So they stayed here."

"Oh." Barry walks back into the bedroom. I follow him. He is sitting on the edge of the bed with the V-8 can in his hand.

"Did you have a good trip?" I ask him.

He doesn't say anything for a few seconds. Then he puts the V-8 can down on the night table. He puts his head in his hands and leans over his knees. "How can you ask me if I had a good time? Of course I didn't have a good time. How could I have a good time? My marriage is falling apart. I couldn't think of anything but you, baby. I didn't want to go to New York."

"I didn't make you go," I say.

It's Saturday night. "Jesus Christ," Barry says. "I haven't seen Ray in six months. He's my best friend, and I haven't seen him in six months. I'm going to go up to the station. Want to come?"

"Okay," I say. I follow Barry out the door. I still have the Joe Namath plate Nellie gave us. I guess we'll never have them over for dinner. I guess Barry will keep the plate if we get divorced.

At the station, Ray looks up and smiles at Barry and me. The tune ends, and Ray's lips move taut and fast, his low mellow voice articulating into the mike, "That was Brubeck, vintage nineteen sixty-one, gets richer with age, baby, like a good woman. And here's a good woman, Sarah Vaughan —" Ray sets the needle down on the record and looks up at Barry and me. "How are you two doing, man? Where've you been?"

"Around," Barry says. "What about you, Ray? How's your wife and your son?"

"They're great, Barry, just great." Barry turns away from Ray and looks at a wall. Ray turns to me. "What's wrong, Sally?" he says.

"What do you mean?"

"I know you are a white girl, but I have never seen you looking so white before."

I am wearing my best clothes, a pink sleeveless sweater and skirt, and the bone-colored high-heeled shoes with the strap that snakes across the instep. Barry and I are in Drayton Burns' office. I have never been at the office where Barry works. It has oak-paneled walls and large windows that look out on the city of Birmingham. I'm surprised that Barry works here, it is so nice.

We sit down across the table from Drayton Burns.

"This is my wife," Barry says. He sounds proud. I wonder why he's divorcing me if he's so proud.

"You have a lovely wife, Barry," Drayton Burns says.

"Thank you," Barry says.

Barry and I sit and stare at Drayton Burns. "She wants a divorce," Barry says.

"*You* want a divorce," I say.

"Are you two separated?" Drayton Burns says.

Barry and I stare at him.

"Are you living apart?"

"No," Barry and I say at the same time.

Drayton Burns leans back in his chair. "All right. I am glad to help the two of you. Barry is working for me here, and he is doing a real fine job. I wouldn't send you away to get a divorce, Barry. But I want the two of you to separate for two weeks before you make a decision. And then if you still want a divorce, come back."

Barry and I nod. Barry is wearing the blue suit his father bought him at Pizitz. We look good together. I wonder why we're getting divorced.

Drayton Burns is asking questions and Barry is answering them for both of us. I don't want to answer any questions. I don't have any answers. Outside the picture window behind Drayton Burns' head, a transparent cloud like a veil looks as though it is being dragged across the blue sheet of sky.

"Did you hear that, baby?" Barry says.

"What?"

"I have to sue you for the divorce because you are not a resident of Alabama."

"I'm not?" I say.

"No. You haven't lived here a year."

"Oh."

"The grounds for divorce in the state of Alabama are adultery and physical cruelty," Drayton Burns says. "Would you seek your divorce on the grounds of adultery, Barry?"

Barry looks at me.

"No," I say.

"No," he says.

"Then you are left with physical cruelty. Barry, you will have to attest that Sally has physically assaulted you and threatened your life."

"I wouldn't do that. I wouldn't say those things about you," I say to Barry. I turn to Drayton Burns. "I'll sign anything. But I won't lie."

Drayton Burns spreads his hands on the conference table. "You two live apart for two weeks. And you have to have grounds for a divorce."

"Well," Barry says on the way out of the office, "let's see if we can trip over some grounds."

"We have to separate," I say to Barry in the car.

"We can't, it's too expensive."

"But we have to."

"I don't want to separate, baby," Barry says. "I'll tell him I'm staying in a motel."

I think for a minute. I don't like the idea of Barry staying all alone in a motel.

"Drayton was divorced when he was my age. He had a beautiful wife who was unfaithful to him," Barry says. "But he's happily married now. Has three kids."

"That's nice," I say.

Barry turns up the radio, then turns it down again when

a commercial comes on. "My dad said it was better for me to get the divorce anyway. If *you* got the divorce, it would reflect badly on me if I go into politics."

"Oh." I wait until the song is over. "Do you plan to go into politics."

"You never know," Barry says.

Bobbie Sue and Caroline and Polly and three or four of the other women at the Department of Relief and Security are crowded around me in the hall outside my office. Bobbie Sue is seven months pregnant now, and as she stands next to me her belly pushes up against my hipbone. I have given Mrs. Cardwell my two weeks' notice this morning.

"But we had no idea you all would be leaving us so soon," Caroline says.

"Why you didn't think this Yankee would stick around Birmingham forever, did you now?" Bobbie Sue says.

Polly is the only one of them who knows I am getting divorced. She stands there, looking at the pointy toes of her high-heeled shoes. Then she looks up. "Life has got to be more excitin' for Sally in New York. I'm fixin' to come visit, maybe by the time I get my Social Security check."

Everyone expects me to say something, but I can't think of anything to say.

Bobbie Sue's voice is low now and serious. "Is Barry going to transfer to a law school in New York?" she says.

The muscles on the left side of my face squeeze together and hold for a second. "What was that?" I say to Polly.

"Why I don't know. Maybe you had a slight stroke."

Barry has come to take me to lunch. We are sitting in a booth at Big Daddy's Chicken Bar-B-Q. On the large menu in small type alternating between barbecued ribs and fried chicken and Coca-Cola are spiritual messages from Big Daddy and quotations from the Bible.

> But from the beginning of the creation
> God made them male and female.
> For this cause shall a man leave
> his father and mother, and cleave to
> his wife;
> And they twain shall be one flesh:
> so then they are no more twain, but
> one flesh.
> What therefore God hath joined
> together, let no man put asunder.
> — St. Mark 10: 6–9

"What are you having, baby?" Barry says. "Whitefish, sturgeon, matzoh ball soup?" He pauses, then puts on a southern accent. "Or the barbecued ribs?" He's smiling. This is the first time we have been out for lunch together since we got married. Our divorce should be final in two or three days.

"Look at this, Barry," I say and point to the quotation from Saint Mark.

"That's the New Testament, baby," Barry says. "I never read the New Testament."

"It's pretty good. Jesus had a lot to say."

"They don't have to tell Jews not to get divorced," Barry says. "They don't get divorced."

"You are," I say. "Your parents did."

"Yeah," Barry says. "But I don't look at it that way. I

don't think of my mom and dad as being divorced. *We're not really getting divorced, are we?*"

"I don't believe in divorce," I say.

The waiter comes to the table. I order the ribs and a Coke. Barry orders a hamburger and french fries.

"This is fun, Barry."

One week from Saturday Miranda will be meeting me at Kennedy Airport. I reach across the table and put my hand on Barry's.

"Look at this weird place," I say. More quotations from the Bible are stenciled on the walls of the restaurant, along with photographs of Big Daddy, a fat man with shifty eyes and a thin mustache.

"Do you think Big Daddy would let me eat here if he knew my name was Feldman?" Barry says.

"He might barbecue you," I say.

On the wall at the side of the booth is a jukebox selector. I flip the pages and look at the songs, then ask Barry for a quarter.

He reaches into his pocket and gives me one. "Do they have any McCoy Tyner on there? Any Pharaoh Sanders?"

I slip the quarter into the slot. I play the Everly Brothers' "Bye-Bye Love," and Ferlin Husky's "Gone." "You play one, Barry."

Barry flips through the songs. He plays Henry Mancini, "Moon River."

I walk into the office in the morning, and I see a crowd all clustered around the receptionist's desk. They seem to be looking at something in the newspaper. I wonder what happened. I am about to turn into my office when Mrs.

Cardwell grabs my arm. "I would like to speak with you, Sally," she whispers.

I follow her inside, and she closes the door.

"Sit down, Sally," she says. "Do you know what everyone is doing out in that hall, looking at the newspaper? They are reading that you and your husband have gotten divorced." Mrs. Cardwell looks straight at me.

"It's in the newspaper?" I say.

"Why, certainly, Sally. The newspaper lists divorces on the page right across from the obituaries, didn't you know that?"

I shake my head. I hope they don't list the grounds for divorce. I don't want people to believe any of the things Barry said about me. I don't want people to think I beat him up or tried to kill him.

Mrs. Cardwell sighs. "I believe you had better think what you are going to tell everyone, Sally. They have seen Barry driving you to work every morning."

I try to understand what Mrs. Cardwell is saying to me. I don't know why it is anyone's business but mine that I am divorced. And I don't know what Barry's driving me to work has to do with it. Barry always drives me to work.

"Sally," Mrs. Cardwell says, "since Barry is driving you to work, everyone is going to think that you and Barry are still living together."

"We are," I say.

"But, Sally, you can't be living with a man who is not your husband."

"Oh."

"You had better think about what you are going to tell everyone."

"Why do I have to tell them anything?"

242

Mrs. Cardwell smiles. "They are going to be asking."

I go straight to my office. I can imply that I am staying somewhere else but that Barry picks me up and takes me to work. Since I don't have a car, it's even logical. When I get to my office, the phone rings. I pick it up.

"Hi," Barry says. His voice sounds dead.

"The divorce came through," he says.

"So I heard."

Several liquor cartons are spread out on the living-room floor. I have taken all my colorful paperbook books from the bookcase and packed them. Barry's law books sit on the bottom shelf. The top two shelves are empty. I take Torts from the bottom shelf and put it on the top shelf, but that looks stupid. I put it back. I take André Gide's *Journals* from the top of a liquor carton and throw it casually on the top shelf. Maybe Barry will read it.

"I won't read it," Barry says.

I take it and throw it back into the liquor carton. "I don't like the way the bookshelf looks now," I say.

Barry doesn't say anything. He is pacing around the living-room floor, smoking a Lark.

"Do you want this?" I say to Barry. It is an avocado green chafing dish with a gold stand that holds a candle.

"What would I do with that, baby?" Barry says.

"You might have someone over for dinner. Your Aunt Rose sent it to us."

Barry just looks at me. I wrap the casserole dish in newspaper and stuff it into a liquor carton.

"Do you want this?" I say to Barry and hold up a pair of wooden salad tongs.

"Take everything," Barry says. "I don't care."

"You don't?"

"No."

I am wrapping a set of steak knives with fake ivory handles. Barry comes up to me. "Who gave us those steak knives?"

"Your sister."

He reaches for the knives. "I'll keep them," he says.

I take out the set of Revereware from the cabinet under the sink. "I'll take the large pot and leave you the large frying pan," I say. "You can have one saucepan and I'll take one."

"Who gave us those pots, baby?"

"A friend of mine from high school."

"That was a nice present," Barry says.

On the kitchen shelf there are two small sterling silver brandy goblets set in a box against royal blue velvet. The initial *F* is engraved in script on each one. Barry's best friend, the best man at the wedding, gave them to us. I hold out the box to Barry, and we both stare at the two small goblets with the delicate *F*'s.

"We never used them," Barry says. His voice is soft, almost breathless.

I put them back on the shelf.

As I pick up the last sheet of newspaper from the coffee table, I see a letter from Barry's father. It's turned over and only the last few lines of the letter are facing me. *Don't worry, Barry, when you get back to Florida, we'll find you a good Jewish wife. Love, Dad.*

I put the newspaper down.

"I see your father has your second wife handpicked for you already," I say.

Barry just looks at me.

I pick up the letter and read him the line.

"Oh," he says. "Ummn, what should I tell your mother if she calls here?"

"Tell her I'm out," I say.

I fold the four flaps over each liquor carton and tape them shut. Then I stack them up and print my name and Miranda's address in the Village on them with a marking pen. "You'll send these REA Express to New York, won't you?"

The front door opens, and Mel and Patsy walk in. Patsy is carrying a bakery cake box.

"What's that?" I say.

"Oh, nothing." Patsy smiles. She takes the box into the kitchen.

Mel looks at me across the pile of liquor cartons. "You're leaving the day after tomorrow," he says. It's a statement, so I don't answer him. "Patsy and I have to say good-bye tonight. We're driving down to Florida for the weekend."

"I know," I say. "You told me."

"I know I did," Mel says. He reaches over and hugs me. I stumble over the cartons. I can feel the warmth of his chest, I can hear his breathing. "Good luck, Edwina," he whispers.

"Hey, what's going on?" Patsy says. She comes in from the kitchen, carrying a birthday cake with white frosting, pink frosted flowers, and in pink script, *Happy Birthday, Sally*. There are pink candles lighted on the top of the cake.

"I'm so surprised," I say. "Especially since today isn't my birthday." I lean over the cake and blow out the candles.

Patsy smiles. "But we won't be here tomorrow, so we wanted to give you a little party."

"That's really nice," I say. "Did you know about this, Barry?"

"It was Feldman's idea," Mel says.

Barry is sitting slumped in a chair with his feet up on the coffee table. He is wearing the same olive drab bermuda shorts he was wearing the first time I came to visit him in Birmingham. Through the gray train window I saw him standing on the platform with one foot propped up on the railing. He looked like he had been waiting there for me all his life. He was smiling, and he looked cool and easy. I was hot, dirty, and my hair was tangled.

I walked towards him, and he was still smiling. "Hi, baby," he said and took my suitcase. My body was limp from the summer heat, but the air was clean, and the sky was blue. Barry put his free arm around me, and we walked to his white car. We got in, and he turned on the air-conditioning and the radio. Music began to play. Everything was cool and clean and safe.

Barry gets up, comes over, and kisses me on the cheek. He gives me a little white box. I open it. Inside is a sterling silver cigarette lighter. Engraved on it are two intertwined hearts and the words *Love forever, Barry*.

I look up at him. "Thanks," I say.

I turn the lighter over in my hand. I am surprised it is so heavy as it lies in my palm.

"Let's all eat some cake," Patsy says and claps her hands together. She cuts four-inch slices and dumps them onto plates. Joe Namath is smiling up at me from my plate.

I sink my fork into a large pink frosting rose, cut away a petal, and put it on my tongue. The frosting is pure sugar. I suck it through my teeth, suck the sweetness out until all that is left is the granules, empty of taste.

In the morning, I am leaving for New York on a 9:00 flight. Tonight, Barry is leaving for Miami on a

9:00 flight. He's going to spend the weekend with his father. We are sitting in the cocktail lounge at the Birmingham airport, waiting for the plane to Miami. I am sipping a whiskey sour through a cellophane straw.

"This is the first time you have taken me out for a drink since we got married," I say to Barry. Barry looks good in the dark light of the cocktail lounge. "I wish you had taken me out once in a while."

Barry looks at his watch. "We have to go to the gate," he says.

We walk side by side down the long corridor.

At the gate, Barry looks at me. I look at him.

"Bye," I say.

"Bye," he says. "Have a nice life."

At the apartment I am sleeping alone on the blue sheets. I hear the front door open. It is still half dark, the morning light barely filtering into the bedroom through the blue drapes. I look at the clock. It's 5:45. Barry walks through the bedroom door, drops his suitcase on the floor, and sits on the edge of the bed. He puts his head in his hands and starts to cry.

"What happened?" I say.

Barry looks up at me. He looks hazy in the half-light.

"As soon as I got on the plane I knew I didn't want to go. I got off in Miami and took the next flight back. I don't want to be away from you, baby. You're my wife. You're my family."

"But you divorced me," I whisper.

"Don't leave me, baby."

"I have to."

Barry lies down in bed next to me. I can feel his tears hot and wet on the back of my neck.

Polly is picking me up at 8:00 to drive me to the airport. I am wearing my pink sleeveless sweater and skirt and the high heels with the strap that snakes up the instep. I brush my hair a hundred times. It has bleached out in the sun, and shimmers in streaks of gold.

"Let me drive you to the airport," Barry says. He's standing in the bathroom door. He is not wearing a shirt, but he is still wearing his pants. They're wrinkled and unbuttoned at the waist.

"Polly is taking me," I say.

Barry goes back into the bedroom. He sits on the edge of the bed and stares at the floor.

I turn and walk down the hall, through the living room, and open the front door. The sun flashes in my face, and for a moment, I can't see anything at all but light. Then the light subsides, and I can see the parking lot and Polly's Dodge sedan pulled up down below. I step out the front door onto the balcony. The air settles on me, and I feel the back of my neck go hot and wet. I stare out into the parking lot, and I see Barry lying on the blue sheets in the bedroom, the blue drapes drawn against the sun coming in the window. I see myself, standing in my pink sweater and skirt, holding a suitcase. An autumn breeze comes from the north and lifts the hair off my neck, and I shiver at the cool surprise of it.